JOURNEY TO
FREEDOM

JOURNEY TO FREEDOM

GILBERT MORRIS

ILLUSTRATED BY ANGEL DOMINGUEZ

CROSSWAY BOOKS • WHEATON, ILLINOIS
A DIVISION OF GOOD NEWS PUBLISHERS

Journey to Freedom

Published by Crossway Books
A division of Good News Publishers
1300 Crescent Street
Wheaton, Illinois 60187

Illustrations by: Angel Dominguez

Cover and interior design: Liita Forsyth

First printing, 2000

Printed in the United States of America

Library of Congress Cataloging-in-Publication Data

Morris, Gilbert.
Journey to freedom / Gilbert Morris.
p. cm.
Summary: Chosen by the Maker to do great things, a dreamer and unlikely hero named Chip leads the Whitefoot Mouse army to protect their royal family and defend their homeland against the invasion of domineering Brown Rats.
ISBN 0-58134-191-1
[1. War—Fiction. 2. Mice—Fiction. 3. Animals—Fiction. 4. Fantasy.]
I. Title.
PZ7.M8279 Jo 2000
[Fic]—dc21
00-009044
CIP

15 14 13 12 11 10 09 08 07 06 05 04 03 02 01 00
15 14 13 12 11 10 9 8 7 6 5 4 3 2 1

To Dixie Morris,
the joy of my life

CONTENTS

Part Four: A Hero's Return

INTRODUCTION

THERE was nothing special about Chip. He was just an ordinary white-foot mouse who always did the chores his father asked him to do. He didn't mind doing them, though they did get a bit boring. That's one reason he liked to daydream so much.

In his real life he was just a young worker who did what he was told. But in his dreams he was a great hero who defeated evil villains and saved the lives of hundreds of innocent white-feet. In his real life he stacked seeds or dug holes. But in his dreams he used a magic sword to win incredible victories.

There was nothing special about Chip—or was there? Little did he know that his daydreams didn't come from his own mind but from the One who had made everything and who ruled over all and who had already decided to battle evil through an ordinary mouse.

PART ONE
Mouse of Valor

CHAPTER ONE
Standing Guard

TWILIGHT had cast its spell over the feebly dying sun, so that only the last cries of day creatures sounded faintly. A brown thrasher babbling in the brush and the sleepy yelp of a farm dog closed out the day. As darkness washed over the fields and hackberry thickets, the night-dwellers began their symphony. From the woods a chorus of tree frogs gave out a shrill melody, and in response heavy bullfrogs grunted sullenly from the whispering creek. A band of wandering coons splashed noisily across the stream, chattering among themselves as they headed for a cornfield half a mile past the trees on the uppermost ridge.

Some sounds were not difficult to hear—the screech owl's

mournful cry or the snap of a branch broken by a mule deer. Other sounds could be detected only by the skillful ear of the hunted. The breathless flight of the downy owl would be noticed too late by the plump hare or the tender unwary mouse—just before the clutch of strong talons ended its life. The soft step of the slender weasel or the muted cry of the acrobatic bat were sometimes felt more than heard.

Night is a time of great drama for creatures of the field and wood. As the light fades and darkness closes in like a fist, out of nests, hollow trees, burrows, crevices, and a myriad of hidden lairs an army pours forth—possums, moles, rabbits, woodchucks, prairie dogs, ground squirrels, mice, rats, skunks. They scurry around their world harvesting seeds, leaves, fruits, berries, nuts, grains, and grass.

But if in their search for food they forget there are others in the air and water and on the land who are also searching for food, they put themselves at great peril from many enemies—the sneaky weasel, the clever mink, the ferocious wolverine, the cunning fox, the wolf, otter, coyote, lynx, bobcat, and a host of others.

Even on the most beautiful night the ancient drama reenacts itself, and the limp and the weak have no choice but to dare challenge stronger creatures of fang and claw. Every night is a time of bloodshed for the wild dwellers, and heroic is the tiny hunted creature who survives such cruel violence.

Late one evening, close to a split-rail fence that divided the woods from a newly harvested barley field, a massive rock covered with shaggy moss tilted skyward. At its base there was a sudden movement, then another, and soon the ground was dotted with a multitude of silver flashes reflecting the moonlight. A high-pitched buzzing broke the silence, like tiny singers in a miniature opera. A small stream of white-footed mice poured out of the opening of the rock-crested den. They raced to the field and began carting heavy loads of barley heads that had fallen during the harvest back to their storehouse.

Two of them stood quietly, keeping a careful watch on the horizon. The way they were dressed showed they were military, and the larger of the two was apparently a seasoned veteran. He was over ten deedles long and weighed over sixteen meets. (In human measurements he was seven and a half inches from his nose to the tip of his tail and weighed about one ounce.) Most young white-feet have a gray back, brownish sides, and white underparts, but this fellow had mature golden brown fur on his back and snowy feet and chest. He wore a simple soldier's uniform with a two-edged sword at his side and a silver helmet with the insignia of a corporal on the front. Corporal isn't a very high rank, but it is just as important as a major or even a general, and this corporal had evidently done his share of leading and fighting.

The other white-foot was younger and smaller—obviously a fresh recruit. He kept moving back and forth nervously, taking his eyes off the sky and casting curious glances back toward the fort entrance. Finally, in the high-pitched voice common to the white-foot tribe, he asked, "Corporal, did you see the king and all the officers going into the Council Room?"

"Peedee, you'd better mind your duty," the corporal snapped. "You haven't been put on watch so you can make guesses about the Council!"

"But General Woodland was there—and all the staff officers, and—"

Peedee was cut off suddenly when the corporal began crying out, "Take cover! Take cover! Out of sight now!" Like magic all the white-feet disappeared from sight, throwing themselves onto the ground just as the shadow of a great horned owl sailed across the very section of field they had been harvesting.

Peedee was trembling beneath a rotten pine tree trunk where the older white-foot had jerked him without apology. "I never even saw a feather of that horned owl!"

"That's because you were wasting time talking about nothing when you should have been doing your job," the corporal whispered. "Wait! Don't go out there yet. He'll come back for a second run to pick up anyone foolish enough to think the coast is clear." In a few minutes the shadow passed over them again, and Peedee heard the corporal sigh. "Now it's all right. He won't come this way again tonight." Stepping boldly into the open he called to the hidden workers, "All clear—back to work, and step lively."

Peedee crept out cautiously, then said a little breathlessly, "How did you know he'd be back a second time?"

"If you live long enough, Peedee, you'll learn *exactly* what they will do. If you don't, they'll get to know *you.*" The corporal leered and patted his stomach. "They'll get to know you as well as they know their own supper!"

Peedee shivered and crept closer to the corporal. He kept his eyes on the sky and scarcely blinked for a long time. The workers scurried to and fro with their loads, and the two guards relaxed as if nothing had happened.

Without taking his eye from the horizon for a second, the corporal said, "That's the way to do your job, recruit. This is easy duty, but you can't let up for one second." He stretched his snow-white forepaws, then said, "About what you said earlier—yes, I saw His Majesty—and all the officers with him. Big doings at the King's Council."

"What's it all about, corporal?"

"I suppose that business over on the West Border with the brown rats."

"What business?"

"You haven't heard about that? I thought everyone knew. Oh, that's right, you only came into the fort a few days ago."

The corporal ducked as a low branch in a persimmon tree suddenly swung toward him for no apparent reason. He relaxed when he saw a possum with three babies hanging on her back. He continued cautiously, "Well, Peedee, there are rats and there are *rats*. On the whole we get along with them rather well, but that's because we stay in our territory and they stay in theirs. But for the past few months, they've been trespassing."

"You mean they've been coming into our condee!" Peedee demanded. The word for *place* or *town* means much more to any white-foot than it does to us. The smell, the touch, the appearance of their home community was *everything* to them. Separated from their condee, they had no sense of safety or peace. And for strangers to impose on their home—why, that was enough to raise the fur on Peedee's neck and to make his tiny fangs gleam in the moonlight. "They're coming into *our* condee?" he demanded shrilly.

"Well, so far just a raid here and there," the corporal admitted, "but there's something about it—something *peculiar*. It's more than food raids, from what our scouts tell me. Those rats are planning something—something—" He tried very hard to find the right words but could not.

Suddenly Peedee stiffened. "What's that out there?" he asked.

"Who's there?" the corporal demanded. "Stand still and identify yourself!"

"Silver."

The one word floated faintly back to them, and the two guards looked at each other, then moved back a step or two as a very large mouse suddenly emerged from the grass and stood before them. He was much bigger than the corporal, and his fur matched his name. The new arrival came to a stop, and as his black eyes met Peedee's, the recruit felt that he was being undressed somehow—as if every long-hidden secret was suddenly on public display. He felt afraid.

Apparently satisfied, Silver looked toward the door of the fort and asked, "Has the Council met, corporal?"

"Yes, sire. I think they're probably waiting for you."

Silver nodded his massive head. "Keep close watch, soldiers." Moving quickly for one so large, he disappeared into the rocky fort.

"Whew! Who is *that*?" Peedee asked timidly.

"Many of us would like to know that—including the king," the corporal answered softly.

"I felt like I was looking a red-tailed hawk right in the eye!"

The corporal directed a guarded glance at the fort. "Silver is more dangerous than a hawk. At least we know what a hawk is and what he's likely to do. That one—well, no one is ever quite sure exactly where he stands, and nobody has yet had the courage to ask him."

CHAPTER TWO

The War Council

SINCE white-feet do not as a rule make their own burrows, the passageway that Silver followed was the work of some ambitious woodchucks. The main tunnel was over fifty feet in length, and many side tunnels led off to sleeping chambers, storage rooms, and other private spaces. Best of all, in addition to the main entrance beneath the rock, there were three other entrances, all sealed and guarded from the inside. There would be no easy trapping of those in the Royal Burrow.

The Royal Burrow was, of course, much larger than any of the many other lairs of the white-feet clan. Here was the court, the guard, the Royal Family, and the many servants of the Royal Family. It was the center of the white-feet kingdom in that part of the world.

Silver moved quickly down the hard-packed tunnel, turning at last into a smaller passageway guarded by a massive door. He was recognized at once by the two members of the Royal Guard and passed without a pause into the inner room.

The Council Room was very large, with a high ceiling covered with large elm roots. All along one wall was stacked an array of weapons—swords, daggers, battle-axes. On another wall were shelves from floor to ceiling containing tidy displays of armor. The third wall was packed with seeds of all sorts, for the burrow had been designed to withstand both winter and siege. There were mountains of acorns, hazelnuts, barley, wheat, and many other foods.

A massive table ran the length of the Council Room, and seated at it as Silver entered were King Halbert and a group of officers and ruling elders. The new arrival slipped into a chair next to Major Meadows—the white-foot he trusted most—without saying a word.

"Well," snapped the king, "I'm sure we're all very happy that you decided to come *at last!*" He was very fat, and his eyes seemed to pop out of his head. His father had been a monarch of great honor and distinction, but all the present ruler excelled in was eating whenever he felt like it, which was often, and pouting whenever people or events inconvenienced him, which to his mind was also often.

"I regret my tardiness, Your Majesty," Silver said calmly. His steady gaze seemed to irritate the king even more.

"Why *are* we here anyway?" the ruler blustered. "We were having a *tremendously* good time at the ball! What could be so important as to drag us away from that?" He looked up at the ceiling and moaned piteously, "The cares of the crown are so burdensome! Oh, the pain of it all!"

Several elders tried to soothe him, saying things like,

"There, there!" or "You are so right, Your Majesty!" Not to be outdone in all the self-seeking, insincere consolation, General Woodland, easily identified by the record number of medals stretched across his broad stomach, boomed out, "Exactly! *I* didn't call this meeting. And I know His Majesty did not. May I ask who has summoned us here? Silver, perhaps you can shed some light on this?"

"As you know very well, I have called for an emergency meeting of the King's Council," Silver said quietly.

"And for what purpose?" demanded the general.

"Obviously, because there is an emergency," Silver said more sharply. "There has been another series of raids on the West Border."

"How right you are!" Major Meadows leaped to his feet. A veteran with more than his share of wounds and bruises, he wore his high rank on a short field jacket. His face was afire with anger, and there was a blazing light in his eyes as he almost shouted, "Look at that map!" He swept his arm toward a large map on the only unoccupied wall. "See those new marks? More and more all the time, ever closer together. If this isn't an organized invasion by the brown rats, I'll resign from the military and go eat grass for the rest of my days!" He smashed the table hard with his paw and knocked over several elders' glasses of beet wine.

"Now, now, my dear Major," the king said impatiently. "There is no need to panic. After all, there has *always* been a lawless element in that part of the kingdom. This is nothing new."

"That is certainly so," the general agreed loudly. "In any case, in a few weeks I'll lead a force over there and thrash the villains—all in good time, you know."

A murmur of assent passed around the table, and everyone except the small group of junior officers flanking Major Meadows and Silver nodded.

"No . . . No. That won't do." Silver's loud words cut

through the room like a knife, and when he stood up, his tall shadow swept across the room, covering the king's face. The monarch flinched as though he had been struck. "We can't wait any longer," Silver continued. "There's more to this than you think. The situation is more serious, and the solution not as simple as you assume." He paused, and there was a sadness on his face that none had ever seen there before. "This time the crisis is worse, the enemy more ferocious. We must take action quickly if we are to save the kingdom at all. I tell you, I hear the sound of a distant drummer—and he is making a song of war!"

"But what about the Maker?" the king demanded. "Why can't *He* take care of things like this? I mean, after all, He is the Maker! Since we are His people, surely He will protect us and will defeat our enemies. Can we not simply depend on Him?"

Silver looked the king squarely in the eye. "The Maker is our source, but He expects us to do more than be stones. He has given us minds and bodies; and most of all, He has put within us a will—the ability to choose. It is for His glory as well as for our own survival that we must use all He has put within us to save ourselves."

Silver's raised voice seemed to paralyze the entire Council. They sat motionless, staring at him. Finally the king muttered, "Very well, the situation seems to demand that we fight. If we must, we must!" He waved his hand, giving Silver and Major Meadows grudging assent.

The major, receiving a nod from Silver, said in his quick nervous way, "The army must be enlarged. A new training program—new recruits—fresh supplies—I have it all planned out—and we must have a press, a draft—we must recruit new soldiers right away—we must order them to report for duty."

"Compel some of the white-feet to serve in the military?" General Woodland said sharply. "No, sir! Perhaps we do indeed need an army, but volunteers are the most capable and loyal soldiers!"

"We must have a press," Major Meadows insisted. "The day is gone when we can field a volunteer army. Our young mice are soft. Too many parties, you know." He did not hear the king huff or see him shut his bulging eyes.

"The major is right," Silver agreed. "We must have a stronger force, even if we have to order in the troops." He rose to his feet suddenly. "Major, perhaps you will show me your complete plan. I'm sure His Majesty would like to get back to his . . . party." Without waiting for a reply, he led Major Meadows and a young junior officer out of the Council Room and into the main tunnel.

"Well!" sniffed a fancily dressed young officer after their departure. "He thinks too highly of himself, I must say. Seems to think he's in charge. What *is* his position exactly?"

"He's the chief troublemaker!" snapped the general.

The king looked at the others with a pout. "He must be as old as the moon!" he said angrily. "My grandfather used to tell me how Old Silver would come around and make a nuisance of himself even when *he* was a pup."

"Why don't we just get rid of him?" a long-faced elder asked.

"Oh no! I can't do that," the king said quickly. "I—I mean, he's a pest all right, but somehow—well, when there's *real* trouble, I—I wouldn't like for Silver *not* to be around. For one thing, and perhaps most important of all, he's closer to the Maker than anyone else." He looked embarrassed, as if he had confessed too much, then leaped to his feet and said loudly, "Come, come, let's get back to the party before all the food and beet wine is gone."

CHAPTER THREE
The Right Recruit

ONE day several weeks later, when many white-feet had already been pressed into service, Major Meadows waved toward a tall tuft of cattails that crested a water-filled ditch and said to Silver, "That's where we'll get our next recruit." He looked curiously at his friend, whom many called a prophet or seer because he seemed to see things, especially concerning the future, that others just didn't see. "You've certainly been interested in all the recruiting, Silver. Perhaps you don't trust my judgment."

Silver shook his head. "It isn't that, major. Not at all."

"What is it then? I believe you've checked every recruit we've enlisted in the past two weeks—hundreds of them. You seem to be looking for something special—or should I say *someone*?"

"Yes, you might say that," Silver answered mysteriously. He had a way of answering questions without really answering them.

"Well, maybe it'll be one of old Brownie's pups. They're all good-sized, and brighter than most." Major stepped up quickly to the elderly mouse who met them by the entrance to a fair-sized burrow. "Greetings, old friend, do you have any recruits for me?"

"Hello, Major," the elderly mouse said with a smile. "Well, sir, I'll let you take your pick. They all want to be soldiers." He gave a shrill whistle, and out of the door six young pups stumbled and formed a rough line as their father named them off.

"This is Scamper, my eldest. Next is Peeper, and that's Tender—then Reek and Jumper and last is Beeper." He waved a fatherly paw at his clan and stepped back. "I don't reckon you'll find a more likely bunch in any burrow!"

"That's very likely true," Major Meadows said heartily. He looked down the line, then glanced suddenly at Silver. "Maybe you'd like to do the choosing this time, sire," he suggested.

Silver nodded and began walking down the line. Each young mouse tried to stand as straight as he could. Scamper, the oldest and largest, waited patiently, fully confident he would be recruited. And in fact Silver did finally again stand before him once more.

But after a long hesitation he asked, "Is this all your pack?"

"Well, they all look fine to *me*, Silver!" Major Meadows said tartly. He patted Scamper on the shoulder in a friendly fashion. "Surely this fine young fellow is one of the chosen—so big and strong and undoubtedly braver than most."

Silver murmured so quietly that only the major could hear him, "It's not his muscles or his size that matters—the Maker seeks not an impressive outer appearance or physical ability but strength in the hidden things of the heart." He again asked Brownie, "You have no other pups?"

Brownie shrugged, "Well, there is the youngest—Chip we call him, but he . . ."

"Where is he?" Silver asked.

"Who knows? Catching sunbeams maybe. That's what he's best at," Brownie answered with obvious irritation. "Where is he, Scamper?"

"He's supposed to be stacking the last of the sunflower seeds in the storeroom, but he's probably asleep—that dreamer!"

"Dreamer?" Silver asked sharply. "Dreamer, eh? I think I'd like to talk with this one, major. Why don't you move on to the next burrow and I'll meet you back at the fort." Without waiting for a reply he said to Scamper, "Which way?"

"Over there by that little patch of blackberries, but he'll do you no good," Scamper said in a pout. "Not a serious bone in his entire body!"

Silver strolled off quickly, leaving the major to calm down Brownie. Soon he came to the base of a small tree, and there sitting on a stump was a rather plump, short, young white-foot. He was somewhat shorter than his brothers, and indeed, judging by the expression on his face, he was dreaming instead of working. As he sat nibbling on a large sunflower seed, he studied a cloud overhead.

Silver stood to one side, and as he looked at the youngster a look of joy came into his eyes, as if a decision long sought had been made, and he said suddenly and loudly, "The Maker is with you, mighty mouse of valor!"

The young mouse suddenly swallowed the seed and began choking terribly. The words he'd just heard made him feel emotions he'd never felt before. He was puzzled. He managed finally to swallow the sunflower seed, then looked wildly around until he saw the old mouse. "What—what did you say, sir?"

"I said the Maker is with you, mighty mouse of valor!"

"Oh—well—what on earth—" Chip stammered. "Well—uh, whatever."

"My name is Silver."

"Pleased to meet you. My name is Chip."

"Yes, I know. You see, Chip, I know more about you than you know about yourself."

"Really?" Chip suppressed a yawn and glanced back up at the cloud. "That's nice."

Silver raised his voice only slightly, but Chip paid sudden attention. "I know, for example, that there's going to be a war, and a white-foot leader will arise and do great exploits."

"Oh?"

"Yes. Great and valiant deeds."

"You say a great soldier will come along?"

"Yes."

"But—how will he—how will the soldier know he's the one?"

Silver's eyes glinted, and he said slowly, "I will appear to him and will say to him, 'The Maker is with you, mighty mouse of valor.'"

Chip said, "Oh." Then after a pause his eyes widened, and he gulped and said rather shrilly, "Oh! Do you mean . . . ?"

"Yes. That is exactly what I mean," Silver said with a smile.

"Not me!" Chip shook his head wildly, but Silver only nodded. "But my pack is the poorest in the kingdom, almost at least. And I'm the smallest in my pack. Why, my own family doesn't trust me to stack acorns!"

Silver didn't say anything but just kept looking straight into Chip's face. Finally he said, "I'll give you a sign, Chip. What will it be?"

The young white-foot wasn't sure of the full meaning of

Silver's words, but he was quite sure he didn't want to be part of it. A crafty look came into Chip's eyes. He smiled and said smugly, "If I'm supposed to be the one you mean, let my father give me Durance."

"Durance?"

"Yes—my great-grandfather's sword. He went on many an adventure with it." Chip grinned. "My father wouldn't let the Maker himself have *that* blade. He'd mortgage the burrow to keep it!"

"Very well," Silver said calmly. He looked back at Brownie's burrow and seemed to be talking to himself about something. He turned to Chip with a smile and said, "Shall we go, my son?"

"Just a minute." The old mouse seemed so sure of himself—perhaps Chip needed to make the test a bit harder. "I want another sign—not that one. This is big business, you know."

"Indeed. And what sign would you like now?"

A grin broke across Chip's plump face. "Well, let Scamper—in fact, *all* my brothers—bow before me and call me Master." He laughed out loud. "*That* would be a real sign." *One that will never happen*, he thought to himself.

Silver cast another peculiar look toward the burrow, then said, "Shall we go now?"

"What about stacking all these seeds?"

"Your brothers will see to it. Come along."

The patriarch and his six pups were waiting for them. Chip stood a little way off. "Father, I didn't finish the seeds . . ." He stopped suddenly because after one look from the seer his father popped into the burrow and returned immediately. He had a sword in his hands, and he thrust it at Chip saying, "Chip, my son, I want you to have Durance."

Scamper cried out, "But, Father, you said that I—"

But then he fell to his knees as if knocked down by a brown bear, as did the other five pups, and their father too. Then

Scamper said in a queer voice not at all sounding like his usual voice, "Master, you will do exploits!" And the others praised him with exactly the same words.

Silver took Chip's arm and led him away saying, "We must go, Chip. You can come back and see your pack later."

Just before they lost sight of the familiar burrow, the only home he had ever known, Chip looked back and saw his father and brothers still on their knees staring at him, and he was afraid. What was happening here? What did it all mean? "Mighty mouse of valor"? He was just one small dreamer who had never been away from home before, and he didn't want to go now. What would happen to him?

"Are they bewitched?" he asked in a frightened voice.

"No, just Silvered a bit," the prophet chuckled. "They'll be fine. Now, sir, you come with me." He gave a rare smile and looked down at nervous, little Chip with something like wonder in his black eyes. "The Maker knows best. But he has surely used strange weapons in the wars of the mighty ones. Come along. The nation is waiting for you, Captain Chip!"

CHAPTER FOUR

New Danger and New Friends

CHIP entered his military training in the same way as the hundreds of other recruits before him. Silver took him to an army camp near a pond where a large fallen, hollow cedar served as cover for about 200 untrained troops. They were broken into squads of ten, each led by a corporal and a sergeant. Silver turned Chip over to a corporal without telling Chip anything more about his special calling. "Do your best," was all he told the frightened recruit, then left without a backward glance. Chip had been expecting a bit more, but the corporal gave him no chance to complain or pout.

"Just do your work and keep out of trouble," he said briskly. "Settle in here while I go check on things in the field. Some of our squad are over there, and the others will be coming in soon." He started to leave, then paused and said, "Be careful about the sergeant. He and his favorites like to pick on the new recruits a bit." He left at a brisk trot, but before Chip could do much more than look around the squad room, four troopers came in, and one of them said at once, "A new recruit—it's time for some fun!" The four gathered around him, shoving him this way and that.

Their leader, an angry-looking soldier, said, "Hey, shorty, do my boots." He ran across the room and tossed a pair of muddy boots at Chip, hitting him painfully on the shins.

"And mine too," another voice demanded. A large black mouse with piggish eyes picked up his filthy boots and threw them at the helpless recruit as well, as did the fourth bully.

"See you get them clean, you little squirt, or we'll cut you with your own blade," the skinny one said. "Right, Blackie?"

The large one grinned. "We sure will. You'd better make sure ya do the job right, me lad!" he roared, giving Chip another push.

Not sure what he should do, Chip looked helplessly at the other members of the squad. One small mouse gave him a timid smile of encouragement but looked away when Blackie scowled at him.

"Well, are you going to spit-polish my boots or not?" the angry-looking one called out. "My name's Rattle, and if you don't do what we say, I'll rattle your brains for you."

"Well, I suppose if that's what new recruits do . . . Otherwise—"

"I don't want to hear none of that," Blackie roared. He grabbed Chip by the back of the neck with his huge paw, almost lifting him off the ground. "You'll mind what I say, see?" He waved a huge paw in Chip's face. "Otherwise you'll get a taste of me fist, understand?"

The four bullies began shoving him from one to another until he felt so dizzy he was sure he was about to fall down. Suddenly a tiny voice said, "Let him alone, why don't you?"

They stopped pushing Chip around and stared in amazement as a small recruit stepped forward, his paws gathered in tiny fists. "He ain't doing you no harm!"

"Peedee, I thought we taught you your lesson last time," Rattle snarled. "You wants some more of the same?" He swung suddenly and knocked the soldier to the ground. Peedee's head made a *thump* against a bunk.

For the first time in his life pure rage ran through Chip's veins and without any thought of his own safety he shouted, "Get back there, all of you! You'd better leave him alone or I'll—I'll—"

"You'll what?" Blackie challenged. He glanced at Rattle with an evil look in his little eyes, and then they both leaped on Chip, striking his face and body with their hard fists. The other two joined the fray at once, all four kicking, biting, and gouging the helpless Chip. Even as he fell under the onslaught he thought, *Someday I'll make it right with Peedee! I'll reward him for trying to protect me.* When he'd endured all he thought he possibly could and was about to pass out, Blackie asked breathlessly, "Now, me lad, will you polish them boots, or do ya need some more beatin'?"

Chip gathered all his strength and said as loudly as he could through his bleeding mouth, "Eat dirt! You're more like the brown rats than any white-feet I ever saw!"

That made the four even angrier, and Rattle said, "You think you're tough, do ya? We'll break every bone in your body!" He picked up a stick, nodding at the others to do the same, and they advanced on the helpless Chip, who could only glare at them in anger.

Just as Rattle raised his club, a deep, slow voice announced, "I reckon that'll be about all from you buzzards."

Chip watched through his rapidly closing eyes as the most

enormous mouse he had ever seen suddenly confronted the four bullies. He was not large—he was *gigantic*. In fact, he was more the size of a woodchuck than a mouse. His face didn't look like a white-foot, but more like a stranger from a distant burrow of another species. He looked invincible as he placed his bulk between Chip and the four ruffians armed with clubs.

"I suspect you'd best be about your business," he said pleasantly, but there was a red gleam in his eyes that seemed wilder, more dangerous than his soothing words indicated.

Blackie snarled, "This ain't none of your business, Budger." He hefted his club and eyed the larger mouse daringly. "Maybe you'd better mind *your* business!"

Now the four surrounded Budger, lifting their sticks high, and it seemed to Chip that despite the imposing size of the new arrival, Budger could not possibly win.

But just as Rattle raised his club and screamed, "All right, let's get them both!" a tiny cheeping voice said in an accent Chip had never heard, "Ah ha! It ease the beeg fight, no? Good, good, my frans. But Trooper, he will also join in, eh?"

Chip saw the strangest figure he had ever seen in his life. A tiny mouse no more than half Chip's size came dancing into the squad room with a happy smile on his face and waving a sword no larger than a needle. He moved like a beam of light, flickering from one to the other of the four bullies, who stood still in amazement as he sang at them and waved his tiny blade under their noses.

"Yes, my frans, we weel fight, no? And who weel be the first to die? Ease eet you, Blackie? No. You, Rattle? No. Ease eet you? Or you perhaps? No." The tiny mouse turned to Chip and said rather sadly, "None of my frans theenk it ease a good day to die." Then he wheeled quick as a striking snake and said sharply, "Perhaps it ease good if you go for a leetle walk, ease eet not so?" He lunged toward them with a swift movement, and they scurried out of the room, stumbling over each other in their eagerness to get away.

No sooner had they left and Chip stood to his feet than he felt his head pulled down and the small soldier kissed him firmly on the cheek saying, "Ah, my fran Cheep, you have *courage*! You spit in their eyes, no? I loves you. We weel be good frans, ease eet not so?"

Chip gulped and said, "Well—uh, thanks—thanks a lot to both of you. I guess they'd have killed me if you hadn't jumped into the fight. I was getting ready to meet the Maker." He ran over and pulled Peedee to his feet. "And thank you, Peedee. I'll never forget how you stood up for me!" The little fellow grinned shyly and ducked his head.

Budger said slowly, "Well, I never did like that bunch. But it was Trooper here who saved the day."

"Not a-tall, my fran, Budger! Not a-tall!" Trooper protested, but with a broad, self-confident smile on his tiny face.

"Why—why were they—that is—why did they—"

Budger answered the question Chip was afraid to ask. "Why are they so afraid of a tiny fellow like Trooper? Well, because Trooper is not a mouse."

"He's not?"

"No indeed," Budger said, settling down into the closest chair as if preparing to give a long lecture to pupils. "He is, in fact, a short-tailed shrew. He is full-grown, but do not be deceived, Chip, for you see before you probably the most ferocious creature on the face of the earth."

Trooper smiled from ear to ear and tried to look modest at this statement.

"Why, Trooper eats three times his own weight every day, and that gives him strength you wouldn't believe!"

Again Trooper tried to remain modest, but he could not. "What can I say? Eet ease true!"

Budger continued his lecture. "And look at his teeth." Trooper grinned obligingly. "See, there are thirty-two of them, and each one is filled with poison, Chip. One bite and a creature will have his nervous system so paralyzed that he can do nothing but be a meal for Trooper. Isn't that right?"

Trooper said shyly, "Oh, you say too much, my fran Budger, but eet ease so." He bared his teeth again, and Chip shivered involuntarily. "I'm the deadliest creature I know," he said with a shocking lack of modesty. "Eet ease so, my fran Cheep."

"Oh," Chip said weakly. "Well, thanks again. Would you really have—have killed them?" He waved toward the door the four had used as an exit.

"Oh, certainlee! With great pleasure, fran Cheep!" The shrew again showed off his poisoned teeth, and Chip was *very* glad Trooper was on his side!

"Well, army life certainly isn't what I expected," he said with a sigh.

"Oh," Trooper said, "eet ease not thees much fun *every* day. Most days eet ease very dull. But we fight soon, you and me, fran Cheep. Ease eet not so, Budger?"

"I expect you are right about that, Trooper." Budger looked at them both sadly. "An army is good for one thing—killing something—and the generals won't be satisfied until we've done a lot of *that*."

"Yes," Trooper said with a smile, "and that eet ease good, no?"

Chip couldn't agree with his new friend. Once again he definitely did not feel like a "mighty mouse of valor."

CHAPTER FIVE
The Maker

BY the time Chip's cuts and bruises had healed, he had pretty well settled into camp life. The routine might have been difficult for a recruit used to the comforts of living in town, but a country mouse like Chip found it more like summer camp. There was plenty of hard work, of course, but Chip found the drills—military activities repeated again and again to teach them how to use a sword, how to march side by side, how to work together during battle, and so on—rather exciting. He discovered that he had a natural talent for the sword, and before long his instructors put him in charge of the new recruits. He loved the change. For one thing he no longer had to perform the menial duties that recruits usually have to do (things like cleaning up after meals or washing the officers' uniforms). Of course, not everyone shared his joy, especially his sergeant and Rattle, whose jealousy made him hate Chip even more than before!

But overall they all were becoming friends and enjoyed being together, particularly during the long marches they sometimes took (some as far away as a quarter of a mile—a long way for a mouse). Chip was feeling closer and closer to most of his squad. He adopted Peedee as a younger brother, and the frail young recruit was seldom more than a foot away from him. Chip looked up to Budger as his example and his teacher—the huge mouse seemed to know *everything*. Since he had been a soldier for a long time, nothing in the army was new to him. And he was the best scrounger around anywhere, so he and Chip and the others in the squad's inner ring had the best food in the whole army. Budger was a scholar too, and he knew the names of every berry, tree, insect, and so on. But he did have his shortcomings. Chip had never met anyone who had so many doubts about the Maker and wasn't shy about saying so.

"Now, I'm not saying there's nothing beyond us or beyond nature," he said firmly one day. "But I say if something or someone is out there, let him show himself!" He snorted derisively, "If this so-called Maker is interested in our doings or if He cares about us, why do young mice get burned up in brush fires or get eaten by hungry weasels? No, sir, if the Maker has any power at all, why doesn't He watch over the good creatures and get rid of all the evil ones? It seems to me that maybe something or someone got everything going in the past, but He seems to be sleeping now."

"But, Budger," Chip protested, "we sure didn't make ourselves! And look at how everything works so well in nature. Yes, sometimes sad things happen, but the stars don't fall on our heads, and we always have enough food to keep going. Surely, this didn't all just *happen*!"

"I think it did. It's all just a matter of chance, that's all, Chip." Budger nodded. "There's no Maker, or if there is, He's taking a nap."

Chip was shocked to hear such awful statements because they disagreed so sharply with what his father had always taught him about the Maker. And yet he couldn't just toss aside what his new friend was saying. He saw Budger as an older brother or even a kind father. Budger's words didn't seem to be true, and yet Chip respected and loved his new friend.

Another recruit in the squad whom he had quickly come to trust was a handsome young mouse named Singer. He was called that because he had a habit of making up songs or poems and humming them almost constantly. Singer considered himself a poor soldier, but he believed himself to be an authority in two areas—art and love. However, his preoccupation with young female white-feet either kept him on a mountaintop emotionally or in the depths of despair. In either case he would write a poem about it.

"He'd write a poem about the end of the world if he got caught in the middle of it," Budger growled. "Romantic young idiot!" But despite his cutting words, he liked the young poet. They all did.

The last member of the inner circle of the squad, a group that the other recruits had begun to call Rag-Tags because they were so different from one another and because they seemed to be poorer and less educated than the others, was a sturdy young white-foot named Ben. He looked quite average, but Chip soon learned that Ben was constantly thinking about inventing whatever was needed or making the best use of whatever was available. Unfortunately, most of his inventions were totally impractical—such as his idea of a flying sentry (he wanted to glue feathers to Peedee's legs and throw him out of a tree). Or his idea to carry leaves or branches that had been sprayed by skunks in sacks so they could spray the enemy with the awful smell. There was madness in his thinking, but there was method too, and some of his inventions certainly had value. In the early morning he would rig a trap to catch grasshoppers and would catch enough to feed the whole squad! "Ben's bug machine," they called it. So whenever anything mechanical was needed, Ben jumped at the chance to come up with yet another invention.

This was the Rag-Tag Brigade—Chip, Budger, Trooper, Peedee, Ben, and Singer. Their sergeant, a large, muscular white-foot named Daggers, was mean and seemed to enjoy yelling at them all the time, but that's what sergeants were supposed to be like, the Rag-Tags were told. Rattle and Blackie, along with the other shiftless pair, whose names were Fish and Hawk, kept to themselves. No doubt they would have made life miserable for Chip and some of the others, but Budger's size and Trooper's poisonous teeth apparently persuaded them to leave Chip alone.

"I'm glad I got recruited," Chip said dreamily one night. They had made a long march, almost all the way to Frog Pond, and now they sat around the campfire eating the huge meal of meat and berries that Budger had discovered somewhere nearby. "I never had any real friends back on the farm."

"Yes, Cheep," Trooper said as he nodded, "eet ease the good life!" He bit into a huge chunk of meat with gusto. "We 'ave plenty of food, and soon we weel be in one beeg fight, no?"

Peedee moved a little closer to Chip and said timidly, "I know we will have to fight, but I'm not sure if I could actually . . . kill anybody."

"Well, now, young man," Budger said sheepishly, "none of us—except Trooper here—actually *likes* fighting and killing. But this is a case of self-defense—we have to protect our condee. It's a law of nature, you know. This Maker that the dreamers are always talking about—why, that's just another name for common sense! If somebody invades your home, you may not want to, but if you have to, you cut him down. That's just common sense."

"You don't believe in the Maker?" The quiet voice that made them all jump seemed to come from nowhere. Suddenly Silver stepped into the light of the fire and sat down on a log.

"Silver!" Chip said. He jumped up and ran over to shake his paw. "It's great to see you. Have some of this meat—it's really good."

"I believe I will," Silver said and began eating hungrily. "Well, Budger, what is your answer?"

Budger shifted uncomfortably, then directed a most serious look toward the stars as he stretched out full-length. "Do I believe in the Maker? I believe that is the question, sire? Well, the traditional definition of 'the Maker' is, according to most dictionaries, 'the force or power that is directly or indirectly responsible for the existence and activity of life.'"

"Yes, that's the common definition," Silver agreed.

"Well, now, do I believe it?" Budger pondered aloud. "Yes—and no."

"Spoken like a true scholar." Silver smiled.

"If you mean do I believe that something or someone made all this—" He waved a half-eaten chunk of juicy meat at the twinkling skies above. ". . . the answer is, probably. They didn't make themselves, obviously." He took another bite before continuing thoughtfully, "But is there any source or power or Maker who cares about what we do? Well, I would say no."

"And why do you say that?" Silver inquired gently. He was talking with Budger, but his eyes went from face to face around the fire.

"Why, there's no justice!" Budger exclaimed. "So many things just aren't *fair*! If there's a Maker, why do we have to worry about these brown rats who want to destroy us?"

"But if, as you say, there is no Maker or supreme power,

why should any one thing be more right than any other? I mean, if there are no rules and no Maker to make them, why isn't it just as right for you to plunge a sword into Peedee's throat as for you to save his life?"

Budger pondered this deeply. "Well, I suppose there are rules we have among ourselves . . ."

"Yes, but when you use the words *right* or *fair* you mean there is a greater law or force than ourselves," Silver argued quietly. "Isn't that so?"

Budger threw his bone away and said, "Well, we just live by common sense, sire. Doesn't take any Maker for that."

"Oh, I see," Silver said softly. "Do you always live by common sense?"

"Always! It's the only way for a man of reason like myself. Most definitely."

"And last month when Peedee was grabbed by that large hawk, was it common sense that made you dash out of your place of safety and risk your life to save him? It looked like you would probably die in the attempt, but you did it anyway." Silver's words felt like a sword to Budger.

Budger sat up straight and gulped. "How did you know about that?"

"It's true! It's true!" Peedee jumped up and ran to Budger's side. "I was already off the ground, and you came out and leaped up and caught that hawk by the throat just in time!" His voice got higher and higher. "Then it let me go, and you fought with him."

"Hmm! Well—I mean—" Budger looked at the sky, obviously embarrassed, then looked at Silver. "Well, I will say two things about that incident. First, you're right—I didn't use common sense, and second, I still haven't figured out why I'm not dead. I've thought about it many times since then. I had no chance at all, but then just as that hawk was about to bite me in two, it stopped for some reason. It seemed paralyzed or something, and then it dropped me and flew away. Why did it do that, do you suppose?"

They all waited for Silver to speak, but he just smiled and finally said to Budger, though once again looking at all of them, "You'll have to decide that sort of thing in your own hearts."

He got up and said, "I'll be going, but I will say one more thing: Before long you'll need to trust in something or someone greater than yourselves. Be sure you put your faith in the right place." Then he was gone, slipping away as quietly as an owl.

"Budger," Singer said, whipping out a piece of blank parchment, "would you go over the details of your fight with the hawk? I believe it would make a good song."

"I will not! Write another sonnet to your precious Peaches."

"Peaches!" Singer said indignantly. "I haven't had any feeling for that mischievous imp for—"

"For nearly 'alf a day, no?" Trooper jested. He plunged into the food zestfully. "Well, I tell you one then—that Seelvair, 'e ease not like other mice, I tell you sure! He ease give me, what you call, the creeps when 'e ease around."

They all thought about that. After all, Trooper had never been afraid of anything that swam, flew, ran, or crawled.

For some reason as the training went on, Silver was seen more often in the vicinity of Chip's squad than any other unit, though none but Chip could guess why.

The training continued, and they all grew tougher and wiser as the weeks went by. Things were going well—until Chip found himself backed into a corner by his old enemies Blackie and Rattle.

They approached him while Trooper and Budger were out on patrol. Chip was cleaning his gear when the two of them came in accompanied by Sergeant Daggers. All of them had been interested at one time or another in Durance, Chip's sword, which was not only a beautiful blade but was obviously valuable, having numerous gems set in its hilt of gold. Once the sergeant had offered to buy it, but Chip had refused so sharply that Daggers had said nothing about it since then. One day Chip had also seen Blackie reaching toward the sword when it was lying on Chip's bunk. But when he saw Chip looking at him, he jerked his hand away and made some weak excuse about wanting to borrow his cleaning cloth.

Now when they entered, Chip saw the look of bold hatred on their faces, and he realized he was all alone. Sudden fear made him gasp for breath. He got to his feet quickly and backed up against the wall.

"Take it easy, recruit," the sergeant said soothingly. "We just want to make you a legitimate offer for your sword. What difference does it make to you which sword you use?"

"That's right," Rattle said with an evil smile. "We'll give you whatever you wants for that purty sword."

"Can't be fairer than that, can we now?" Blackie added. He reached for the blade, but Chip beat him to it and pulled it out of its sheath.

"I've told you, it's been in my family for many generations, and it is not for sale at any price."

"*Anything* is for sale if the money's right," the sergeant said. "I'll tell you the truth, recruit, there's a gent in the next company who has a special appreciation for gear such as this. Comes from a wealthy pack he does, and he told us we could have a pocketful of gold if we'd give this blade to him. Now then, you're our comrade, ain't you? And we'll all share the profits equally, right, chum?"

At this point Rattle made a serious mistake, grabbing for the sword but missing, causing Chip to throw himself into a position of defense that he had learned very well by this time. "Just leave me alone," he said. "I don't want to have to hurt you!"

Instantly Blackie drew his blade, as did Rattle, and they

began to thrust and parry in the confines of the small room. Perhaps the sergeant only intended to stop the fight, but when he drew his blade and rushed toward them, he ran onto Chip's blade and received a slight wound in his left arm. He dropped his sword and began to scream loudly, "Guard! Guard! Come here, at once!" Almost as if they had been waiting for a signal, three tall veterans rushed in and disarmed Chip.

"Arrest the recruit!" Sergeant Daggers said. "Take him to the guardhouse. I'll take care of his sword. Rattle, bring the doctor to my tent." He looked angrily at Chip. "We'll teach you what it means to attack an officer without a good reason. I'm glad there are witnesses who can verify your terrible act against me."

Chip was dragged off to a dark, cold hole in the ground to await a court-martial or worse. In his despair he could not even remember what Silver had said to him earlier: "The Maker is with you, mighty mouse of valor." All he had now was cold and dark silence.

CHAPTER SIX
Warden of the Petticoats

THE royal family was bored. King Halbert was bored with his parties. Queen Halloo was bored with the king. Prince Hal was bored with getting his own way. And Princess Hallee was bored with everyone and everything. No one afterwards could remember who first thought of what turned out to be not such a good idea, but actually it was the general's fault. He had been listening to the king complain for a week that there was simply *nothing* for a gentleman of honor and birth to do, and the general finally said in sheer desperation, "Well, Your Majesty, I suppose you *could* take a tour of the kingdom."

"That is the very thing!" shouted the king.

"Yes," agreed his wife. "Anything to get outside of these four walls."

"Sire," Prince Hal said quickly, "wouldn't this be a good time to review the army in the field? Perhaps we could even watch some of the fighting."

"Splendid suggestion, my boy! If you're going to be a soldier like your father, it's high time you began your preparations." Actually King Halbert's father had been an able soldier, but Halbert's own military experience had consisted of being uncomfortable while sitting still long enough to have his portrait painted in a gorgeous uniform and holding a golden sword. Nevertheless, he always assumed he would be a fierce warrior if he had only had the chance. There had been too much peace during his reign!

They were all somewhat shocked to hear Princess Hallee suddenly announce that *she* would be a member of the party as well. The king frowned and said, "Nonsense! Some things in army camps are simply too gross for you and your court maidens to see or hear."

Prince Hal snorted "Ha!" in agreement, and that, of course, settled it for the princess. Now she just had to go along! So she did what she always did when the king said no—she threw such a tantrum that he gave in after a brief struggle. Then she gave him a kiss and said just the right sweet things so that he felt quite pleased with his firmness and compassion in handling the situation.

Actually they would not be able to leave for almost a week. The waiting ladies had to have new touring clothes, and Prince Hal had to have a set of armor, and Princess Hallee simply would not be seen dead in the old rags she had worn for ages! But after days of preparation, all was ready.

The expedition that finally left was nearly fifty strong with attendants for the royal family, a company of the Royal Guard, friends of the prince and princess, General Woodland, staff officers, and anyone else who could find an excuse to make the trip.

At the army camp, when Major Meadows saw the parade coming he groaned, then put on the best face he could and went to greet the royal party.

"Sire, we are honored to have your Majesties in our camp," he lied with a smile. "I trust you will pardon our second-rate food and uncomfortable lodgings."

"Spare the ceremony, my dear major. I want no ceremony!" The king wheezed as he stepped down from the royal carriage, which was pulled by a pair of hired ground squirrels. "I am an old campaigner myself and am used to the hard life, you know."

"The hard life" consisted that evening of having a small army of cooks set up a kitchen where they prepared a supper worthy of a royal banquet hall. Another crew set up the tents and portable beds and mattresses also worthy of royalty. The family watched real soldiers go through their paces, and by evening they were almost as bored with army life as they had been back in the Royal Burrow.

The prince and princess and their aides wandered about the camp, getting in the way and making a general nuisance of themselves, when they saw a young mouse in chains. "What's this?" inquired the prince. He stood directly in front of the prisoner, who was flanked by two armed guards.

"Who is this, and why is he in chains?" Princess Hallee asked the guards.

"This prisoner will be court-martialed this very evening, Your Majesty."

"Court-martialed? Whatever for?" Princess Hallee asked loudly, taking a step closer, as did the others, not at all mindful of how the prisoner might feel about all the negative attention. To them he was not one who could be offended but was merely a piece of equipment belonging to the Royal Family, as did all the realm.

"Attempted murder is the charge, Your Majesty."

"Murder?" laughed the prince. "He doesn't look dangerous to me." He stepped closer to Chip, placed a small stick under the prisoner's chin, and lifted his head so he could see his face. "Why, he's just a pup." The prince laughed.

"What will they do to him if he's found guilty?" Princess Hallee asked. She had no stick to poke him with, but her condemning stare felt even worse to Chip.

"He'll be executed at sunrise, Your Majesty."

Some of the party gasped, but the prince and the princess merely looked more interested. This certainly wasn't boring. The princess asked Chip directly, "Well, prisoner, what do you have to say for yourself—are you guilty?"

Chip remained silent, and the prince poked him in the ribs with his stick. "Speak up, fellow—the princess speaks to you."

Chip had lost most of his plumpness during his training, and his suddenly blazing eyes seemed dangerous, so much so that the princess and several of her attendants took a step backwards. Chip still did not speak, and the prince grabbed the insolent prisoner's coat. "If you won't speak when you're commanded, I'll have you whipped!"

Chip knew that saying what he was thinking would get him into even more trouble, but he didn't care. "I am sure the whole world will admire the courage of a royal prince who dares to have a helpless prisoner flogged."

The prince went pale, and he began to draw his sword. What would have happened will never be known, for Major Meadows suddenly appeared and intervened.

"I must insist that you have no communication with the prisoner, Your Majesty. It is against military laws." That was not true, but the major was concerned for Chip and could not stand by idly. He had spoken earlier with Chip about what had happened, but he had heard also the testimony of the sergeants and their witnesses. There was no doubt in his mind as to who was lying, but he could only act on clear evidence, and he could not yet see any legal way to free Chip. The major knew that Silver had a special interest in the young recruit, but the prophet was away on one of his unexplained journeys and would be back only when he chose.

"Very well!" Prince Hal said angrily. "But I *insist* on attending the trial."

"That is impossible," said the major.

"Is it?" the prince smiled. "Very little is impossible for a prince, the only son of the king."

Though he didn't like it, not at all, the major knew the prince was right. He tried to prevent the prince's attendance, but the prince told the king, and the king told the general, and . . . So late that night in a large open space underneath a large overhanging rock where they would be safe from owls, Chip was brought out for his court-martial. He was surprised to see not only the small group of officers who customarily hear such cases but over fifty civilians! He saw the triumphant sneer on Prince Hal's face and the look of victory on the face of the princess, and he knew they wanted him punished for his behavior earlier that day.

Major Meadows read the charges quickly, and Sergeant Daggers gave his testimony, which was of course corroborated by Rattle and Blackie word for word. Then the major announced, "Prisoner, you have heard the evidence. You may give your defense."

Private Chip rose and faced the court. He looked straight into the eyes, not of his accusers or his judges, but of the prince and princess of the realm and said in a ringing voice, "I am innocent! I will say no more."

The judges looked at one another. The major said quickly, "Have you no more to say in your defense?"

Chip looked at the major and said sharply, "I have done no wrong."

"Your life is at stake. You must defend yourself," the major said gently.

"What defense is there against liars?" Chip asked as he looked directly at his accusers. "The Maker will be their judge. I have nothing more to say."

After a long, uncomfortable silence the major said with a voice filled with sadness, "In the face of the evidence the court has no choice but to find you guilty. The sentence is death."

There was a silence and then a slight commotion as the princess ran to her father and whispered in his ear. The king shook his head, but she persisted, and finally a small indulgent smile appeared on his face. He rose to his feet and said, "Major, you have done your duty. You have shown justice. Now as the king of the land I will show mercy. Prisoner, you have been condemned to death. At the request of my daughter, the Princess Hallee, I am changing your sentence. You will not die."

"But, Your Majesty," General Woodland said with concern and a touch of irritation, "this will set a bad example for future court-martials. If we let this white-foot get away with . . ."

"General, I have made my decision." The king was now using a tone of voice that everyone knew meant "Shut up! I have made up my mind!" The general quickly sat down.

"So is the prisoner to be set free, Your Majesty?" asked the major.

"Absolutely not. Not at all. As the general indicated, that would encourage similar offenses. No, no, he is to be assigned to a new office, a new task, and he will fulfill his duties or the sentence of death will yet be carried out."

"And what is the office he will fill, my king?" the major asked.

The king said with a mischievous smile, "He will become the Warden of the Petticoats!"

The young females who served the princess giggled and nudged Princess Hallee. The prince's followers laughed out loud. Chip, who had been ready for death, went blind with anger at this humiliating turn of events.

"The Warden of the Petticoats will be in charge of the wardrobes of the ladies of the court. He will also be available to do any small services they might require."

"I won't do it!" Chip suddenly cried out. "I'd rather die!"

"Shut up, you young fool!" the major whispered furiously. "At least they're letting you live!" He turned to the court. "It shall be done, Your Majesty. The prisoner would like to thank you and the princess, of course, for your mercy." He nudged Chip viciously. "Do it, soldier. You must make the best of a difficult situation, Master Chip."

Though it was indeed the hardest act of Chip's life, he walked straight to the king and said with his head bowed, "Sire, I thank you for your great mercy." Then he walked over to Princess Hallee and bowed even lower. He picked up the hem of her gown and gave it a ceremonial kiss, then looked right into her face. The crowd had fallen completely silent, and he waited so long that the princess grew a little frightened. Finally he spoke. "I thank you for your gracious mercy, My Princess. Let all the world take note that we have in our kingdom a princess who is not only lovely and learned but who is filled with generosity and kindness."

Chip's gracious words, even if a bit insincere, somehow made the princess feel ashamed. She turned swiftly and ran from the scene. From that point on, whenever she thought of that moment, she felt as if she had been on trial and not Chip.

CHAPTER SEVEN
The Royal Tournament

TROOPER, as usual, was eating when Silver walked hurriedly into the squad room. "Ah, I have not seen you in so long, my fran. You 'ave heard of our young fran Cheep?"

Silver did not look worried as he glanced around the room. "Yes, the major just told me about it. How's the lad taking it, Trooper?"

Trooper swallowed the last fried grasshopper and began nibbling at some wheat that lay close to his bunk. "I tell you, Meester Seelvair, first 'ting I say is dat Cheep gonna *die* with humiliation. Ho ho!" The tiny shrew laughed heartily. "Dat princess, she make heem do dis, den do anodder theeng til

Cheep he about go crazy. Every day he come back and say, 'I can't stan it no more!' But he keep on makin' heemself do it."

"He's very proud, you know."

"Sure, like me. You know what he do? Every day when dey feenish wid him at the court, he come to camp and get his sword, and he practice, practice, practice!" Trooper jumped up and whipped out his own tiny sword to demonstrate. "Lunge—parry—sweep—over and over until he nearly drop! And you know what, Meester Seelvair? He get so *good* with dat blade he beat de instructor!"

Silver relaxed with a faint smile. "That's good news. I was afraid—"

"You was afraid he maybe run off, no?" Trooper said with a wink. "Not dis one. He stubborn as can be! Hey, we go see heem now, no? Come on." He jumped up and led the seer to the section of the camp reserved for sword practice. They heard the clash of blades and soon saw Chip giving instruction to one of the advanced students.

"How you like dat, eh?" Trooper whispered in delight. "Cheep is de best blade in da whole camp. Better even dan *me*!"

Silver nodded, and when the other recruit was dismissed he said softly, "Hello, Chip."

"Silver!" Chip's face lit up, and he dropped the sword into the sheath and ran to greet his old friend. "Where have you been?"

"Official business," Silver answered. "I hear you've had a busy time of it." He looked at the young cadet and saw lines that had not been part of his face a few days earlier. "I have been proud of the reports I've received about you."

"Oh," Chip said awkwardly. "Well, it's not—it's not *too* bad." He walked around, avoiding the prophet's glance. "The princess and those females had a lot of fun teasing me at first, but I just did everything they asked without a fuss, so they got tired of mocking me. I don't really do much at the court anymore."

"And Prince Hal?" Silver asked softly.

"Well, he doesn't like me much."

"And you, Chip? How do you feel about him, or about what's happened?"

"What difference does it make? I'm just a common soldier, and he's the prince." He attempted to change the subject. "How are things going—with the enemy, I mean?"

"Not at all well," Silver said. "In fact, it couldn't be much worse. I expect you'll see action soon."

"We weel be magneeficent!" Trooper cried out, pulling furiously at his sweeping mustache. "But first, my frans, we have a leedle fon, ease eet not so?"

"Fun?" asked Chip, acting as if he had almost forgotten the word.

"Ease eet not the Royal Tournament, Cheep? And weel we in our squad not win all the best prizes, eh? Weel we not show these puppies what eet ease to be a real soldair?"

Silver suggested with a small smile, "I think you might be interested in the Order of the Blade, Chip, my son."

"What's that?"

"The most important prize of all—a sack of gold and a gold medal for the best swordsman in the realm."

"Well, I'm not that good." Chip shook his head.

"Cheep, do not think so. Eef you want it bad enough, you will ween eet!" Trooper cried shrilly.

"I don't think I want to enter," Chip said. "There is no reason to do so."

Silver added with a twinkle in his eye, "There's a little more to it, Chip. The award will be presented by the Princess Hallee—and she has to proclaim the winner to be the most noble blade in all the kingdom."

Chip said nothing, but his eyes began to glow, and a firm look about his mouth said more than his words. "Well, maybe I should compete—for the honor of the squad, you know."

"For the honair of the squad, yes, eet ease so," Trooper cried out. All the way back to the squad room he kept listing the honors and prizes he planned to bring home from the tournament.

†

The day had come, and it felt like a holiday in spite of the crisis at the West Border. Flags and new clothes could be seen everywhere one looked. Small bands had been playing, and singing had been heard day and night leading up to the tournament. Somehow the necessary work still got done, but the tournament was ever the topic of conversation.

On the day of competition, Chip's squad brought itself great glory. They won the tug-of-war, mostly because Budger was so big, no other squad could pull him and his friends across the line! The Rag-Tags came in second in tracking, and first in the climbing drill. Singer won second place in archery, despite facing competitors who had much more experience than he. Chip made it all the way to the finals in swordsmanship, and late in the day he stood before the other finalist—a scarred veteran of many battles who glared at him as if he were some sort of beginner who didn't even deserve to be in the finals. In fact, the entire army and the court and all the spectators were amazed at the unexpected success of the young soldier.

"I don't understand it myself," Budger said to those standing near him. "I mean, Chip, I know you're good with a sword, but you're so inexperienced. For you to be in the finals, well, it's not—logical."

Silver touched Budger's arm and whispered for his ears only, "Perhaps, my learned friend, there are more things in heaven and earth than you have ever dreamed possible."

"Humph!" sniffed Budger. "We'll see about that. I know about his opponent—a tricky swordsman if ever there was one! It'll take a miracle for Chip to get past him—and I don't believe in miracles!"

At the signal to begin, the older soldier, whose name was

Mace, attacked with such fury that the crowd gasped. He was like a maniac, moved to frenzied action by the rage of battle.

"That ease not play!" Trooper said angrily. "He is out to keel the boy!" Trooper started to join the fray, but Silver pulled him back.

"Let it go," the prophet said. "The rules must be followed. If Chip can just last a while, he'll win—no one can keep up the pace his opponent is waging."

Chip fell back before the onslaught, almost helpless under a shower of deadly blows. His opponent seemed to have a dozen blades, and Chip could not even think about going on the attack—staying alive for one more moment was all he could hope for at the moment. He parried and dodged and tried to think of a way to get control of the battle. Slowly his enemy's attack lost some of its fury, and Chip began to hold his own. Mace's eyes eventually glazed over with weariness, and his arm began to get tired. *If he tries one more of these high lunges*, Chip thought, *I think I can get in a hard thrust.* He continued to defend himself, patiently awaiting the hoped-for move, and when it came, Chip was ready. He parried the lunge, and in one movement he shot forward and gently placed Durance on Mace's throat. "Yield!" The cry rang from his throat.

Mace hesitated only an instant, then acknowledged that he had no choice but to accept defeat. "I yield," he said reluctantly.

"For the king and for the Burrow!" Chip shouted as loudly as he could. Early in the fight he was certain he would be beaten, but now victory was his. He knew the Maker had helped him—there could be no other explanation.

Hearing the cry of the winner, amazed at what they had just witnessed, every soldier echoed Chip's cry, making the air shake. "For the king and for the Burrow!"

Silver cried out in a voice louder than any, "For Chip—Chip of the Burrow!"

The rest should have been so simple. All that was left was for Chip to walk over to Princess Hallee and receive the prize.

But then something shameful happened. Princess Hallee, dreading the humiliation of having to publicly reward the white-foot she had enjoyed mocking, said audibly, "I *won't* do it! I will not give *him* honor!"

Her brother, Prince Hal, wanted to support the princess in her defiance. Leaping in front of Chip he said, "I challenge you for the honor of the blade." This was a grave and dreadful error. In the first place he was not eligible for the tournament and so could not issue such a challenge. In the second place to challenge a soldier when exhausted by the labor of a battle just concluded was just not done. And worst of all Prince Hal drew his sword and lunged at Chip without a word of warning.

A gasp went up from the crowd, and Chip barely had time to raise Durance and fend off the Prince's blade. Chip would wish many times afterwards that the incident had stopped right there, but the prince's lunge carried him further forward, right onto Chip's blade. Chip felt his sword enter Prince Hal's breast and saw a sudden rush of scarlet stain the prince's white jacket. Chip couldn't breathe.

There was an awful silence as the prince slumped to the ground, blood spreading like a hideous scarlet flower over his chest.

The king rose and ran to his son. As he held the prince's head, he looked wildly at Chip and screamed, "Arrest the traitor! He has murdered the crown prince of the realm!"

Within moments, Chip of the Burrow found himself, for the second time in his brief life, in a dungeon awaiting trial and execution.

CHAPTER EIGHT
A New Hope

NEVER had anyone seen King Halbert so angry! Indeed, his temper raged so furiously that his attendants feared he might have a heart attack. "Execute the traitor!" he roared over and over again. "Are we to allow rebels to strike at the royal throne and go scot-free? Execute the traitor!"

"But, Your Majesty," Silver said, "the prince isn't dead. He is badly wounded, but he is still alive."

"You mean we're going to let that traitor go free just because the prince might get well? I am glad my son lives, but . . ." the king screamed illogically.

"Have no fear, sire," General Woodland snorted. "If Prince

Hal dies, I'll have the traitor's head set on display for the entire world to see."

Silver shook his head and whispered to Major Meadows, "This is dangerous business. How badly is the prince injured?"

"I don't know," the major said. "The women are swarming over him so much, it's hard to tell. But I don't think his wound is fatal. The young bully! I'll venture he's the most spoiled brat who ever stood in line for the crown."

"I'll go see to him," Silver murmured. "I have some skill in these matters. You stay close to the king and keep him from cutting poor Chip's head off before morning." He hurried down the tunnel, now crowded with confused white-feet all trying to look important. When he arrived at the royal apartments, he found an assortment of doctors disagreeing violently on the treatment of the young prince and a covey of females who wrung their hands and generally got in the way. With effort he made his way through them all and stood beside Prince Hal's bed. Drawing the prince's garments aside, he examined the wound carefully. His face brightened, and he said, "Bring me some boiling water."

Once it arrived, he took a leather pouch from his inner pocket and removed several leaves, then crumbled them and dropped them into the water. Despite onlookers' cries of alarm he helped the prince into a sitting position and held the tea under his nose. The first moment Hal breathed the aroma, he opened his eyes, and a cry of delight went up from the queen. "Sip some of this, My Prince," Silver commanded. After two or three swallows the prince sat up with a new light of alert concentration in his eyes. "I'm all right, My Lady," he said to his mother, and she broke down in a glad series of sobs.

Meanwhile, as Silver was seeing to the prince of the realm, in the deepest dungeon of the Royal Burrow, Private Chip was receiving attention from the Princess of the White-feet, attention he would have rather done without.

Princess Hallee had demanded entrance so she could see

"the vile traitor," and Chip, sitting on the single stool in the tiny room, stood up to face a barrage of charges.

"You—you murderer!" the princess cried. "I wish I had let them cut your beastly head off after your court-martial!" She was so furious, assuming her brother had died, that she could hardly speak. "I wish I hadn't shown you mercy before. Now my—my b-bro-brother . . ." The princess fell onto the cot, beating it with her tiny paws and crying inconsolably. She wanted to throw something at Chip, but her sorrow was overwhelming.

Chip felt terrible! As far as he knew, he *had* killed the prince, for so he had been told, and he knew no reason to believe otherwise. He stood helplessly, a forlorn figure. Finally he cleared his throat and said hesitantly, "Perhaps he won't die, princess. I—I hope not. I'm not a murderer . . . I . . ."

She wiped the tears from her eyes. "But you *are* a murderer! You are!" She rushed out of the cell, and he could hear her shouting, "I hope they cut your head off, you traitor!"

Slowly Chip sat down on the cot, the darkness of the dungeon adding to the deep sorrow in his heart. He felt defeated and alone. He longed to be back in his burrow with the rest of the Rag-Tags—anything to be out of this desperate situation! He sat there for what seemed like hours, each one more gloomy than the last. He was tempted to throw himself on the cot and cry like a pup, but he did not. He sat trying to endure the loneliness and fear that threatened to overwhelm him. Later he would perhaps face something worse—torture or even death. But sitting in the silent darkness, not knowing his fate—he couldn't imagine feeling more abandoned than he felt right now.

Chip lay down but had little hope of sleeping. Nevertheless, he soon began to doze, and suddenly he heard a voice. It seemed to come from far away, and it was the most gentle—and yet the strongest—voice he'd ever heard. He opened his eyes, and there in the cell he saw someone dimly. He could make out little of the man, for he was clothed in brilliant light.

I'm dreaming, Chip thought. He tried to move but could not, and that frightened him.

"Who—who are you?" he whispered.

"Can you not guess?"

Chip blinked at the shining figure but could only shake his head. "I don't know," he said finally.

"I am the Maker, Chip."

Chip felt so afraid, and yet so excited, that he was afraid his heart would stop beating. Surely this had to be a dream! He managed to gasp, "Why do you—why are you appearing to me?"

"To give you courage. I have great tasks for you, my son, so do not fear. You will not die, for I have chosen you to be My servant."

Chip blinked with astonishment, and then he suddenly found that he could move again. He leaped to his feet and peered around the dark cell. "Maker?" he whispered, but there was no answer.

Finally there was a very tiny sound, and light came into his cell as the door opened just a crack, then swung open. Chip turned, expecting the executioner. But then he heard a familiar voice.

"Cheep? Eet ease me—Trooper!" The tiny shrew sprang into the room, and behind him were the rest of the Rag-Tags—Budger, Peedee, Singer, and Ben. They all crowded into the cell and pounded his back and chest as they excitedly cried, "Here we are!" "No fear, recruit, we'll take care of you."

Chip's throat was uncomfortably dry, and he had trouble seeing because he was so overcome with emotion. After clearing his throat he questioned, "What on earth are you doing here?"

"Why, we are breaking you out of here," Budger said calmly. "And I think we'd best hurry. That guard won't be out for very long."

Chip looked out and saw the guard stretched out on the floor. "Is he—is he dead?" he asked timidly.

"No. I only bite heem a leetle." Trooper grinned. "Pretty soon he be wakin' up again."

"But—but you can't do this," Chip said. "This is treason! We'll all end up in the dungeon!"

After a moment of silence, Budger replied, "I reckon this is one of those times Silver talked about. Common sense and reason didn't bring us here, but you're our friend, so here we are!"

"Indeed!" Silver said, and he stepped inside so quickly that none of them could move. He glanced at Budger with a smile. "You're going to have to revise your philosophy if you keep on being this 'unreasonable,' friend."

"Silver," Chip said, "the prince is dead, isn't he?"

"No, nor likely to be. But some of *you* probably will be if you don't get out of here. Now you five had better get going!"

"But what about Chip?" Peedee asked.

"He'll be all right, I promise. You get out of here while I try to think of some way to cause that guard to think he's had a nightmare. Quickly now! You'll have Chip back soon—I promise."

There was a hurried exodus as they left, and Silver said, "Chip, how are you? Have you been afraid?"

Chip dipped his head and said, "Yes." He thought about it for a moment, then added, "But I didn't give in to it!" He thought about telling Silver about the vision he'd had, but somehow he knew that was meant for him alone.

Silver clapped him on the shoulder and gave a sudden laugh. "That's my brave fellow! Now, it will take a while, and there will be some difficulties to work out with the king, but you must leave here, Chip. Your training is over; now you will begin your work."

"Will you be there—wherever I go?"

"I will never be too far from you, Chip, though at times you may not see me."

"Silver," Chip confessed, "as I've been sitting here, I got to wondering about it all—I mean about all you've said and the mission and the Maker and all of that." He said slowly, "Well, I got to wondering if it was really true or if it was just people's ideas or wishes or coincidence or something."

Silver grew still, and his penetrating eyes looked deep into the young white-foot's face. "Well, my son, what have you decided? Is there a Maker or not?"

"Yes, there's a Maker all right. I don't really understand it all, but I know that something's happening, and I—I feel like I'm a part of something bigger than anything I've ever imagined. Before you led me away from my father's home, I did a lot of dreaming. But this is different—this is based on who the Maker really is and what He has shown us about Himself and His plan."

Silver nodded slowly. "You will do great exploits, Chip. You will walk in paths of wonderful light. But remember these dark hours because there will be others, perhaps even darker. You will get through these, and you will get through those." He turned, went to the door, and pulled it shut without another word. Chip sat down on the stool. But this time there was a song in his heart, and it soon rose to his lips. There in the darkness Chip of the Burrow knew the Maker was real and that he would serve Him forever.

For several days there was still talk of executing the prisoner, but the miraculous recovery of the prince made that seem less and less advisable or just. Certainly something must be done to Chip, but what? Finally there was a hearing in the Council Room. Chip was there with Silver standing by his side, and the king ranted and raved until he had to take a large glass of beet wine to calm his nerves.

The king insisted, "I want this dangerous criminal placed back in his dungeon until we go to war, and then he is to be assigned to the most dangerous section of the fighting, where he can either help bring victory to his nation or die in payment for the suffering he has brought to the royal family!"

Major Meadows and Silver glanced at each other with a grim nod, and then Silver said, "Your Majesty, we have news for you."

"What news? What is it?" the king demanded.

"We have just received a message, Your Majesty," Silver said. "The war has begun."

"What!" demanded General Woodland. "Why wasn't I informed?"

"The messenger only got here five minutes ago, general," the major said. He handed him the message.

"Why—why, this says we have been overrun at almost every position, and our territories have been invaded in force by the brown rats!" He looked dazed as he continued, "There must be some mistake."

"I'm afraid not, general," the major said. "The war is on, and we are all in great danger. We must move at once, for they are marching toward the Royal Burrow even now."

A cry of fear sped around the room, but Silver's clear voice cut through it like a knife. "We must not panic! Are we not white-feet? Let us defend our kingdom! Your Majesty, we will indeed place this young soldier in the front lines as you have decreed, where he and many others like him will no doubt die for our cause." He looked around and said more softly as he placed his hand on Chip's shoulder, "Who knows, friends, perhaps he has come to the kingdom for such a time as this?"

As the officers left at a run, all heard the sound of rapid drums and blowing bugles.

The war had indeed begun. A threat that few had taken seriously now loomed over the kingdom like an evil and monstrous presence, and no one—not even Silver—knew how it would end.

PART TWO

Warrior Under Fire

CHAPTER NINE
Battle Tested

ALL the maneuvers during their training had been orderly and with no effort wasted, but the Rag-Tags, and all the other raw troops, soon learned that war is not very much like training camp at all. They had learned how to march, but their leaders always knew exactly where they were going, and nothing got in their way. But now the entire group of reserves rushed to the west, sometimes actually cutting each other off in their haste, sometimes not sure if they were even going in the right direction as they made their way to the Royal Army, which was holding the enemy back by sheer determination. But somehow they all made it to the deadly destination.

All night long they had driven straight across the fields at the fastest pace they could keep up. To keep the men going, the sergeants slapped them with their swords—not in a way that would injure anyone, but enough to keep them moving at breakneck speed. Across creeks that were so cold their teeth shook—up hills that took all the wind out of their lungs—through thickets they hoped didn't contain a hungry wolf just waiting for tender white-feet—all through the night, with only a few brief stops, the troops drove toward the west gap at top speed.

When they finally stopped for more than a minute or two, most of the cadets fell to the ground to rest. Budger and Trooper began pulling food out of their packs, chatting away as if they had enjoyed a moderate evening stroll.

"Do you have anything fit to drink, Trooper?" Budger asked. "I have plenty of dried grubs and some fresh berries, but all I have for liquid refreshment is some of that old ale from last season."

"No, I have nutheeng but this rainwater they call wine—fah!" exclaimed Trooper. "Who haves some good wine, eh?"

After a long silence Peedee gasped, "I—I've got—some of that—good wine—we had last night—but I'm too tired to move."

"That ease good wine," Trooper exclaimed as he hopped over to retrieve Peedee's water bag. "You better eat now, my frans. Eet may be a long time before we rest again."

"We can't go on like this," Singer complained. "We'll all be dead before we get to the blasted war!"

"Don't be too concerned about that," Budger said as he tossed huge chunks of meat down his throat. "I suspect we're very close to the front line now. They're letting us rest and eat here before we go into battle."

The cadets were quiet, all thinking more or less the same thing. Finally Chip forced himself to say, "Budger, you and Trooper have been in battle before, but none of the rest of us have. What—I mean—what will happen—what if we . . . ?" He stammered around, unable to finish his question.

"I expect you're all thinking what everybody thinks the first time they go into a battle—will I fight or run away?" Budger didn't wait for a reply but continued quietly, "Some will run, some won't. There's no way to tell what one will do when he faces bare steel. But when you're actually in the battle, you'll probably do what you were trained to do without thinking about it much."

"There is dangair, oh yes, but there ease also the glory!" exclaimed Trooper. "The clash of the steel, the parry, the thrust! Ah!" He kissed his tiny paw eloquently. "Eet ease a life of bravery and honor, no? And if eet ease my time to die, then I have no worry for the next battle, ease eet not so?"

The sergeant soon began to call them back to the march with his shrill cries, and complaining they fell into rough lines and floundered on through the last shreds of darkness. Soon the east behind them was streaked with red, and the light grew stronger as they drove westward almost at a run.

Much sooner than they'd hoped, they heard the first sounds of battle—steel on steel, faint but clearly ringing through the morning's air. Chip's heart began to beat faster as the sounds grew louder. He wasn't sure if he was excited or afraid.

"Ready now, lads," the sergeant shouted. "Close ranks—stand close together, lads—closer now. That's the way!"

Looking around, Chip realized he was boxed in. In front of him was a squad of cadets he didn't know, to his right and left the other members of the Rag-Tags marched proudly, and behind him he heard the scrambling of many other white-feet. All were moving forward, kept in place by the shouted commands of the officers and sergeants, and Chip knew he could not run away even if he wanted to. Strangely enough, that was a sort of comfort to him, for he dreaded nothing so much as being a coward in front of his comrades, perhaps even endangering them by his fear.

His world had narrowed down to the ground immediately in front of him and to either side. The majesty of the trees, the dew-dripping flowers, and the innocence of lively bees landing on tall flowers—such beauty in a scene of battle and death struck him strangely. *I don't think I'll ever take a flower for granted again—if I live through this*, Chip thought.

Suddenly the cadets around him parted like water that had struck a rock. In between the two streams of recruits Chip saw a dead white-foot. His eyes were open but were covered with a fine layer of dust. His front forepaw was stiffly raised in a salute, and beside his mouth a red ant was carrying some sort of burden. The stench of death could almost be felt by the cadets, but then they saw other bodies too—some of them enemies, some of them not. Some of the dead had limbs raised as if in devout prayer. Chip felt too afraid to go on, and yet unwilling to go back. Fighting against their evil foe was no longer a possibility—the time was here.

Without warning, they marched over a small rise, and there before them Chip saw a field of blood. All along the floor of a small ravine, dotted at intervals with blooming flowers, two waves of warriors were face to face in a death struggle. The brown rats wore red uniforms and helmets marked by a red circle around a pile of bones. Many of them lay still, dead or nearly so, but others were driving fiercely at a thin line of white-foot soldiers, who were slowly falling back as they left bleeding comrades lying on the ground. Seeing that the brown rats were overrunning the position, Major Meadows cried out, "Sound the charge! Archers, keep them busy ducking your arrows so we can attack! Recruits, line up in full ranks! Prepare to advance!"

A tinny cry of many tiny horns sang like the hums of huge insects, and the reserves surged forward as one mighty beast. A hail of arrows whistled through the air, and all along the line red-clad rats fell to the ground. The more experienced soldiers held out their heavy blades, and the first wave of brown rats attempting to resist were pierced at once. Chip saw the front ranks of white-feet disappear among the foe, cutting and hacking like mad. He wasn't sure whether he should follow them into the frenzy or lag behind. Suddenly a large rat waving a bloody sword stood in his path, towering over him. Chip saw eyes red with fury focus on him, and he felt powerless to move as the sword began to swing toward him. Then a tiny form jumped in front of Chip, and Trooper attacked the enemy with his razor-sharp sword. A thin, red line appeared on the rat's throat. He dropped his sword and grabbed his wound. He fell to the ground, kicked wildly for a moment, then was dreadfully still.

"Now, Cheep, you do eet like that." Trooper's grin helped Chip to not be so afraid. He saw Peedee giving ground before a huge rat. His friend was in the same perilous situation he had been in moments earlier. Chip lunged and watched his blade disappear into the furry breast of the enemy. The light in the rat's eyes went dark, and he gurgled once, then fell to the ground. Now Chip knew what he must do, and he fought with confidence and boldness. Parry, guard, thrust—over and over he met the charge of the enemy. He saw a rat getting the best of Ben and thought, *I can take care of him with one stroke, then take a sweep at the pair that have Budger tied up*. Soon he found that the path before him was all clear, and the Rag-Tags were cheering his name. "Hooray for Chip of the Rag-Tags!" Suddenly realizing that no enemies were at hand, he looked around and saw that the tide had turned—the enemies had turned tail and were in total disarray in their retreat.

Trooper was trying to persuade the officers they should pursue them, but the order came to take up positions in the gap instead, and all of them set to work at once digging in.

The sergeant came by and asked, "Everybody all right? Any wounds?" Aside from a few bruises or cuts received during the scramble to the front, none of the Rag-Tags had a scratch. In their excitement they all began to talk loudly, as if everyone were deaf. "Did you see Budger when he got pinned up against a tree?" "No, I wasn't running away—I just got confused!" "We showed those rats, didn't we?" There was also a great deal of scuffling and rude joking in the manner of adolescents who want to blow off steam. It was, Chip would realize later, always the same after every battle, no matter how many a soldier had been in.

They worked hard all morning, moving large stones to use as barricades, constructing platforms for the archers to sweep the gap in case of a fresh attack, and, the detail they had all already grown to hate, taking care of their dead comrades. Collecting the weapons and gear and putting the bodies into a deep gulch took more courage than to charge the enemy line. They were sad at their friends' loss of life but were also proud and appreciative of their sacrifice.

"Do you think the rats will be back again?" Chip asked Budger as they lay down in the shadow of a boulder late that afternoon.

"You can count on it, Chip," Budger said sleepily. "Maybe not tonight, but from what I hear, they seem to have an endless supply of troops. No one can figure out where those rats are coming from. Or why they're invading our condee."

"We'll beat 'em," Peedee said shrilly. "Why, when we showed 'em what we're made of today, they ran away."

"Yes, but they were caught off guard. They know we're here now, and I'd say that by tomorrow they'll be back with a striking force big enough to give us more trouble than we can imagine."

"I wonder if it's like this all along the border?" Chip said.

"Pretty much the same, I hear," Budger said. "I can't see that we've got much of a chance—unless—"

"Unless what?" Chip asked.

"Oh, I don't know. Unless *something* happens, I guess. They've got us outnumbered pretty badly. They're larger than we are too. There's no reason why we *should* win—unless we get . . . lucky."

They all thought about that, and then Chip said, "Budger, I know it looks pretty bad, but I'll bet we *will* win!"

"That's right, Chip." Budger nodded. "Put a good face on it. We'll just do our duty—that's the line to take."

Singer said suddenly, "You know, I was talking to one of the squirrels today, after the battle, and you know what he said? He said there's an invasion of all kinds of animals, not just the brown rats. He said that there's a bunch of squirrels that are moving in, and you know what? They wear the same kind of helmet with the circle and bones that all the rats have."

"Really?" Budger responded. "I wonder what that could mean? Nothing good I expect."

Late that night Major Meadows came into their area and talked with them briefly. He always liked to visit cadets after their first action, and he wanted to compliment the squad on how well they'd performed. "I was watching you today," he said warmly. "Good job, all of you. You're doing well, Chip. Yesterday in the dungeon, today a hero!"

"That's right, Chip," Singer teased. "How many folks did you jab with that sword before the war?"

"Two of 'em, wasn't it?" added Ben. "Counting them both, that is?"

"Now, now," the major said with a pat on Chip's shoulder. "Never mind them. You did well, Chip. I'm beginning to understand why Silver was so interested in making you a part of our unit. As a matter of fact, I have some news for you, for all of you. Your corporal is leaving you—I'm sending him over to replace one we lost in another squad. Now who would you all like for your new corporal?" The major was a strong believer in letting units choose their own leaders, and he felt pretty sure who their choice would be. He had seen the fire in Chip's eyes during the battle, and he knew that leaders are born leaders.

"Chip! Chip!" They all caught up the cry, and as he began to protest, Budger smiled and held up his hand. "I nominate Chip of the Burrow as corporal. All in favor, so indicate. Unanimous! Congratulations, Corporal Chip of the Rag-Tags!"

Chip stood there helplessly, but inside he felt proud, and as his friends cried his name he made a silent vow. *I'll never let them down. Death first!* He whipped out Durance and cried out shrilly, "To the Rag-Tags—together to the end!"

And that became their motto, their creed, and their battle cry. They all raised their blades high and said as one voice, "To the Rag-Tags—together to the end!"

So it was that a legend was born.

CHAPTER TEN
The Perils of Pride

BUDGER had been wrong. Over a week went by without another attack by the enemy. The white-feet managed to strengthen their defenses and enlarge their quarters but otherwise avoided work as much as possible, which, according to Trooper, was the practice of soldiers everywhere.

Silver visited them late one night with news. He appeared, as usual, without warning as they sat around a fire.

"What sort of guard is this when someone can walk right up to your camp without you knowing it?" he said with mock severity. "Corporal Chip, is this the way you command your squad?"

"The enemy is still over there and not over here, sire," Chip said, pointing at the gap. "Sit down and tell us whatever news you can."

"Sit down? Gladly. I've walked many a step today." He helped himself to some of the stew and then began to tell them about the battles along the front. "The enemy is strongest in this area, though there have been a few attacks to the north. We think they won't try to get across the river there, for our defenses are strong. Right here at the West Gap is where the main battle will be."

"When?" Chip said quickly.

"I don't know," Silver said. "Major Meadows has been expecting it for several days. He thinks they may be waiting for us to attack them."

"Ees 'zactly what we *should* do!" Trooper said forcefully. "Sweep the swine back into the reever!"

Silver listened to the cry of approval by the others. "What do *you* think, corporal?" They all turned to hear the new corporal's reply.

"Well, I'm no expert, but I don't believe in doing what the enemy *wants* us to do. I say we should dig in, and when they cross the gap we can cut them down without risking too much."

Budger nodded approval. "True! We've got the right mouse for our corporal, eh?"

Silver nodded slowly, and his eyes gleamed as he regarded Chip fondly. "Yes, I'd say so." Then he got up and said, "General Woodland will be here tomorrow with the main force."

"What's his plan? Do you know, sire?" Chip asked.

"I'm not sure, but—well, the general may be a bit hasty. There's been a lot of pressure at home to get on with the war. The general wants a quick victory, and that's usually dangerous."

"Aye, dangerous for us!" Budger agreed. He grinned at Silver. "But as long as the Maker is with us, all will be well, eh?"

Silver knew Budger didn't really believe in the Maker and just wanted an argument, but he refused to take the bait. He simply answered, "Good fortune to you all," and then he was gone as suddenly as he had come. For a long time they sat there without saying a word. Finally, reluctantly, one by one they dropped off to sleep, each thinking of home and the dangerous adventures they would soon face.

†

The general arrived at dawn with row after row of fresh troops, all arrayed in new uniforms and marching stiffly. "Now, sir, here are some *real* soldiers!" he bellowed at Major Meadows. "See how well they keep in line? Much better than your rag-tag slouches!"

"Well, general," the major said, "they look impressive, and we can certainly use them here. I suggest that we reinforce the lines heavily here at the West Gap , for this, in my judgment, is where the main attack will—"

"Reinforce?" The general swelled up like a huge frog. "Reinforce indeed! I have not brought my army here to reinforce anything!" He raised his voice loudly enough for all the troops to hear him and pointed directly at the gap. "The enemy is over there, and that is where I intend to meet him, sir!" A cheer went up from the army he had brought, and he lifted his hat in a token of recognition.

"But, general, surely you don't plan to attack?" the major asked.

"Certainly, and at once! We have come to teach these villains a lesson, and we will. After today there'll be no rat left alive in our land. Now, are your men ready for the attack?"

"General," the major said earnestly, "I know you have authority over me and that I am responsible to obey your orders, but I beg you not to do this. If we wait until the enemy comes through the gap, we can cut him to pieces—easily—with hardly any loss at all to our forces."

"I see you prefer to sit here and pretend to be a soldier of war, major! Go ahead. But I am not made of such poor stuff, nor are my men. Are you ready?" he bellowed out at the top of his lungs, and his army answered him with a well-rehearsed cry. "We are ready, general!"

"Sound the charge," the general commanded. Without further ado the charge rang out, and the army, led by the general in his carriage, moved forward. The major and his forces remained where they were.

It was, they all admitted later, the most magnificent sight of the entire war. Usually the war was fought in small actions or in deeply wooded country, but here the entire army was visible as it marched across the flat ground into the gap, exactly as they had been doing for weeks on the flat ground of the training camp. The sun caught their swords as they were raised in salute, and every soldier was in step as the army marched in perfect cadence toward the enemy. Up to the gap they went, and through it. But suddenly from the other side came the sound of horns. The major saw waves of red-clad rats attack the general's force from both sides. Like grain being cut by a huge scythe, the white-feet fell in large numbers. Troops specially trained for close fighting hit the general's army with full force, catching the bewildered general and his officers off guard.

Major Meadows called out, "Officers, get your troops up to the gap! Quickly now!" Chip got his squad into position as the attacked white-feet returned to the gap at a dead run.

"Get into the high places," Chip ordered. "We can get them as they come through." They began to find logs and rocks to use for cover as the frightened troops, led by the general himself, came back through the gap in wild retreat. General Woodland was white-eyed as he urged his driver to get the squirrels to pull the carriage faster. Just behind him came evil rats with the red circle and bones. They came at a full run with blood lust in their eyes. If the major had not been there with his troops, it would have been a sad day for the kingdom. The general had made a tragic error.

As it was, the brown rats ran into the arrows of the well-hidden Rag-Tags and other squads. They fell in waves, clutching the arrows that pierced their throats and chests, and then were suddenly swarmed by hundreds of what appeared to be demented white-feet screaming with rage. But above all the rest could be heard, "Rag-Tags! Rag-Tags! Together to the end!" For long afterwards the white-feet soldiers remembered a vision of a huge mouse, an insane shrew, and a corporal called Chip who swept the field and led a countercharge that forced the rats to retreat. In fact, the enemy lost more in the field that day than they had during the entire war. And it was the reports of that battle that caused the burly commander of the brown rats to put a bounty on the head of Corporal Chip of the Rag-Tags.

The general, humiliated and terrified, had not stopped at the field camp but had rushed all the way back to the safety of the Royal Burrow, where he spent a great deal of time telling the king how the day had gone against them and that it was perhaps time to talk with the enemy and make compromises for the sake of peace—a suggestion that disgusted both the prince and princess. "Compromise!" raged Prince Hal, now fully recovered. "Never! I think it is time for me to join the forces at the front, along with my friends, the Black Cavaliers! We'll win this war!"

The Black Cavaliers were young nobility who'd had some training but mostly liked to dress up in fancy black uniforms and run around the countryside pretending to be heroes and getting into mischief. But in their own mind they were great soldiers, and the prince figured he might as well take advantage of that to gain himself some fame in the war.

"You'll be careful, won't you, Hal?" Hallee asked quickly.

"You've been wounded in peace, and you haven't actually had any experience fighting a war."

That was the wrong thing to say, for it pricked the prince's pride. "If that—that *peasant* can fight, I would think a royal prince can do even more." He turned and walked away, and Hallee was seeing for the first time that war was not the game she had considered it. Her heart ached with worry and fear.

All might have gone well if Major Meadows had been in camp when Hal arrived at the West Gap. He would have been able to restrain the fiery young prince. But he was away inspecting various units at other locations. Only a relatively low-ranking officer with a weak will was there when the prince came charging in obviously wanting to see some action.

The Black Cavaliers did look impressive with their fine uniforms and silver helmets. It so happened that Chip and several of his squad were posted on watch that day, and the prince picked him out at once.

None of the Rag-Tags took any notice of what they wore, and their group name described their appearance. Hard use had honed them down to a fine fighting trim, but they looked scroungy to the prince.

The prince and Chip looked at each other, and Chip tried to make matters more bearable. He gave a very correct salute to the prince and then said cheerfully, "Welcome, My Prince. We are glad to see you and your forces. Can I make you comfortable until Major Meadows returns?"

The prince studied him and then curled his lips and said insolently, "See to the needs of my troops. Food and drink for all." Chip bit his lip, then said respectfully, "Yes, sir. If you'll follow me, I'll show you to the most comfortable quarters."

When he had shown the young prince to the best place available, he said slowly, "Your Majesty, may I say a word to you—without offense?"

Prince Hal looked at Chip sharply, then said, "What is it?"

"My Prince, I wish to beg your pardon for—for the incident

at the tournament. I should not have been so clumsy. Will Your Majesty pardon my offense?"

This was an opportunity for Prince Hal to show the nobility so appropriate for royalty, if he could simply take the earnest young corporal at face value! He almost did because there was an appealing quality about Chip, and they were the same age, though there was a vast difference in their roles in society. Suddenly the prince felt here was a chap who could be trusted, unlike most of those who followed the prince because they hoped he would share his wealth with them.

"Well, now—" But just as he was ready to accept Chip's apology, one of his assistants walked in, and the prince did not want to look weak in front of others.

"Watch yourself, corporal," he said to Chip with a forced sternness. "I haven't forgotten how you almost killed me, and I have my eye on you. You may go."

Chip looked at Prince Hal sadly, then said quietly, "Yes, Your Majesty." As he walked out, Hal looked with a quick stab of regret at the soldierly form of the young corporal. He knew he had lost something by his unwillingness to forgive.

Perhaps because he felt he had to prove something to himself, or to others, that afternoon Prince Hal insisted on leading his forces on a raid against the enemy. He knew that every day a party of brown rats would emerge from behind a wooded hill and carry out some puzzling maneuvers. No one knew what they were doing, but Trooper suggested, "Ah, they are trying to get us to come and fight with them—like before, no?"

If Hal had seen the rout of the general and his troops, he would have known better, but he was sure this would be an easy victory!

"Come on, men!" he ordered the untrained Black Cavaliers as he led them toward the small force of brown rats. He would make them his prisoners and show everyone what a great military leader he was!

Knowing the prince was rushing into danger that was more than he or his men could handle, Chip began to hurry after him. But Budger's grip held him back. "Chip, not now. You have to learn when to attack and when to wait. Would you lose Peedee and Ben and all of us for nothing?"

Slowly Chip calmed down, and then he said, "You're right." But his back stiffened as he watched the enemies surround Hal, then close in on him. The prince was doomed. "They'll kill him," he said.

"No." Budger pointed at the scene. "They see his rank—they're trying to capture him. See there—yes! They've got him, but he's alive."

"Why did they want him alive?" Chip said bitterly. He felt he should have done something. He blamed himself for the prince's capture, thinking that because he had handled his apology badly, Prince Hal had tried to show off to get back at the lowly corporal!

Budger tried to explain. "Most likely they'll trade him for some prisoners we've taken. Come on, Chip, now's a time to help by believing," Budger said in a kindly voice.

"Believing?" Chip said. "But you don't believe in anything, Budger."

"No. But *you* do, and I guess if you've got faith in you, you're bound to use it, eh?" He patted Chip on the shoulder and wished he had more to say to the young corporal, for Chip was more discouraged than the large soldier had ever seen him. *He'll just have to learn to live with his doubt—like the rest of us*, Budger thought without comfort.

CHAPTER ELEVEN
A Terrible Choice

DEEP in their bones all living creatures recognize the end of summer and the coming of fall. As the hot summer days grow shorter, instincts that had been dormant since the last approach of winter awake again. Beasts scurry about eating all they can stuff into their throats, adding to the layer of fat that will carry them through the long winter sleep. Or they scour the fields again, looking for that extra acorn or bit of food that will fill the last niche in their stuffed storerooms beneath the sod.

Now the white-feet had more to worry about than the war,

for impulses deep within their brains warned them that winter would stalk the land soon, and it was time to make final preparations.

The Rag-Tags were on their way back to the Royal Burrow for a leave, a short break from their duties. Two weeks had passed since the capture of Prince Hal, and there had been much sending of messages back and forth, but no real fighting. As they approached the burrow, Singer looked up into the familiar trees. "Look!" he said. "It looks like the martins are getting ready to leave for the winter."

Above their heads the purple acrobats did seem to be getting ready for a long journey. They dipped and rose through the air, chattering earnestly about serious matters. The whitefeet knew it would not be long before some invisible signal would come to the birds, and they would rise like a cloud and strike through the cool autumn skies to some far destination.

Singer watched them and began a little song.

> *"Where is that summer sun?*
> *Where are the skies of May?*
> *Faster and faster do they run,*
> *It's time to go away, away!*
>
> *Soon the fields beneath the snow,*
> *Will turn to frozen ground,*
> *It's time, it's time for us to go*
> *Before the winter snow comes down!"*

He sang it several times, and before long they were all joining in:

> *"Faster and faster do they run,*
> *It's time to go away, away!"*

Ben kicked at the ground as they marched along. "The approach of winter doesn't usually bother me, but with all this fighting and marching, I wonder if there's enough food to last us through the winter."

"I'd guess it'll get a little scarce this time," Budger said. "The young ones and the females have done what they could, but that probably won't be enough. Well, at least if we die in the war, we won't starve to death this winter."

"Now *that's* a cheerful thought!" Chip exclaimed. "Anyway, there hasn't been any fighting for the last two weeks—at least no real battles."

"But why not?" Budger asked, then answered his own question as he dearly loved to do. "Because the brown rats have discovered who Prince Hal is, and that's to their advantage."

"How so?" Ben inquired.

"Silver says they want us to pay a ransom for him."

"What do they want?" Peedee asked.

"Oh, nothing much!" Budger said mockingly. "All they demand is that we lay down our weapons, surrender our kingdom, and become their subjects."

"What!" Chip said in astonishment. "Why, they must be *crazy!*"

Budger did not answer but just kept walking at a brisk pace, and Chip scurried to catch up. All of them were thinking about how hard the dilemma must be on the Royal Family, for they had to choose between the life of the Crown Prince and the freedom of the kingdom. Chip was glad he did not have to make that decision.

That very moment in the Council Room King Halbert was in a terrible state, and Queen Halloo was worse. The king was shouting and waving his arms about in a totally useless way, but the queen was practically in a coma. Since receiving the news of her son's capture, she had scarcely spoken a word or eaten a morsel of food. Princess Hallee sat beside her mother, urging her to take a sip of beet wine and telling her she must be brave. The princess herself was thin and had a tired, worried look on her pretty face. Being a princess is sometimes a life of special privilege and comfort, but she is seldom prepared to face the harsh realities of life-and-death decisions. What color a new dress should be—that was the hardest decision Princess Hallee had ever been called on to make. Now her brother's life hung by a very flimsy thread, and she was so frightened for him that she could barely keep herself from throwing a screaming fit.

The king had been screaming almost without a pause for the whole two weeks. Now the walls of the room echoed as he waved his fist in General Woodland's face and bellowed, "You are the general of my army! You are the top officer—no one is over you, except me of course. I have commanded you to rescue my son from those filthy beggars—so do it!"

"But—but—"

"Don't *but* me, you moron! I command you to obey my orders!"

"But, Your Majesty, as I have explained, the situation—"

"The situation is that if my son is not back in his room in two days, you will have no head!"

"Father—" Princess Hallee said hesitantly, "I'm sure the general is doing all he can to get poor Hal set free." She did not feel nearly as calm as her words indicated, but she also knew that her father's ravings would accomplish nothing.

"Whatever he's doing, it isn't enough!" The king took a huge drink of beet wine from a clay bottle. "And I mean what I say, general! You have two days! If you do not want to be court-martialed or imprisoned or both, you had better . . ."

Princess Hallee tried hard to keep from crying, but the tears she had held back for so long began to run down her face. She turned to leave the room so her parents would not see her weep, but just then Silver and Major Meadows came in, accidentally blocking her way. Silver looked into her face and took her by the shoulders. "Princess, talk to me."

"I'm—I'm sorry, Silver, but with Hal being a captive of those awful rats—it all seems so—so hopeless." She placed her head on the prophet's shoulder and sobbed desperately. Finally she shook her head and wiped the tears from her face. "I'm sorry—I'll try to be brave."

"That's good. I know it's not easy—these are indeed terrible times, but we must not lose hope," Silver said gently. He kept his arm around her as he asked the king, "Your Majesty, are you well—as well as can be expected?"

"No, I am not well!" the king snapped. "What are we to do?" he said with defeat in his voice, and any remaining trace of hope disappeared from his fat face. "What ever are we to do? Is my poor boy lost from us forever?" He twisted his face in a desperate attempt to keep from crying.

"We must not give way to our fears," Silver said. "It is very discouraging, I know, but we are not alone."

"Oh, the Maker, you mean," the king sighed. "Well, I see no hope where you do. I am not religious, Silver, as you know."

"I think you should learn to believe, Your Majesty. If one does not believe in anything, there is a vast emptiness in him. And if one does not trust in the Maker, he has no hope. The greatest tragedy of life is to die empty and alone."

"That all sounds well enough," the king said heavily, "but we need more than fancy religious talk. Can't we *do* something to help my son?"

Silver looked at Major Meadows and nodded. The experienced soldier stepped forward and said in a promising voice, "Sire, there is one thing I would like to propose."

The general, who had been barely listening to the conversation after being rebuked by the king, suddenly stirred and cried, "Attack! I knew it! It's the only way! We must attack!"

"No, general," the major said quickly. "We must *not*

attack. King Halbert, every day the enemy parades the prisoners back and forth in full view of our troops. The prince, of course, is their most treasured prize, and he is always put out in front, where all our soldiers can see him."

"Then why can't you simply go over there and take him back?" Princess Hallee cried. She longed for the solution to be so simple.

"That is exactly what they want us to do, princess. But the raid would surely fail, and then they would have even more prisoners. I have another idea. Look at this—" The major drew some lines on a large white paper on the table. "Here is where our forces are—and this is where they have the prince. There is a deep gully in between. We would have to go down a steep incline, then climb almost straight up, and they would be looking down our throats all the time. We would be easy targets for their arrows and spears."

"Could you sneak around behind them?" the king suggested.

"Impossible, sire. The canyon is too long, and it is guarded all along the rim. We have tried time and time again to get around their flanks, but they know as well as we do the importance of keeping us from getting behind them."

"It's impossible then?" Princess Hallee asked. "Is there no way?"

"Nothing is impossible, princess," Silver said confidently, "if we believe and then act." He waited and looked straight at the king. "I think there is one small chance, Your Majesty. It is very small indeed, but desperate situations call for desperate remedies."

"Anything!" the king cried. "We must do whatever we can. Even if it fails, we must try!"

"Very well, sire. We will proceed." He got up to leave, but the princess followed him outside to question him further.

"What is this plan?"

Silver looked at her with a strange light in his eyes, then

said, "I think, princess, it would be well if you came with the major and myself. Then you can return and tell your parents what you see and learn, for it may be hard for them—and for you—to accept what we intend to do."

He and Major Meadows hurried on without waiting for a response, and the princess ran to keep up with them, confused to say the least. They left the Royal Burrow and made their way through the field that was now filled with soldiers, workers, and young mice, playing the typical games of white-foot youngsters. Finally they came to a shelter where a number of rather weathered soldiers were resting. All in the group stood at attention and saluted the major. Princess Hallee was shocked to see that one of the soldiers was none other than Chip! Their eyes met, and both of them looked away in embarrassment.

The major told the soldiers to stand at ease and then said sternly, "Cadets, you know the situation. What would you think about a direct attack to rescue the prince?"

"Ah, eet ease a fine way of committing the suicide." Trooper grinned and twirled his whiskers, and the rest nodded in agreement.

"Too right," Major Meadows agreed. "Our only hope is to catch the enemy off guard. Every day they parade the prince in full view right on the edge of the canyon. Now, if a small force could somehow get across the canyon during the night without being seen, hmm, do you think they could creep close enough to grab the prince, take him down into the canyon, and bring him up the other side?"

They all looked at each other hesitantly, and finally Budger said, "Major, what you need is a sorcerer!" He grinned straight at Silver, as if daring him to say something. "And we're just soldiers. What you want is impossible."

"Would you do it if you were commanded?" Silver asked suddenly.

"Yes!" several answered at once, and Chip's voice was the loudest.

"But it wouldn't work," Budger insisted stubbornly.

Ben began pulling at Chip's arm. "Chip, do you remember what I told you last night?"

Chip tried to ignore him, but Ben kept pulling. "It will *work*! I know it will!"

Chip kept shaking his head stubbornly. Princess Hallee stepped forward and said softly, "I know it's asking too much for you to do what the major has suggested, but—well, the prince is my *brother*." Her eyes met Corporal Chip's. "I can't do anything myself, but if you can do anything, I would never forget it!"

Chip suddenly felt light-headed, though he wasn't sure why. He looked at the princess, then at Silver, who was studying him intently, then at his squad. He hemmed and hawed a few times, kicked at a lump of dirt, then looked the princess straight in the eye and said firmly, "Your Majesty, your brother will be saved."

"What!" Budger yelped.

"Ah, eet ease wonderful!" breathed Trooper.

"Eet ease suicide!" Budger mocked loudly with a furious look on his face.

"Princess," Silver said warmly, "you have had your answer—and I for one believe it."

"And I also believe it!" echoed the major warmly.

"And—and I believe it," breathed Princess Hallee. Her eyes suddenly filled with scalding tears, and she turned and ran away.

Chip looked around him—at Silver, at the major, at his squad. Then he grinned feebly and said in a small voice, "Wait until you hear my plan."

"*Whose* plan?" Ben demanded.

"Okay, okay, you can have full credit, Ben," Chip agreed. "Now don't stop me until you've heard it all," he said. They all sat down, and Corporal Chip unfolded a plan to save the prince of the kingdom. He could barely keep from laughing at the wild thing he was proposing, but as he looked at his comrades' faces he saw that they were not laughing, and to his amazement he spoke with such assurance and courage that he found himself falling under the spell of his own eloquence. *Thanks for Your help, Maker. I think this plan will work, even if it kills us all. Just so the prince is set free!*

CHAPTER TWELVE
Flying Rag-Tags to the Rescue!

"WHERE do you think they've gone off to?" Major Meadows asked nervously as he stood in a line of tall pine trees on the edge of the canyon.

"Well, I would guess they're rounding up the *secret weapons*, as Ben called them," Silver replied.

"Do you really think this plan will work?" The plan that seemed so logical when Chip had explained it back at the burrow two days earlier now seemed like some sort of fantastic fairy tale to the old soldier. He had done what Chip asked, which was to have a large company of commandos ready to make an attack on the enemy lines just as they were parading the captives on the lip of the canyon—not to defeat the enemy but to distract them. Now the attack force was ready, and they saw the prince and the Black Cavaliers, so called because of the all-black garments they wore, escorted out of the woods and forced to walk back and forth in plain view.

"Yes, I think the plan will work," Silver finally answered, "but of course that all depends on how well Ben and Chip persuade our—allies."

Chip and the Rag-Tags suddenly came dashing out of the woods and ran up to them.

Major Meadows said at once, "Well, were you successful?"

"I think so," Chip said. "Are you ready to get the enemy's attention so they won't see what we're up to?"

"All ready," the major said, "but where are your *weapons*?"

Chip shrugged his shoulder and grinned. "The flying squirrels finally agreed to help, but I never had to talk so hard and fast in my life. They thought I was crazy, but finally they agreed."

"It'll work, major!" Ben said for the thousandth time.

"Well, let's get at it," the major said. "They're already on the rim of the canyon."

Chip whistled, and almost at once there was a soft scuffling in the air and almost fifty squirrels came scampering up to the group. One of them, obviously the leader, quickly said, "Well, Corporal Chip, they all think I've lost my mind, but I don't care—at least I got them here."

Chip grabbed his paw and said warmly, "I knew you'd come, Frisky! This is Major Meadows and Silver, a mysterious prophet we all respect."

Frisky introduced his staff and then said, "Now that we're here, I think you'd better go over the plan again."

"Well, you see over there—across the canyon?"

"You mean those evil rats and their prisoners?"

"Right. All we have to do is get over to where they are and take the white-feet prisoners away from them. But the canyon is too steep for us to do that without being massacred by the brown rats."

"So you want us to get you over there, right?" Frisky's nose began to twitch. In fact, his whole body twitched—from nose to tail. "That's a long way," he said measuring the distance. "And you want each of us to carry a white-foot soldier on our backs? I decided we would help you, but now, seeing the actual canyon, well, I'm sorry, but it just can't be done."

"They don't *fly* actually." Budger began a lecture in his accustomed fashion. Perhaps that was his way of making himself less nervous, or maybe he just liked to show off his knowledge. "They glide downward by spreading their limbs and stretching those loose folds of skin that you see between the ankles of the front and hind legs. "You see," he continued, "their true name is *Glaucomys volans*, and they are found—"

"Who is *he*?" Frisky asked, rather insulted by Budger's apparent arrogance. "We are called *flying* squirrels, you know!" He looked back over the canyon and shook his head. "But we can't fly or glide or whatever you want to call it *that* far!" he said firmly.

"No, I didn't think so," Chip said. "But look there . . ." He pointed upward at the towering pine trees overhead. "What if we climbed *those*—then could you make it across with us aboard?" he asked hopefully.

Frisky and his friends did a quick survey, then went off to one side and had a rather heated conference. They chattered loudly for some time, and Chip and his friends began to fear that the squirrels would refuse to help.

Finally Frisky came back and said, "It'll be a piece of cake!" He was a cocky fellow, and the light of adventure was in his eyes. "You see, we've been having some trouble ourselves. Some rather strange squirrels from somewhere else have been causing us trouble, and since they wear the same mark as these here rats you're fighting, why, if we can help you against them, it sure won't do us any harm!"

"Fine!" Major Meadows said. "Now then, as I understand it, as soon as you're ready, we'll attack from the sides and when the enemy is busy, when you get the signal, you'll *fly* across. Then the Rag-Tags will kill the guards, but then what? How will all of you get back?"

"No problem," Frisky said with a grin. "Some of us will carry Chip and the Rag-Tags, and the rest will go alone. Then when the guard is taken care of, the Rag-Tags and the others will mount up, and we'll sail back."

"But their side of the canyon is lower than ours," the major said. "You can't sail *up*, can you, especially with a burden on your backs?"

"Too right," Frisky agreed. "But we don't have to. All we have to do is get away. We'll land on the floor of the canyon, and you can have a guard there waiting for us. Then we can just scramble back and thumb our noses at those beggars!"

"I believe it will work," Silver said finally, "but it will be very dangerous work for those who go."

"That's what we came here for," Chip said. "After all, we're soldiers. Let's get at it."

The hardest part for the Rag-Tags was climbing to the very top branches of the tall pines. They were good climbers, as all white-feet are, but as they got near the top, the swaying trees caused Chip to feel a little dizzy, and when he looked down at the tiny figure of Silver far below, his stomach did a somersault. Gritting his teeth, he made himself move onto the top branch and crouched there beside Frisky.

"Better get on," Frisky said, "The attack is beginning." The squirrel was a handsome fellow, with a silky, reddish-brown coat and a creamy-white tummy. Chip, drawing Durance, was ready for action. From far below he heard Silver cry, "All teams away!" He felt Frisky gather his muscular body into a small ball, then give a tremendous kick as he launched them both into the air.

Chip dug in with his claws as the squirrel's legs spread, and the animal resembled a flying pancake, the air rushing through his fur. Chip looked around and saw the other Rag-Tags—Ben, Singer, Peedee, Budger, and Trooper, along with twenty other white-feet—all in flight! It was a stirring sight, with the ground far below, rushing beneath them faster than he could have imagined. Just ahead was the lip of the canyon. The enemy guards had not seen them; they were watching the fighting that was visible on both sides as the major led his best troops up the steep mountains. Chip could see some of the white-feet falling as they were cut down by the rats, who had the advantage of higher ground.

Chip could hear nothing except the rush of wind and the far-off cries of the fighting. Seeing that they were approaching the small group of prisoners, he braced himself for action. He saw the prince look up and saw his jaw sag as he spotted the Rag-Tags flying in on the sailing squirrels. At first the prince looked as though he was doubting his sanity, but then he did the right thing. "Down!" he shouted and threw himself to the ground. His arms were bound, but when his fellow prisoners saw Prince Hal fall to the ground and heard him command them to do the same, they instantly obeyed.

That left the rat guards as perfect targets, and the flying Rag-Tags hit them full-force! Frisky rammed the tall rat standing closest to the prince and knocked the wind out of him. Chip rolled off Frisky's back and cut down a dark, hairy rat who simply stared at him in disbelief. But the rats, realizing they outnumbered the Rag-Tags three to one, quickly rallied. If the Rag-Tags didn't act fast, the mission would fail.

"Quick!" Chip shouted to the prisoners. "Get over there away from the fight—by the edge." Then he called out, "Peedee, untie them. Frisky, get your troops in position—we'll keep the rats away from you."

They all obeyed at once, and Chip and his Rag-Tags formed a wall to keep the charging rats away from the prince and the others. Chip's blade darted in and out like a deadly serpent, and many of the foe fell at his feet. All of the Rag-Tags were screaming, "Rag-Tags together!" Chip received a cut on his right forearm but hacked down the huge rat who had wounded him. Blood from a wound on his forehead ran into Trooper's face, but he was singing as merrily as if he were at a fancy party.

Despite the Rag-Tags' fine sword work, after a while they found themselves being forced back, and Chip saw that enemy reinforcements were running toward them, the brown rats yelling angrily.

"Frisky!" Chip shouted. "Leave! Take the prisoners away while you can!"

"We're ready," Frisky yelled. "But there are too many—we can't take you all."

"Leave!" Chip commanded. "A few of us will stay behind for now. We'll make it back through the canyon. Trooper, Budger, go with the others—they may need your brave help."

So a few held back the enemy as the squirrels leaped into space bearing either a black-clad Cavalier or a Rag-Tag. Only Chip was left, along with Peedee, Singer, and Ben. A wave of red-clad brown rats charged them like an avalanche rolling down a mountainside, threatening to destroy everything in its path.

"Come on!" Chip yelled. "Over the side!" Grabbing Peedee, he went over the edge, and the others followed. It was not a straight drop, so they slid and rolled wildly, clutching at trees and rocks to slow their descent. Chip heard the whizzing sound of an arrow close to his ear.

"Don't stop!" he yelled. "Archers!" Desperate to escape, they slid down the canyon wall as quickly as they could, not caring about the scratches and bruises gained in the process. Many arrows thudded into the ground, but none hit them, and in a short time they rolled onto a flat spot and scurried into a small grove of short oak trees where a force of white-feet was waiting for them.

"Go on up!" their leader said, a stern-looking sergeant. "We plan to give the beggars a surprise party when they come after you." He waved them past a line of white-foot archers waiting to ambush the pursuing rats.

They were all totally exhausted, and Peedee suddenly fell. Chip called out, "Singer, Ben, help me with Peedee!" Then he felt something wet, and when he looked at his paw, he saw it was red from fresh blood. "Be careful! He's been hurt!"

They carried him up the steep bank, with help from the others who had flown down with the squirrels and were now rushing to meet them.

Finally they got to the top, where the major was grinning from ear to ear. "Chip, my boy, that was magnificent!" Silver took him by the shoulder and whispered, "There's my mouse of valor!"

The prince saluted Chip, and his companions said in a choking voice, "Your prince thanks you!"

But Chip heard none of that. He knelt beside Peedee, holding him in his arms. The tiny mouse was very still, and Chip's heart seemed to stop beating, then race with a stab of fear.

"Peedee!" he cried out in pain. "Peedee, don't die! Don't leave me, Peedee!"

And slowly—so very slowly—Peedee opened his eyes and then said, so softly that Chip had to almost put his ear to Peedee's lips to hear him, "Chip?"

"Yes, Peedee?"

"Chip—did we do it?"

"Yes, Peedee, we did it! You were great!"

He felt his friend's small body sag. Peedee's eyes opened wide as if in surprise, and then he said, "Chip?"

"Yes, Peedee?"

"I stood up for you that time, didn't I? Against Rattle and Blackie."

Chip couldn't answer, his eyes were so blurry and his throat so dry. Finally he whispered huskily, "Yes, you did, Peedee. You were my friend."

"That's—that's good, Chip." Peedee sagged even more into Chip's arms, and he said, "I'm so tired, Chip."

"Peedee!" Chip cried. "Peedee, don't leave me!"

But despite his friends' earnest wishes, the littlest Rag-Tag opened his eyes one more time, then said, "I'll be waiting for you, Chip. I—I'll be—"

Then Peedee left them all and went to his rest far away in the Deep West.

CHAPTER THIRTEEN
A Growing Shadow

NEWS of the daring rescue of Prince Hal by the Rag-Tags spread like wildfire throughout the kingdom. There were victory celebrations in every burrow, and the names of Chip, Budger, Trooper, and all the other heroes were on the lips of every pup in the land. Triumphant songs were sung about Peedee, the Rag-Tag who had given his life to bring the prince back into freedom. Chip and the other Rag-Tags felt proud of their fallen comrade every time they heard Peedee's praises, though their deep sorrow over their friend's death often felt like it would overwhelm them.

At the same time the Rag-Tags' new fame helped take their minds off their loss. Now it was *Sergeant* Chip who was mobbed whenever he showed his face, so much so that after yet another banquet in the Rag-Tags' honor, where he heard the story of the raid told for the fiftieth time, he said, "Budger, let's get back to the front—I can't take much more of this!"

But since Major Meadows didn't want to send them back to the war just yet, Chip had to put up with the attention. The public was hungry for heroes and for victory, and the tattered uniforms, the brave Chip of the Burrows, the colorful Trooper, the romantic Singer, and so much more made the Rag-Tags perfect candidates for public affection.

In fact, an official banquet was given to honor the Rag-Tags. The Royal Stateroom was packed wall to wall, and everybody who was anybody was there. There was the usual gluttony, and several boring speeches were made, but when Silver rose the room grew quiet.

"My fellow white-feet," he said in a solemn tone, "it is fitting that we have met to honor those who have dared so greatly to win so worthy a victory. So often the awards of the state go to those who deserve them least. Tonight, however, there is an honor to be paid to one who, though he does not seek it or need it, must receive it because a grateful nation needs to recognize the merit of its faithful defenders." He looked toward the table where the Rag-Tags were seated and said, "Sergeant Chip, will you come to the front of the room please?"

To Chip that short walk, with so many eyes upon him, took more courage than the flight across the canyon on Frisky's back. His knees were unsteady, and he felt shaky, but he finally stood in front of the king and his family.

Silver took a leather box out of his pocket and turned to the Royal Family. "Prince Hal and Princess Hallee, as representatives of our nation, I ask you to make the presentation."

The prince and the princess stepped forward, and Silver handed the long case to the prince, who opened it and took out a beautifully crafted gold chain that supported a circular golden disc set with precious stones spelling out the word *COURAGE*. He held one end of the chain and gave the other to his sister. They approached Chip and together placed the chain around his neck, then fastened it. Following an ancient white-foot custom, the prince said in an apologetic voice, remembering his earlier treatment of Chip, "Your Sovereign Majesty pays tribute to your dedication and courage." Placing his paws on Chip's shoulders he gave him a ceremonial hug. Then he stepped back, and Princess Hallee, her face red, kissed Chip softly. "Thank you, Sergeant Chip."

The large crowd broke into an ovation so loud that if Chip had said anything right then, no one would have heard it. He flushed and looked helplessly around. When the crowd had quieted, he said, "I thank you for this honor, but as you all know, it was not one mouse that brought rescue and victory—it was the courage of all of the Rag-Tags and of the flying squirrels and of those who died in the attack. I accept the medal for all of them."

"To ze Rag-Tags forever!" Trooper sang out, and everyone cheered thunderously until every ear rang. Only Silver heard what Chip murmured during the jubilant uproar—"I wish Peedee could hear all this."

"Are you sure that he can't?" Silver asked quietly, and Chip gave him a warm smile.

†

That was the last happiness in the kingdom for a very long time, for the brown rats, infuriated by the loss of their prize captive, attacked the border at several points with a new fury, and the defenders were driven back a little further day by day. The Royal Burrow soon had to be turned into a hospital, and the females, wearing white headbands and veils, worked until they almost dropped with exhaustion from tending to the steady flood of wounded soldiers.

Chip and the Rag-Tags went back to the front lines, and Prince Hal, along with the most promising and capable of the Black Cavaliers, was serving under Major Meadows—with great distinction according to Silver's reports.

The seer was in and out of the burrow almost daily, and it was his swift journeys from one end of the kingdom to the other that kept the white-feet forces from being totally disorganized. Princess Hallee watched for him carefully, always seeking news of the war—about Hal and about someone else, though she wouldn't admit it to anyone. She began to wonder how Silver could be on the east border one day and yet the next day be back with a report, obviously from firsthand experience, about the western front.

Silver was growing thin, she noticed, and the creases in his aged face grew deeper as the lines of their army were driven back more and more. But it was not until Chip and Budger brought messages from the major to the home office that they all learned how dark the situation really was.

Hallee saw Silver leaving the Council Room and asked, "Did you see the prince on your last visit to the front?"

"What? Oh, princess, I didn't see you there. My mind is occupied with so much . . . Well, we can't talk here. I have to give some messages to Chip for Major Meadows."

"Oh, really? I have written a letter for Hal. Do you suppose he would deliver it for me?"

"I'm sure he would. Come along." She followed Silver, and they found Chip and Budger waiting at the supply depot, from which food and other equipment were sent to the front.

"Silver and Princess Hallee," Chip said, "I'm glad you're here—I thought we'd have to leave without seeing you."

"I have some letters for the major, and the princess has one for her brother."

Chip took the letters and stuck them inside his jacket. "We have some fresh fruit here. Would you join us? Don't ask me where Budger got it."

"A professional secret from an expert scrounger," Budger said. They sat down at a little table and began enjoying slices of apples and pears, then washed them down with juice from some late-bearing blueberries.

"Delicious!" Silver exclaimed. "Trust an old campaigner to take care of his stomach. Thanks, Budger."

"Yes indeed, but winter is coming, and things are going to get harder for us all," Chip said with a worried look at the gray sky. "What does the situation look like, sire? Can we hold out, do you think? We soldiers only see one part of the war, and if we win our particular battle, we think all is well, but overall I don't think that is the case."

Silver sipped at his juice and looked across the fields as if he could see the battlefield far away, then said, "Do not repeat what I will tell you now—not to anyone! I am afraid that the kingdom is—" He was obviously searching for just the right word, and Chip supplied *Doomed* in his own mind. But the prophet finally said, "The kingdom must be ready for hardship worse than any of us has ever seen."

"Do you think we'll lose the war?" Hallee asked fearfully.

"The war," Silver answered, "is bigger than any of you know. As Chip says, you each see only a small part of it. We think only of the kingdom of white-feet, but there is a power that is growing all over the world, an evil shadow that is everywhere. I tell you, all creatures and even man himself are in danger. There is much at stake, and incredible perils to face."

"This power, this shadow—what is it, sire?" Budger asked. "I have seen, or *felt*, that the world has gone astray, that something is not as it was intended to be."

"You are discerning, my friend," Silver said with a nod. "I cannot tell you much, but I fear that none of us will ever again see the peaceful world we have loved. We must be ready to faithfully perform our duty, no matter how difficult or costly it is."

He got to his feet, overcoming the aches of fatigue, and said, "Give the major those letters as soon as you get back, Chip. They may help to stem the tide—for a while." He left them, and they looked after him with a touch of fear.

"I must go," Hallee said. "Tell my brother to be careful. We had all better be careful."

"I'll tell him, princess." Chip smiled. "But being careful doesn't come easy for a good soldier."

Day after day, week after week, the white-feet had no real victory. No matter how many dead rats they left on the field, the next day there seemed to be even more to take their place. Slowly, though making the enemy pay for every inch of ground, the white-feet fell back. It was as if a blunt and massive hammer was striking constantly against a finely-wrought shield, and the shield was slowly being battered and gradually destroyed by the constant blows.

Chip saw many of his friends fall, some of the Rag-Tags among them, but sadly there was no time to mourn their passing, for always there was the red wave of the enemy to be delayed at all costs.

Finally, the brown rats advanced so far that the entire white-foot army had to retreat into the Royal Burrow. The kingdom was teetering like a rock on the edge of a cliff, and no one could say whether it would stand or fall.

CHAPTER FOURTEEN
A Special Visitor

IT was a time of desperate siege. Every day the numbers of the white-feet defenders dwindled, while reinforcements for the brown rats seemed to increase limitlessly. Daily in every burrow within the inner defenses there was a shrill cry of mourning over a lost son, husband, or brother, and the entire burrow was like a hospital, with the wounded stacked like firewood in any shelter that kept out the cold wind and dripping rain.

Chip lost track of the days. His world was the clash of battle, a hasty meal, a few brief moments of sleep, and a quick return to the lines.

One day he was trying to fight off sleep as he stood guard outside the stockade—a large rock-lined cave where captive enemy soldiers were kept. There were not many, not more than two dozen, for in their battle fury almost all the brown rats refused to surrender, fighting to a bloody death even when overwhelmed by the defenders.

Chip looked at the prisoners curiously as they walked around the small space allowed for their hour of outside exercise. One of them was apparently some sort of officer, for he wore the all-too-familiar red circle and bones on his jacket, and whenever he issued orders the others obeyed him instantly.

He was larger than usual, and his right forepaw was in a dirty sling. With his left paw he managed a clumsy crutch that had been whittled out of a piece of pine, necessary because his left foot was seriously injured. There were terrible gashes all over his face, and his eyes were angry as he glared at Chip. He spoke suddenly, and his voice was as rough as his exterior. "Why don't you all give up?"

"What did you say?" Chip jerked awake and stared at his enemy in amazement, for none of the rats *ever* talked to their captors, only to each other.

"Why don't you give up—surrender?" he repeated. "You can't win."

"What's your name?" Chip asked, primarily to give himself time to think. Silver had said once that if some of the captives would only talk, it might be possible to discover something about the enemy's plan.

"I am called Murkon, and I am an officer in the service of the Dread Deliverer." He touched the red circle on his breast with special respect.

"The Dread Deliverer? Who is that?"

Murkon laughed, exposing yellow fangs. "You poor fools! You are doomed!" His eyes seemed to glaze over, and his raspy voice fell into some kind of incantation.

> *"The Dread Deliverer has come to earth!*
> *He will set us free from bondage;*
> *No more will rats be slaves,*
> *Nor prisoners to the hateful Maker!*
> *The sword is laid at the throat of all*
> *Who trust any other than*
> *the Dread Deliverer!*
> *Freedom for the servants of*
> *the Dread Deliverer!*

Chip asked cautiously, "But if this Dread Deliverer is setting everyone free, why are you making war on us?"

"You are *blind*!" Murkon said. "We must make you servants of the Dread Deliverer so he can free you from the bondage of the Maker."

"We like what we are, and we know whom we serve," Chip said. "Why don't you all go back where you came from and leave us alone?"

Murkon laughed again. "Where we came from? You do not understand! We are *everywhere*. The Dread Deliverer is not a local being! The entire world—every rat, mouse, every animal and bird, even man—must bow the knee to his mighty power or die!"

Murkon grew quiet, and he looked at Chip curiously. "Sergeant Chip they call you, is that not so? Do you not see what is happening to your nation? You have seen your country shrink to *this*! Every day you grow weaker, while the servants of the Dread Deliverer pour in like waves. So what if you kill a thousand of us? There are many other thousands waiting to fill those places."

"It does not matter—we love the Maker, and we will fight to the end," Chip said slowly.

Murkon shook his head. "Don't you have any love for your nation?"

"Yes, I do!"

"Then why do you insist on seeing them all butchered? I have heard of you, Sergeant Chip. We servants of the Dread Deliverer have been told that *you*, and not the king, are the real hope of the white-feet."

"Me?"

"Yes." Murkon nodded. "The Dread Deliverer knows all hearts, and he has told his staff officers that if *you* can be convinced to join his cause, the war will end. And then you, Sergeant Chip, will be the ruler of the white-feet!"

"I'm just a soldier," Chip protested.

"Is there not a prophecy about you?" Murkon put his face so close to Chip's that the young soldier drew back from the enemy's foul breath. "You would be second to none among your nation—you would be subject only to the will of the Dread Deliverer. That is no small honor, I tell you! What power you would have! You could save your people from certain death!"

Chip shivered, for a terrible desire to take this path seized him for a moment. *I could do it—I could be the ruler of my race and stop this awful war!* he told himself. And yet deep within, he recognized his enemy's lies, and he knew he would not betray the Maker. If only he could keep Murkon guessing until he talked to Silver . . . He smiled and said, "I'll think about it."

"I knew you were a reasonable mouse." Murkon grinned. "It could all happen so easily. Tonight you can come here and relieve the guard. Then you can take me through the lines—I am sure you know the secret passages. We will go to *our* lines, and then our forces can sneak back through the defenses. We will take the Royal Burrow and set up a government with you as chief under the Dread Deliverer. What could be easier, or more rewarding?"

Chip said, "Here comes my relief. I'll be back tonight and we'll see."

Murkon clapped him on the shoulder. "You are a *very* wise white-foot, sergeant. You will lead your people well in the ways of the Dread Deliverer!"

"Relieving you, sergeant," the guard said, and Chip left as quickly as he could.

He was out of breath when he got to the tiny room where Silver was, and he was so excited that Silver had to calm him down. "Easy, Chip. Have some of this cider and catch your breath!"

Chip gulped the sweet cider down, then forced himself to be calm as he related the words of Murkon as accurately as he could.

Silver did not interrupt, and when Chip had finished, the aged prophet bowed his head as if listening to a voice deep within. He remained still for so long that Chip was about to shake him. But then the seer raised his head, and suddenly Chip was aware of a third presence in the room. There in the shadows was a figure glowing with a strange light, and Chip whispered, "Maker, it's You!"

Silver knelt, and Chip too fell to his knees, his eyes fixed on the face of the being of light. He had never seen such compassion or such strength, and he dropped his head, unable to bear the brilliant light.

"Rise, and listen to Me," the Maker said. His voice was soft but powerful, and as the two white-feet rose, they could not tear their eyes away from His face.

"You must lead the white-feet out of here, Chip," the Maker said with an intensity that shook Chip to the heart.

"What! Leave the burrow?" He could not have been more shocked if he had been told to jump over the sun!

"Yes! There is no hope here, but if you can get through the rat armies there is a place where you will be safe."

"Where is it, Maker? Is it far?"

"Yes, it is far from here—a place in the wilderness. You must go there with all the others at once—tomorrow at the latest!"

"Tomorrow! Why, that's impossible!"

Silver looked at Chip in a way that seemed to scorch the very soul of the young white-foot. "Nothing is impossible with the Maker, Chip," he said. Then he repeated the words he'd spoken to Chip on their first meeting: "The Maker is with you, mighty mouse of valor!"

The Maker said, "You have come to the kingdom for such a time as this, My son. Your people need you, and I have called and prepared you. Will you trust Me?"

Suddenly the two white-feet found themselves alone, but they had no doubt about what had just happened. Chip swallowed and shook his head. "I'm just an ordinary mouse, Silver."

"There are no ordinary mice in the sight of the Maker, my boy!" Silver said firmly. "The Maker has spoken, and we know what we must do!"

†

Convincing the king, the ruling elders, and the military leaders was not as difficult as Chip had feared.

It was much worse.

"Leave the burrow!" the king roared. "This is *treason*! Arrest them!" He waved wildly toward Chip, Silver, and Major Meadows.

The three had forced the leadership of the nation out of bed, hastily assembling them in the Council Room. Silver had spoken first, hoping to prepare them for what was to follow, and Chip then told them about his conversation with Murkon.

The king erupted with the wrath of a raving maniac when the plan to leave for the West was revealed.

"Your Majesty," Silver implored loudly, "no one *wants* to leave, but we have no choice. Major, how long can we hold the enemy off?"

"A week—no more."

"So we must leave tomorrow night," Silver said. "Tonight Sergeant Chip will dig out of this Murkon the gaps in the rat defenses, and then the Rag-Tags will lead us out! *All* of us, every pup, the old, the wounded—*everyone* must go."

"Go where?" a statesman demanded. "Show us on the map!"

Silver looked at him gravely. "Places of safety or security or happiness," he said, "are not always seen on a map."

"Ha! You and Chip," the king snorted angrily, "are proposing that we leave the safety of the burrow and follow you all over the dangerous countryside to a supposedly safe place without being able to tell us where it is?"

Chip spoke before he thought. "Your Majesty, the Maker gave us life, and He will not allow us to perish. We will find our place—no matter how far it is!"

"You are a traitor!" the king screamed. He leaped to his feet and began running around the room waving his paws wildly, his face growing bright red. "Arrest them! *All* of them! They shall die for this! Why don't you—why don't you—" But then his screams were cut off, and he said in a whisper, "I feel very fu—" Without another word he collapsed, falling to the floor in a heap.

"Help him!" Princess Hallee screamed. Silver was the first to reach the still form. He lifted the body into a sitting position, lifted an eyelid, let it drop, then felt for a pulse. Breathlessly they waited. Slowly the prophet laid the body down, then looked at the distraught princess, then straight at Hal.

"The king is dead. Long live our next king!" he said.

Automatically a murmur went around the room—"Long live the king!"

Hal looked at the body of his father, then bent to raise Hallee who was weeping as if she would never stop. He looked at Silver, at Chip, then swept his gaze all around the room. Everyone was waiting for his decision.

"My parents have called you traitors," he said to the three standing before him. And once again Hal failed a crucial test of character. "I will go along with my father's saying." His voice rang out in his first royal command—"Arrest those three!"

The guards did not move, stunned at the new king's foolishness, looking to Silver, Major Meadows, and Chip for direction.

Silver shook his head sadly. "Nay, sire, we are no traitors. We are your true and loving subjects."

"Will you not obey me?" the new king demanded. "Am I not now the king?"

"We had hoped," Silver said, "that Your Majesty would lead the nation to the place prepared in the West. But you are not ready to assume the crown." His voice rose with the sound of command. "*Prince* Hal, you will one day be king of all the white-feet! But until you are fit for the throne, I appoint as the Regency myself, Major Meadows, and Sergeant Chip of the Rag-Tag Brigade!"

All waited in awe. After a long pause, taking time to settle his thoughts, Captain Chip drew Durance from its sheath. He walked directly to Prince Hal and said, "Sire, I am your servant. Will you accept my service until the day when all of us can say, 'Hail to King Hal, Ruler of the White-feet'?"

Hal's face was dark with anger, but he looked around the room. Realizing he had no other choice, he touched Chip's blade and said, "I accept your service, *Captain* Chip."

And thus it was that the white-feet chose to leave their native soil and to begin the terrible journey that led to a dim and uncertain spot in the West—a wilderness of peace. But it was good that none, not even Silver, could see the dark road that lay before them or they might never have had the courage to begin their journey.

PART THREE

The Journey West

CHAPTER FIFTEEN

A Desperate Plan

"I KNOW I agreed to leave the burrow, but the enemy has us surrounded. If there's a way to get out of here, I'll eat my sword!" the major shouted.

Deciding to leave was one thing, but to actually move the entire nation of white-feet into the wilderness was another. The tension in the Council Room was already tense, and the major had just issued a challenge that made Chip look at Silver in alarm.

"If *he* feels like that," he whispered, "so will the rest, and we'll *never* get away!"

Silver gave him a reassuring nod, then spoke to the council. Almost all the council members were brand-new because nearly all the former elders had refused to have anything to do with what they called the madness of moving the entire nation. "Major Meadows, we recognize that the proposed venture will require all our resources. Indeed, we will need more than our own strength."

"You refer, I presume, to the Maker?" Budger asked.

"If I did not believe He was guiding us, I would be against this mission myself. Surrender would then be the only alternative."

"Surrender? Never!" Chip broke in. "We'll die in the wilderness before we submit to this Dread Deliverer and his evil followers!"

"That is exactly what will happen if we follow your plan, Captain Chip. We will die in the wilderness," the major said sadly. "Have you thought at all of how we are to move the wounded and the elderly and the young pups? Can some of them even survive such a move in itself, let alone the attacks of the enemy? What you suggest is impossible!"

This brought a most uncomfortable silence into the room. Even Silver had felt perplexed about how to make their plan work, and yet he knew it was the only way. For a long time they all argued and discussed whatever anyone could think of to lead their people to safety, but after an hour they were no closer to a solution than at the beginning.

When they finally lapsed into a rather sullen silence, Ben spoke up. "I know I'm not a member of the council or anything like that, but I think I know a way to move all the wounded and the others."

Silver turned his piercing eyes toward Ben, as if to say, "The experts can't figure out to do it, but you can?" But the plucky white-foot refused to be intimidated. "I wanted to mention it before, but—well, I guess I was afraid to suggest it in front of such a knowledgeable crowd, but now— Anyway, a few details still need to be worked out, but my invention will—"

Mutters of "Oh great, another of his childish ideas" or "His inventions usually don't work, do they?" could be heard around the room.

"Wait a minute," Chip said suddenly. "One of his ideas did work, remember? Using the flying squirrels to rescue Prince Hal. What's your idea, Ben?"

Ben stood up and began pacing the floor, waving his paws around as he always did when he was excited. "I've been thinking about a way to use this particular invention for a long time, even before the war. And last night Chip and I were talking and trying to find a way to move everyone who couldn't walk. Well, I thought about it, and just before I went to sleep, why, the idea just popped into my mind! That's the way my inventions usually come, you know, they just—"

"Never mind that now," the major snapped. "What is your idea?"

"Well, have any of you ever been to the farmhouse next to the big cornfield?"

"I have," Silver said.

"Did you ever go by the fence behind the house, almost in the woods? If you did, you saw a big pile of stuff that the men who live there have thrown away."

"Yes, I know that place. Did you find something there we can use?"

"It's where I get almost all my material for my inventions. And this one is *big*, bigger than anything I've ever done before."

"What is it, Ben?" several of them asked in exasperation. "Get to it, son."

"It's a—a—well, I don't know what they call it, but I saw them use it once a long time ago when I was just a pup. There was the littlest man there, just a pup, and he was pulling this *thing* along. It's red, and it's big—*very* big! I'd say it was about five or six times as large as this room, and it must be about five times as high as Budger."

"How did the pup pull it?" Chip asked.

"It's like a big square room, and it has round things on each corner. When the pup pulled it, it rolled along the ground quite easily."

"So, what's your invention, Ben? What does it have to do with what you are telling us?" Silver asked.

Ben looked surprised. "Don't you see? We can put all the wounded and the mothers and the pups in this room, put some kind of a top over it to keep the owls and hawks away, and move them along in it."

"But how can we *pull* it, Ben?" Singer asked. "It must weigh as much as a mountain!"

Ben squirmed and looked around nervously. "Well, that's one of the details I haven't figured out yet."

A cry of disgust went up from almost everyone. "Just a minor detail!" Budger groaned. "It's just like all the rest of your stupid inventions—it just won't work!"

Silver waited until the room had quieted down, then put his paw on Ben's shoulder. "Wait a moment—what other plan do we have?"

"None!" Budger snapped. "And this is no plan either! We can't pull the silly thing ourselves."

"No," Silver admitted. "But there are others—other animals, I mean. I think our only hope is to do what we did with the flying squirrels. We must persuade some large animal to pull this thing—*Ben's Chariot*, we can call it."

"Oh, fine!" Budger snorted. "Maybe we can persuade a bobcat or a fox to help us. They'd love to be within striking distance of a whole nation of tender white-feet! Any big animal you can name loves mice well enough—for breakfast, lunch, and dinner!"

"We'll just have to make a vegetarian out of one of them then," Singer said. Then he paused, and a strange light came into his eyes. "Wait a minute," he said slowly. "Wait a minute—I think—" He suddenly jumped straight up and yelled, "I've got it!"

They all stared at him, and Chip said, "What animal are you thinking of, Singer?"

"I'm not sure if I can get—*him*," Singer said. "And I don't want to tell you about it yet in case . . . If you'll go get the—the, uh, chariot ready, Ben, I'll meet you tomorrow at sundown in the junkyard."

"It's all nonsense. We're doomed!" Budger said hopelessly.

They all looked at Silver, and after a long pause the prophet looked around, then announced, "I think we have found a way. Now we have to begin to trust each other. Singer, go now and try to persuade your—friend. Ben, you get whatever help you need to rig up your chariot. The rest of us will make the preparations for our exodus. Any questions?"

"What if Singer's friend won't help?" Prince Hal spoke up suddenly. He had kept in the shadows, as had his sister, but now he stepped forward. "What if this chariot is gone? What if—"

"My prince," Silver said firmly, "never make decisions based on your fears. We *will* survive, and as our prince you must set an example of courage and wise action."

Hallee crept forward, took Hal's paw in hers, and whispered something in his ear. The prince slowly nodded and said firmly, "Very well. What can I do to help?"

"Oh, you can do a great deal." Silver beamed with pleasure. He was delighted, as indeed they all were, to see the prince and princess throw their support behind the plan. "You must convince everyone that we must make this move. Only you can do this, Prince Hal, and we are all depending on you to have everyone ready to leave tomorrow night."

Hal blushed, looked around the room, especially at Chip, and said firmly, "It will be done." He left the room with a spring in his step.

"Well, that's a change!" Budger murmured. "I wonder what made him stop acting like a pup?"

"I think the prince may be growing up, Budger," Silver said. "Now we must all work hard, for the time is short. Budger, you see to the supplies—we'll need all we can carry. Chip, you have a difficult job—I want you to go visit that rat, Murkon. You have to convince him you are a traitor. We may be able to take advantage of that to buy ourselves some extra time!"

"I don't think he'll believe me for very long," Chip said.

"Put him off until tomorrow if possible, the next day at the latest. By then we'll either be on our way or—" Silver didn't finish, and a cold look came into his eyes. "You can do it, Captain Chip."

With new hope in their hearts and determination on their faces, they all sprang into action.

CHAPTER SIXTEEN
Singer's Friend

SHRILL cries from the tree frogs were echoing loudly, and the owls and bats were beginning to stir as darkness fell as a small group of white-feet gathered by the pile of junk, looking for Singer and wondering who his friend might be.

Noting the nervousness of the others, Silver said, "Ben, you've done a fine job on your chariot. Tell me again how it works and how you accomplished it."

Ben perked up and began to point out the advantages of

his invention. "Well, as you see, it's certainly big enough. We'll have room for all our wounded and sick, our mothers and pups, and the old ones too. Furthermore, look at this!" He led them up a board that rested on the edge of the vehicle, and once they were inside he waved at the interior and said proudly, "See that? Plenty of compartments for food and supplies."

It was impressive, they all agreed. Ben had found some large boxes and had installed them in rows across the front of the compartment. On the floor there was a green rug Ben had found. But the best feature was the roof. In some way that none of the others could grasp, Ben had placed wire in several arcs over the top of the chariot, and over this he had stretched a piece of cloth so there was an arched roof over the entire chariot. "See, this will keep most of the water out if it rains," Ben said, "and the hawks and owls won't bother us."

"You've done wonders, Ben," Silver said proudly, and all the others agreed. But one thought kept coming into their minds—where was Singer and his friend?

"Silver! Chip!" a shrill voice called.

"There's Singer now!" Chip announced with relief and led the rush down the gangplank. There was Singer all right, but he was alone as far as they could see. "Where's your friend, Singer?" Chip asked.

"Oh, he's on his way," Singer said cheerily. "He *does* move a bit slowly, so I thought I'd come on ahead so you wouldn't worry."

Singer began to look over the chariot, oohing and ahing at the cleverness of it all. "Ben, you've done a magnificent job!" he exclaimed.

"Do you think your friend will be able to pull it?" Budger asked suspiciously.

"Pull it? Of course he can!" Singer said, then looked into the growing twilight. "I think I hear him coming."

They all strained their ears, and then they heard a most peculiar sound. It was a sweeping sound, or a rustling. It gradually got louder, then there was a snuffling, grunting wheeze, and then into the clearing lumbered a large bristly porcupine!

"This is Porky," Singer said in introduction. They all tried to say hello or whatever, but only garbled sounds came out, for they were intimidated by the *huge* animal. He weighed at least thirty-five or forty pounds and was covered with thousands of needle-sharp quills. He moved so slowly that he was no danger at all to the lightning-like white-feet, but all of them had seen wolves and other large animals dying in agony as the quills worked their way in deeper and deeper.

Budger's curiosity finally drove away his fear, and he said in his scholarly tone, "*Erethizon Dorsatum*, I believe. Sometimes called a quill pig. His name means 'one who rises in anger.'"

"Does—does he eat mice?" Braveheart asked in a shaky voice, not living up to his name at the moment. He was one of the younger soldiers assigned to help Ben, and his eyes were big as moons as he looked at the fearsome Porky.

"No, no," Budger assured him. "Mostly leaves, twigs, and bark." He gazed at the porcupine. "Sir, we're mighty grateful to you for coming all this way."

Porky replied in a slow, rather vague voice," Oh, it ain't nothin'—no bother at all."

Ben raced around and picked up the rope he had found somewhere to use as a harness. "Porky, I hope you can pull it with this."

Ben, keeping clear of the dangerous quills, slipped the noose over the porcupine's head and said, "There . . . Can you pull it?"

Porky leaned into the harness, and Ben's chariot moved behind him perfectly! A cheer went up, and Porky gave a shy grunt. "Oh, it ain't nothin'. Ain't no bother to me."

"This is excellent!" Silver said. "Do you think you can pull the chariot back to the burrow tonight, Porky?"

"Oh, yes!" Porky mumbled "Ain't no bother." He moved out into the darkness, pulling the chariot effortlessly.

Budger looked after him and shook his head. "Well, I'm amazed! I have to admit this looks mighty good. You did fine, Ben!"

It's better than I'd hoped," Silver agreed. "We can even travel in daylight if we have to. No creature will tackle a customer like Porky."

"Well, there is one animal that kills porcupines," Budger said. "The fishers—they're cousins of the weasels, you know. They're so quick, they can reach under and flip the porcupines upside-down and then rip open their stomachs."

"But there are no fishers around here," Silver said, not wanting Budger's realistic comments to make the others more afraid than they needed to be.

"True, but one of them just might come around for a visit," Budger said gloomily. "But until he does, I'd say we're all right."

†

Two days later the rain that had been threatening came with a roar. Lightning stretched across the dark skies, and thunder deafened the already frightened white-feet. That night the little band met in the Council Room for the last time. There was a hint of desperation in all their faces, but Silver said, "This is our hour, white-feet! Tonight we leave for our new kingdom in the West!"

"But won't the rain make traveling difficult?" Major Meadows asked.

"Actually it will help us, I'd say," Chip ventured. "I've been trying to trick that awful rat Murkon for information for two days now, and I've found out that they hate the rain worse than we do. There won't be any enemy lines out tonight; so we can get away before they even know we've left."

"And the rain will wash away our tracks," Silver said. He turned to the prince. "How many are willing to go?" he asked.

Prince Hal shook his head sadly. "Most of them are refusing," he said. "All of the wounded we'll simply take with us, but the rest—what's the count, princess?"

Hallee mourned, "Twenty-two wounded, thirty-nine mothers with their pups, twenty-seven old ones."

Silver frowned. "Is that all?" he asked. "Don't they know what will happen to them if they stay?"

"They've convinced themselves they'll be all right—that the brown rats aren't so bad."

Silver said, "They'll regret it, but we must allow them to make their choice. How many soldiers, major?"

"Well, sire, I'm ashamed to tell you, but many of them are staying too. We have just under 200 who will go."

Prince Hal gave a hollow laugh, "My kingdom has shrunk."

"It will prosper, My Prince," Silver said sharply. "It is time for us to be on our way. Chip, you know the route we have chosen, so you go with Porky. Major, I assume you have a plan of march."

"Yes. Corporal Budger, you take the rear guard. You take the right flank, Ben. Singer, yours is the left flank. I will take the forward scouts. Let's go."

Silver offered a prayer for the journey. "May the Maker of all things—He who begins all things and gives all things meaning—be our guide." Several responded, "So be it."

There was a flurry of activity, and all was confusion for a time. Chip asked Porky, "Are you ready, our new friend?"

"No fear! It ain't no bother to me, Chip." And he lumbered forward into the darkness, following the captain.

Once again a tiny band of hardy adventurers were leaving their homeland, risking everything for a new life in some dim and distant place. As the lightning pierced the darkening skies, as some of the rain fell into Ben's chariot and nearly soaked the courageous defenders, the white-foot nation headed for the wilderness and the West. They were few and small, but courageous. As they left the Royal Burrow and disappeared into the woods, only one tiny cry from one group of soldiers was heard—"Rag-Tags forever!"

CHAPTER SEVENTEEN

A Dangerous Retreat

THE officer with the gold star on his breast was puzzled. The brown rat had led his company to the white-foot line of defense, determined to break through if it cost him every soldier he had. But surprisingly there had been no resistance—none at all. He turned to the sergeant at his side and said, "What do you make of it?

"I can't make *anything* of it, Captain Tedor," the sergeant said. "Before the storm we made an attack here and lost twenty good fighters. Those mice fought like wolves! Now they've all vanished!"

"It may be a trap. We'll go in but we'd better keep two squads out here just in case. Move on in."

Dodging from tree to boulder, the brown rats edged closer and closer to the entrance to the Royal Burrow. Still there was no response. Finally the officer stood at the very door and looked around in bewilderment.

"Captain! Over here—by the big log."

Captain Tedor made his way to the door of the prisoner's cave, barred with heavy timbers. He looked inside. "Colonel Murkon! We all thought you were dead! Sergeant, get some help and get this door cleared."

In a few minutes Colonel Murkon hobbled out of the cave followed closely by the rest of his men. He had thrown away his crutch but still limped heavily. He looked furiously at the cave and said, "They've all gone, Tedor."

"Gone, sir?"

"Yes. They pulled out during the storm. They left us some food and water, but they've got three days' head start on us."

"But, colonel, where have they gone? No place is safe for them now."

There was fury in the colonel's eyes as he screamed, "Where have you been, Tedor? You could have walked in here any-time and walked over them. Why did you delay? I'll have your head for this!"

"But, colonel, it's been raining so hard that the creeks are overflowing. We knew they couldn't get away—"

"You idiot! They *have* gotten away. But not for long!" Colonel Murkon forced himself to be calm. "We'll catch them."

"But perhaps—why not just let them go, colonel? We've captured the burrow, and they can't get far. The hawks or the foxes will get most of them."

"No!" Colonel Murkon whispered. He struck the captain's shoulders with a hard paw and said savagely, "They are a sym-bol of the world we must overcome. They have rebelled against our Dread Deliverer and therefore they must die! Do you hear me, captain? They must die if it costs us every soldier we have. Those are my orders, given to me by the Dread Deliverer himself!"

"But, colonel, how can we kill them? They could be anywhere. And the rain has undoubtedly washed out their tracks."

"Your orders, captain, are to search and destroy. I want these white-feet made into an example—especially this—this *Chip*!" The colonel began to tremble and almost lost his voice, so great was his rage. "I want him taken *alive*!" He smiled evilly and said softly, "Believe me, I have several interesting things in store for Captain Chip! Send scouts in every direction. Interrogate every animal in this part of the world. Someone must have seen them! Then when—" He broke off suddenly as a rat came running up.

"Colonel Murkon!" He raced up and saluted. "There's a large group of white-feet hiding in the burrow. They say they want to surrender to the Dread Deliverer."

Colonel Murkon stood motionless for several long moments, and then a smile touched his lips, and an unholy light burned in his eyes. He squeezed his paws together and murmured, "They want to surrender, do they? Captain Tedor, we can begin our search right here. I'm sure we can find some way to persuade these new servants of the Dread Deliverer to inform us about the plans of Captain Chip and those who are with him, eh?"

The captain grinned. "You've never failed to get cooperation, have you? I'm sure they'll be helpful."

"Get the fire started," Captain Murkon said. "Do we have anything that can be used for a branding iron?" They gathered the necessary items, then walked quickly to their unsuspecting and defenseless victims.

†

Finding the cave had lifted all their hearts, for after three days of hard traveling they were all falling down with exhaustion.

Chip had driven them as long as the rain lasted, pausing only a few times for food and short naps. Though they took refuge under logs and trees at those times, they were quickly soaking wet, except for those in the chariot.

"We *have to* go on!" Chip had said a hundred times. "We must put all the distance we can between us and the brown rats."

"Maybe they won't follow us," Singer said unconvincingly.

"They will. You can bet on it, Singer," Chip replied. "I got to know Colonel Murkon pretty well those last few days, and you can be sure of this—we made a fool of him, and he'll risk the life of every soldier he has, and his own life too, just to get back at us!"

"We're going to die anyway if we don't stop to rest," Budger complained. "You can only drive a mouse so far!"

"We have to move on," Chip insisted. "When the rain stops, we'll try to find a safe place to rest. Can you go further, Porky?"

Porky momentarily stopped nibbling some tender bark and said in his shy fashion, "Oh, sure, captain. It ain't no bother."

"You see," Chip cried, "Porky has had it worse than any of us, pulling that chariot. But not one word of complaint! You're a real hero, Porky."

"Ah, yess, eet ease so!" agreed Trooper. He danced around Porky and said, "I would kees you, my fran, but dere ease no place to do eet!"

"Aw—" Porky ducked his head modestly. "Ain't nothin' much." He leaned into his harness, and they trudged muddily onward.

Late that day Major Meadows, muddy all the way up to his eyebrows, had approached Chip. "Captain, we've *got* to rest! The rain is about to stop, and I've found just the place for us. Just bear to your left there—it's not too far ahead."

Soon they came to a small opening that led to a very roomy cavern that went far back into the bank. When Chip and

Budger followed the major in, Chip said, "Why, this is perfect! It's big enough for all of us."

"And then some," agreed Budger. He walked onward but stopped suddenly. "What's *this*?"

"Careful, Budger!" the major called out. "That rock is balanced on the edge of some kind of deep hole. Wouldn't take much to tip it over, and you with it."

Chip walked carefully up to the rock, picked up a stone, and threw it down into the darkness. There was a long pause before there was finally an echo from far, far below. "We'll have to keep everyone away from here."

"No problem—there's plenty of room in here," Budger said. "Let's get everyone inside. We'd better hide the chariot—cover it up with brush. We may be here for a day or two."

Soon they were all in the cave. Cooking fires were burning, and the smell of hot food made them all feel a little more relaxed. They ate all they could hold and lay down for needed rest. They all slept so soundly that if an enemy had found them right then, that would have been the end of the white-feet! But no one came, and only moans of comfort and the crackling fire broke the silence.

CHAPTER EIGHTEEN
Discovered!

I SAY it's not natural," Budger insisted. He was sitting inside the cave, gnawing on a succulent morsel of fresh sugar-cane he had discovered while foraging that afternoon.

"Oh, you're always looking at the dark side of things," Singer said.

"Not the dark side—*realism*, my little friend. After all, we've had it so good these last few days, something real bad must be about to happen."

Silver glanced over at the portly Budger and smiled. "You have no confidence about happiness?"

"I'm confident it's pretty *rare*!" Budger said. "Oh, we have our moments—brief moments here and there. But trouble comes more often, don't you think, sire? You've seen enough of it, I'd think."

Silver nodded slowly. "That's true enough, Budger. But we must have hope."

"Hope, eh?" Budger waved his sugarcane like a pointer. "Well, all I can say is, when things get *too* good for *too* long—well, you just better watch out!"

Singer sat up suddenly with a faraway look on his face. He began to weave slightly, and little murmurs came from his throat.

"Look out, Budger warned, "he's about to compose another poem."

And sure enough, after walking back and forth for a few minutes, finally clearing his throat, Singer began to recite in his poetry voice—a low, rhythmical tone:

> *"The road winds on through darksome trees,*
> *And as the weary traveler plods along,*
> *The trees reach out with skinny claws*
> *And sing a broken, hopeless song."*

"Just what we need!" Budger complained. "A sad song!"

"Hush, now," Silver said quickly. "Sometimes a sad song is better than a happy one."

Singer just kept singing.

> *"The winter winds that come in blasts*
> *Of heavy snow and downy flake*
> *Will freeze the stoutest chap*
> *And cause the strongest heart to break."*

Budger began to mumble a complaint, but then Singer's song set a lighter mood.

> *"But when the snows of winter melt,*
> *And from the earth the flowers spring,*
> *Every heart of every mouse*
> *Lifts up his voice and then he sings.*
>
> *The road winds ever on the way*
> *Round many a dangerous bend.*
> *But those who keep their courage high*
> *Will come at last to the journey's end."*

Budger nodded and said, "That's beautiful, Singer, but I still think trouble's coming."

And sure enough, it did—that very night, silently and deadly.

As the mice drifted off to sleep, they tossed and turned, trying to rest. Sleep reluctantly came, but as they all breathed deeply and dreamed, though fitfully, a weasel came into the camp.

If Budger and the others had been awake, he would have undoubtedly explained that next to the shrew there is no more bloodthirsty animal than the long-tailed weasel. Its scientific name means "those who carry off mice," and it looks like a snake with legs. Worse, the fully grown male who had discovered the cave was larger and heavier than most weasels. His dark brown sides and back were set off by a cream-colored belly, and his long tail had a black tip. He had once sneaked into a henhouse and killed sixty chickens in just a few moments.

The white-foot sentry at the cave entrance awoke only long enough to feel the weasel's needle-sharp teeth in the base of his neck. The weasel sensed the large number of living creatures inside the cave and trembled with delight. Silently he glided into the shadows and had sliced the necks of nearly a dozen sleeping white-feet before the alarm was raised by a female who lived only long enough to utter a short, piercing cry.

All the others were awake instantly. Chip, seeing the intruder, cried out, "Rag-Tags, stand with me!" He rushed straight toward the monster, who was reaching for a new victim.

Chip felt like a grasshopper charging a bull elephant, but he did not hesitate. He looked with horror at the bloodstained throat and razor-sharp fangs, then plunged Durance right into the enemy's black nose.

The weasel cried out in pain and stood on his back legs, determined to kill the one who dared hurt him. But at that moment something pierced one of the weasel's feet, and he saw a tiny shrew grinning up at him, poised for another thrust and screaming wildly. With a snarl the invader bent down and grasped Trooper in his jaws. But now not only did he have a small sword thrust into his nose again, but suddenly the floor was swarming with white-feet, all jabbing and slashing at him with daggers and knives.

This was too much for the beast. He had never retreated from anything, much less a pack of mice, but feeling like a grizzly who was being swarmed by hornets he turned and fled into the night.

"Rag-Tags forever!" Chip and his comrades cried, and they sang a victory song that would be remembered in white-foot history for many years to come. After all, to their knowledge, this was the first time a weasel was defeated by mice!

"We drove off the enemy," Budger sighed finally. "But what about these?" He pointed to the bodies of those who had been killed by the weasel "They'll never make it to the West."

"Some of us are bound to die on the way, sad as that may be," Silver said. "But better here, Budger, than in chains back at the burrow."

"Maybe so, but I say we have chosen more trouble than we can face or conquer."

"No, Budger," Chip said firmly. "We will finish our journey—all the way to the West."

"That's pie in the sky," Budger snorted even as he laid a friendly paw on Chip's shoulder. "But it would be kind of nice, wouldn't it?" He shook his head as if embarrassed by the emotion he had let show. "Well, maybe you and Silver and the others will get to the West. But not me, I reckon. It's not logical to even believe in such a place. These bodies, on the other hand, they're sad and they're real. We'd better get to work."

But he was right about one thing—more trouble would come—the next day just as they were preparing to leave the cave and head west to the river.

Before they had gotten more than 200 yards from the cave, the forward scouts encountered a party of brown rats, and a fierce battle ensued. Soon a dozen wounded white-feet lay near many more dead rats.

"Did you get them all, major?" Silver asked anxiously.

Slowly Major Meadows shook his head. "No. At least one of them got away. I'm sorry, sire."

"Couldn't be helped," Silver said at once, knowing the white-feet had done their best, and yet afraid of the consequences of one of the rats' escaping. They all realized that once Colonel Murkon knew where they were, he would lead a force there to surround them and finish them off.

"I think we had better move out as quickly as possible," Silver said.

"Yes, but that won't really help, will it?" Chip said slowly. "More brown rats will be here in about two days, I'd guess."

"Maybe sooner."

Gloom assaulted all their hearts, and even Silver looked defeated as he slumped against a large root.

An idea suddenly began to form in Chip's mind. He waited, and it fell into place almost as if it had been given to him somehow. In fact, he was quite sure it had. "I think," he said slowly, "that I know what we can do."

Silver looked up quickly, and his face had new hope in it. "What is it, captain?"

Chip said, "The rest of you—all except me, Ben, Budger, and Singer—move on as quickly as you can. Head for the river."

"But what will you do?" the major asked.

"I'd rather not tell you, but we'll catch up with you soon. Just leave us a trail, and as soon as we can—well . . ." He hesitated, wanting to use the right words, words he couldn't seem to find. "As soon as we can, we'll meet you."

Prince Hal said, "Captain, I'd like to go with you."

Chip looked at the prince with a nervous smile. "My Prince, I thank you for this—it's not that I don't want you at my side. But your place is with the main party—they need your support."

Hal's face grew dark, and he said, "But I want to help!"

"You must put the nation first," Princess Hallee said. She added, "Captain Chip, you will be careful? You know how I—how we all depend on you."

Chip gulped and said, "We don't intend to take any risks we don't have to."

Budger grunted, "I'll see to *that*, princess!"

Trooper, wondering why he wasn't remaining behind with the other Rag-Tags, said, "My good fran Cheep, is eet not a good idea for your most brave warrior—me—to also stay here?"

"No, Trooper, you must guard the prince and help the major any way that is needed." He continued nervously, "Major Meadows, we'll meet you to the west. Take care of the prince," he whispered. "I think he's growing up to be a *real* king."

"I'll eat my sword if he doesn't!" said the major. "All right, everybody move out now. On with you, Porky!"

The four watched the caravan make its way into the deep woods. Then Chip turned to his three friends and said timidly, "Wait until you hear my plan!"

CHAPTER NINETEEN
A Rattrap

NEARLY twenty-four hours had passed since Major Meadows led the white-feet toward the river, and the four Rag-Tags had worked furiously during most of that time. Confident they were ready, they threw themselves down wearily in the cave waiting for the morning.

Chip looked at the others and thought about what a struggle it had been to get them to agree to his plan. Now that it was dark he was afraid they were right—his idea would never work! But now they had to go ahead with it—there was no other choice.

He had explained the plan to the others as soon as Porky

and the chariot lumbered out of sight trailed by the rear guard. He began, "Sooner or later the enemy will come down that trail, perhaps in two days."

"More likely one, I'd say," Budger added.

"When they get here, we have to be ready for them. We need a rattrap that will catch them all, one they can't escape from. If none of them can get word back to their commanders, we'll have time to get away. Then we can meet the others at the river."

Budger prodded the dust with a stick, then looked up. "How do you propose to trap an entire company of rats? Why, there may be a hundred of them!"

"I don't think so. I believe Murkon will send out the fastest unit he has, a small one, and then send a larger group later to finish their dirty business."

"Maybe," Budger replied nervously. "But how can we trap them?"

"That will be up to Ben," Chip said. "Come with me." He led them into the cave and then to the brink of the chasm where the huge rock they'd noticed earlier extended out over the pit. "What if we were standing here and this rock suddenly tilted toward that hole?" Chip asked.

"I see what you mean, Chip," Ben said at once. "We get them to come to the edge here, then we tip the rock, and boom—good-bye, rats!"

"One little detail bothers me," Budger grunted. "Just a trifle perhaps. Eh, how do we get them to stand here?"

"I've been thinking about that, but first—Ben, do you think you can rig up a way to tip this rock at just the right moment?"

Ben began to scurry around, muttering under his breath. Finally he said, "Shouldn't be too hard. We'll use a rock for a counterbalance, and then we'll use a pole for a fulcrum—"

"We don't need the details," Chip said hurriedly. "You can show us later. Now, Budger, how *do* we get the rats to stand here? Any ideas?"

"Let's see, they'll have to all line up here at the same time . . ."

Chip swallowed and then said much more calmly than he felt, "I'll have to let them capture me."

"What!" "No way!" "Oh, that simply will not do," they all began to argue.

"Wait a minute!" Chip shouted. "At least listen to my suggestion. I'll let them capture me, and then I'll pretend to be a traitor. I'll promise to lead them to our secret hideout—a very difficult place to get to. Then I'll lead them into the cave and right to this spot."

"And then what?" Singer demanded. "You'll go over with them!"

"No. I'll get them here, and then I'll call out a signal. Then Ben will count to four, or however long it takes me to get from here to the opening. I run out of the cave, and they fall into the pit! Simple, eh?"

"Simpleminded!" Budger snorted. "That's the craziest plan I've ever heard, and I've heard some crazy ones, believe me! I can think of a dozen things that could go wrong!"

Chip waited until Budger stopped talking, then added quietly, "Can you think of another way, Budger? Can any of you?"

"Well—" A long silence followed.

"Neither could I. Any plan is dangerous at a time like this. But it's the only one I could come up with that has even a slight chance of succeeding."

Ben murmured, "Well, I have no doubt I can fix the trap so it will work well—the tricky part will be Chip's getting away at just the right moment."

"No, the tricky part will be when they get their hands on you, Chip. They won't want to risk losing you," Singer said. "Colonel Murkon himself may be leading the party. You've already outsmarted him once. I'd say your chances of doing it again are very small. Even if Colonel Murkon doesn't lead this unit, they know who you are, Chip, and they'll want to take you back to headquarters for questioning."

"He's right, Chip," Budger said with a frown. "So your plan just won't work."

"Oh, it'll work," Singer said. "We just need a different bait."

"A different bait?" Chip inquired.

"Me," Singer said. "They don't know me—there's no special prize on my head. Chip, you know I've always been a ham—always behaving like I'm onstage. Well, this will be the greatest role of my life! The sniveling white-foot traitor promises to tell everything. Our audience of foul-mouthed brown rats will love it! And then as they fall into the deep—" he waved his arms theatrically—"I'll compose the most tremendous ode ever written!"

Chip looked fondly at the beaming Singer, weighing the merits of the new plan. But he shook his head. "No. It's my place to take the risk. I can't possibly ask anyone else to do it."

Then began an argument that went on for two hours. Finally Chip was convinced, though secretly he had huge doubts, that it would be safer for all if Singer were the bait and the captain himself sprang the trap.

"If we did it my way, you'd probably be so busy thinking of a rhyme that you'd forget to tip the rock and would let me go into the chasm with the rats," Chip said fondly with a playful swipe at Singer's head. "All right, I agree, but we're going to go over the plan again and again and again, to make sure we get it right. Agreed?"

Ben and Budger began gathering materials for the trap, and Chip and Singer practiced the plan step by step over and over again until they knew exactly how many times Chip could say "Rag-Tags together" from the time Singer called that same phrase until he made it to the door at a dead run. They finally agreed on six times.

"Singer, when you call, I'll start counting, and on the sixth time I'll cut the rope. That means I'll have to cut the rope *before* I can actually see you, and you'll have to dive through the door the best way you can."

"It'll be a piece of cake, Chip," Singer grinned. "Enough practice and planning. I'm hungry. Let's eat something."

"No, we're going to practice some more. I'll be the colonel or whoever, and you try your story on me." They went on for several more hours, and Chip had to admit that Singer did a much better job of acting than he could ever have done. But because it was such a dangerous venture, they kept at it most of the night until Singer finally rebelled.

"It'll be all right, I tell you. We have it worked out perfectly." He rubbed his stomach and said, "Now can we eat?"

But now, tired of thinking about how this had all come about, knowing Singer had gone out into the woods so the brown rats could capture him, lying in the darkness and feeling fear in his throat, Chip could not help thinking about the many ways the plan could fail.

"Budger?" he whispered.

"You can't sleep, eh, Chip?"

"No. Budger, what if—"

"Now just a minute, captain," Budger said, "we've decided on the plan, and we're committed to it. There's no use going over what we should have done or could have done."

The light was beginning to break in the east, and Chip could see his large friend's kind face.

"You're worried about Singer, eh?"

"Yes, I am!"

"Nothing can be done about that, Chip. That's the way it is when you're in command!"

"Then I don't want to be in command!"

Budger chuckled deep in his furry chest. "I reckon you don't have much to say about it, according to what Silver told me."

"What do you mean by that?" Chip was surprised that Budger ever listened seriously to the prophet.

"You know—how you've been chosen." Budger had a mysterious look in his eyes. "He told me that business about a great deliverer being raised up, and I guess you're him, Chip."

"But I don't want to be!" Chip cried. "Why does it have to be *me*?"

"It has to be *somebody*," Budger said. Then he shook Chip's shoulder with a strong paw. "Chip, I—" Just then they both heard the unmistakable sound of approaching soldiers.

"It's time, Budger! Ben, wake up, they're here!" Ben sprang up and took his position beside Chip. They had agreed that if for any reason Chip could not cut the rope, one of the others must do it. So now the three stood scarcely daring to breathe, their hearts threatening to jump out of their chests as a company of rats passed out of the woods and into view.

"Look! There's Singer, right in front!" Chip said. "It's going to work! Everything is going just like we planned it!"

But Budger sighed heavily. "No, no, it's not, Chip."

"What do you mean, Budger?"

"A rope is tied around Singer's neck, and a big rat is holding the other end of it. He'll never be able to break away and make it to the opening!"

They were all filled with horror at this turn of events! Singer's paws were tied behind his back, and the rope around his neck was firmly in the grasp of one of the biggest rats any of the white-feet had ever seen!

CHAPTER TWENTY
An Agonizing Decision

CROUCHED beside the tautly strung cable made of vines, the white-feet could hear the enemy voices clearly.

"Wait a minute," the leading officer said. "I don't like the looks of this. It could be a trap." He stepped closer to Singer and grasped him cruelly by his slender neck. "You'd better not be playing any tricks or you'll get some more of what you got last night."

Singer's voice was very feeble as he gasped, "No tricks, captain! This is the place, I swear it!" It was clear to Chip that the quiver was more than an act. He chanced a look at the group and saw that Singer was barely able to stand, and there was dried blood—and some not dried—on his face. Chip ground his teeth in helpless rage and swore a vow against the enemy captain.

"Why are there no guards?" the captain demanded. "They wouldn't leave the entrance to their lair unguarded. You're lying!"

"No, no, I'm not. There's no need for a guard here because this isn't the main entrance. They keep *that* guarded day and night! You wouldn't get past that one!" Singer said. "This is an escape passageway, and it's very steep, so you'll have to be very careful, captain!"

"And it leads to their main burrow?" demanded the officer.

"Yes, yes, it does!" Singer cried. "Please don't hurt me any more! I've done all you want."

"Corporal, hold on to that rope. We'll make him go first just to be sure it's safe. Keep your sword on his back. Keep your eyes open, all of you."

As the rats cautiously entered the cave, Budger whispered, "*Now* what can we do?"

"We can't spring the trap," Ben said. "That's for sure. Singer can't possibly get away."

Thoughts were running through Chip's head faster than a flooded river. He felt like throwing his sword down and running away. He wanted to be anywhere except here!

"Maybe—maybe we can get them one at a time as they come out," he said, knowing how foolish that sounded but not having any better idea.

"Not a chance!" Budger snorted. "We might get one or two, but they'd get us before we could finish the job."

"Let's get away while we can," Ben said. "We can't help Singer anyway. He'll just be a prisoner of war, won't he? I mean, they wouldn't do anything worse?"

"But what about all the others?" Chip asked. "This patrol will catch up to them and find them for sure!"

'But, Chip, there's nothing we can do!" Ben said rolling his eyes.

They stood there silently, until finally Chip said what all three were thinking. "We have to cut the rope—we have no choice!"

Budger looked Chip in the eye for a long moment, then said slowly, "As a soldier I've had to take many gut-wrenching actions, Chip, harder than you know. But—but I can't do *this*—" He motioned toward the rope. "I just *can't*!"

"Me either!" Ben said quickly. "Not to Singer! He's our friend, Chip, a good friend."

Chip drew his sword slowly, and the morning sun turned it blood-red as he extended it toward the rope. The others saw the glazed look in his eyes, and his voice did not sound like his own when he said, "The rope must be cut!" He looked at them so strangely that they became afraid.

"How can you seriously propose such a thing, Chip?" Budger asked.

"It's better that one white-foot die for the nation than for the whole nation to perish," he said very quietly. His face was old and worn.

Out of the depths of the cave they suddenly heard Singer's voice! It was not feeble now. They heard the words echo triumphantly through the cave and out into the rosy dawn. "Rag-Tags forever!"

Budger and Ben stepped back as Captain Chip of the Rag-Tag Brigade raised Durance and repeating in a choking voice, "Rag-Tags forever—Rag-Tags forever—Rag-Tags forever." Each time he said it, his face grew more strained and his eyes filled with enraged sorrow. As he said the familiar phrase the sixth time, with all his strength he brought the razor-sharp sword down on the straining rope, and it gave way instantly.

From the cave there came a frantic cry of rat voices screaming in wild terror, and then the crashing of the huge rock. But over the sound of all came the voice of Singer: "Good-bye, Captain Chip! Don't grieve—I'll see you in—" A tremendous crash of falling rock drowned out the brave white-foot's last words, and then there was only an awful silence.

CHAPTER TWENTY-ONE
A Sad Reunion

SOMEWHERE far off in the west a wolf howled, and two small figures under a towering oak froze for a few seconds, then began to gather acorns quickly. A sense of urgency, due to more than the frosty air, drove them to move more rapidly than usual.

"It's getting cold," Prince Hal said. He lifted his nose in the air and sniffed cautiously. "I wouldn't be surprised to see it snow before too long."

"You may be right," Silver said. "We've made good time, but we started late in the fall."

"What will we do if it snows? We won't be able to keep

moving so easily, and we don't have enough food to stay in one place very long."

"Don't think about that, My Prince. We have enough of a burden without adding to it."

"You mean Chip and the others?"

"Yes."

"They should have been back by this time, shouldn't they?" Prince Hal asked. He stopped gathering the acorns and looked with concern at the seer. "Do you think something terrible has happened?"

"Perhaps. Theirs was a dangerous task—suicidal, some would say. Maybe I shouldn't have let them do it." The wrinkles in Silver's face were growing deeper almost daily, it seemed to Hal. It startled him to think that even Silver was having doubts about what had happened, about what would happen.

Hal didn't ask any more questions, but as they finished the job and made their way back to the camp, his thoughts were gloomy and fearful. The past few days had been hard for the prince. He had been a spoiled royal son one day, and on the next he was forced to begin a dangerous journey and to make sacrifices that were making him grow up faster than he had wanted. His simple life of privilege was gone, probably forever.

He looked around as they entered the camp and was pleased as he remembered how the major had made him chief of the scouting party to find a safe spot. When Silver saw his choice, he said with a smile, "You have done well!" Hal had realized on that day that the approval of mice of character was worth far more than all the two-faced applause he'd ever received from his old followers at the royal court in his pampered days!

Ben's chariot sat in front of a large rock that covered a sandbar, part of a streambed. Most of the white-feet were under the rock. A large fire burned brightly, and the fragrant smells of hot food filled the area. The creek that ran nearby each spring was now just a trickle. The white-feet were glad to have fresh water close by for drinking and cleaning. Their hard journey had been dusty and exhausting, and they had not had time for proper clothing. But now there was a frenzy of bathing, brushing, and cleaning.

"Ah, you are back, my frans!" Trooper cried out. "Seet down and have some of thees most delicious food." He ushered them to a place near the fire and pressed some of the freshly roasted meat into their paws. "Eet ease hot but gooood!"

Hallee came and sat next to Prince Hal, patting him on the arm. "We were getting a little worried about you. You were gone so long." Since leaving the burrow, Hallee had grown closer to her brother, and he to her.

"We found an abundant supply of acorns, and it took a while to gather them," Hal explained. He looked around and asked hesitantly, "Did they get back yet?"

There was a silence, and Hal did not need any further answer. He looked at their faces, then added, "We had hoped to see them here."

Major Meadows said quickly, "Well, don't lose hope, my boy. They could be back at any time. It was a most perilous task, but if there's anyone I'd trust to bring it off, it's Chip and his squad. I tell you, there's something about that Chip. I wish I knew what it was. Perhaps—" He shook his head.

Silver was concerned about the deep sadness that was becoming more obvious every day. He looked around the circle and saw the porcupine almost asleep with a stalk of wild alfalfa in his mouth. "Porky, wake up—I want to ask you something."

"Wot's that?" Porky gave a little jump and gulped as he swallowed the morsel whole.

"I've been wondering how you came to be such good friends with Singer. Without your help we wouldn't have been able to escape, you know, and we're all tremendously grateful to you."

"Ah, it ain't nothin'!" Porky said in a muffled tone.

"Yes, it is, sir!" the major disagreed quickly. "What other animal would have pulled that thing across the wilderness?"

"Eet ees true! And who else but you, my dear fran Porky, would have been so good at keeping the hawks and wolves away from these white-feets!" Trooper insisted.

"You have saved us all," Princess Hallee said warmly. "I'd kiss you, but there's no place!" She laughed.

"Ah now, none of that!" Porky protested, embarrassed to be the center of attention. "Did you ask about Singer and me? Aw, that was a time, that was!" He stopped and began to go to sleep again, but everyone began urging him to tell his story.

"Well, it was like this. I'd gone and stuck me foot in a trap, I had." Cries of concern went up, and he nodded slowly. "It was one of them little 'uns, but I couldn't get out no ways. I ate every blade of grass and every stick I could reach, but after a while they was gone, and I was mighty thirsty, don't you see? Well now, I was about ready to give up when I hears this little voice, and I was thinkin' I was dreamin' or delirious, but then I looks up and there he is—this little white-foot with a twinkle in his eye."

Porky reached out and took one of the fresh acorns that Trooper handed him. Silver was relieved to see that the porcupine had taken their minds off their worries—for a while at least.

"He upped and give me a bit of wild onion—mighty welcome it was—and then he kept draggin' in all sorts of stuff for me to eat. And all the time he was sayin' things like 'Heads up, Chap!' or 'Come on now, don't let it get you down!' I tell ya, he just wouldn't let me quit! Finally he came draggin' a little cup made out of some kind of flower, and it was full of water!" Porky smacked his lips. "I tell you, it was the best drink I ever had in me whole life!"

"But how did you get loose, Porky?" Prince Hal asked.

"Why, Singer done it all hisself! First off, he tried to open the metal jaws around my foot. When he couldn't do nothin' with that, he went to work diggin' like crazy, and finally he got to where the trap was tied onto a root, and he gnawed the root until I was loose! Then he got some kind of lever and got the thing off my foot." Porky sighed fondly and said, "He's a real clever one, ain't he now?"

"Yes, he is," Silver agreed warmly. "I suppose that's why you've been willing to leave your home and drag that thing all over the world."

Now rather enjoying the attention, Porky continued, "Aw, it ain't nothin'." He curled up into a ball so that all they could see were thousands of white-tipped barbs. All they heard was a sleepy little voice saying, "He's a good 'un, that Singer!"

Most of the others left, falling into a weary sleep. Hal remained, and Hallee stayed close to him. Major Meadows and Silver talked for a long time about supplies, food, and possible dangers. Trooper nodded, taking a sip from a little flask from time to time.

"Well," Silver said finally, "we'd all best get to bed."

"Silver," Hal said, "I don't understand quite—well, where are we going?"

"We are going west," the seer said. "Right now that's about all I can tell you. But I will say this—we'll have to make a decision soon, because the river is not too far away."

"The river?"

"Yes, the Great River—the one that flows into the sea."

"The sea?" Hallee asked.

"Oh, yes! The most water you ever saw, princess!" the major said. Then he asked Silver, "What do you think we will do then?"

"Well, we must either cross the river and continue west until—" He lifted his face to the skies, and they all watched him quietly. It was one of those times when the old white-foot seemed to be listening to something, or someone, they could not hear. "—until the way is made clear to us."

"Until the way is made clear—can you be a bit more specific? No, probably not. So what's the other choice?" the major asked impatiently.

Silver got up and stared westward. "I don't want to say yet. I see something—but it's rather vague. Something about the river, but I'm not sure what—" He shrugged, and they started to say something else but decided not to. "Did you hear that?" the prophet asked sharply.

"Yes. There ease someone coming!" Trooper whispered, drawing his sword. "It ease maybe those rats!"

They all drew their weapons and made a line across the woods in front of the entrance to the cave-like refuge. It was a long time before they heard the sound again, and this time they recognized a voice.

"That ease Ben!" Trooper cried, and they all ran forward as several weary figures emerged from the darkness.

"You're back!" Silver cried with joy. "We were afraid something had happened!"

Budger limped in wearily. He was holding Chip's arm, seeming to lead him. Ben walked a few paces in front of them.

"Did it go well?" the major asked. He looked around and then asked, "Where's Singer?"

Budger shook his head sharply, and Ben said very quickly, "Do you have anything to eat? We're starved!"

There was a quick flurry as the three sat down close to the dying fire and food was set before them. Budger and Ben began to eat ravenously, but Chip sat still holding his food in his lap for a long time, then slowly raised it to his mouth. He had not said a word.

Finally Hal could stand it no longer. "What happened?"

"Well, we got them rats off our trail," Budger said slowly. "That bunch won't give us any trouble."

"Were there any survivors to carry a warning back?" the major demanded.

"No survivors!" Ben said shortly, seeming to lose interest in his food. He suddenly bowed his head, and his shoulders began to shake.

Silver waited for a long moment, then said, "Chip? How is it with you, my boy?"

Chip did not even move his head. He was holding some food in one paw, but his eyes were fixed on something far-off that none of them could see. He seemed not to hear Silver—indeed, he seemed unaware of everyone and everything around him. His eyes had no expression whatsoever. It was as if the real Chip was gone, and his body was functioning on a physical level only.

"What's—what's *wrong* with him?" Princess Hallee whispered.

"He's been like this ever since we lost Singer," Budger said in a normal tone of voice. "Oh, you don't need to worry about him hearing us! I only wish he *would*!" He told them quickly about how they had destroyed the rats and how Singer had been lost.

Throughout the telling, Chip paid no attention. "And he hasn't said a word since," Budger concluded. "He does what we tell him to right enough, but he isn't right somehow, you know?"

Silver's wise old eyes were filled with pain. He sat down beside Chip, taking one of his paws. He sat for a long time looking into the expressionless face. Finally he turned with a weary sigh to the others and murmured in a hopeless voice, "I think—I think that our Captain Chip has paid too high a price."

CHAPTER TWENTY-TWO
Hallee and Chip

FIVE days had dragged by since the patrol returned, and the countryside had become more difficult each day, making the travelers more and more weary. Several times they had to make long detours to get around bluffs or thickets. Porky's feet were getting quite sore, but he never grumbled, and they all sought the tenderest and freshest bark and shoots for him. Each night he would simply eat until he fell asleep, looking like a dead porcupine until the major woke him up the next morning.

Sickness was also becoming a problem. Several soldiers grew ill and had to be placed in the chariot with the wounded, the children, and the elderly. Eight of the wounded had died, and when a litter was born during the third day, every pup died. "It's not natural—perhaps it's a sign that we're not doing the right thing!" many protested. In addition, it was getting colder each day, and Major Meadows and Silver knew that if a blizzard should hit them, most of them would die.

"Look," Silver said one day, pointing upward at several crows sailing high in the air. "They've been up there off and on for the last few days."

"They're just crows, sire," Hal said in surprise.

"I think not. They're scouts."

"Scouts! Scouts for who?"

"For the enemy. The Dread Deliverer uses all kinds of beasts to accomplish his dark purposes. He captures their minds. These crows are crisscrossing in a way I've never seen them do before. They're looking for us, I think. If the woods weren't so thick, they would have spotted us already."

Hal looked up with apprehension. "What should we do?"

Silver thought, then said, "We must keep under deep cover and not cross any open spaces where we can be seen. See to it, My Prince." Silver had learned to depend on Hal, and now he scurried off, leaving the prince to carry out the order.

Hallee was already overburdened with the care of the sick and the elderly in the chariot. But now she added another task to her responsibilities. Someone had to watch Chip at all times. He would sometimes just wander off, and then a patrol would have to go fetch him. They would find him sitting down and staring into space, but he would come quietly when they asked him.

Hallee thought this was like caring for a grown pup. She even had to tell him when to eat. Indeed she found that unless she put the food in his paw and ordered him to eat it, he would simply walk off and leave the meal behind. She also had to tell him when to sleep and when to get up.

And he never spoke a word. Day after day he opened his mouth only to eat. Worse, the emptiness in his face was more sad than anything she could remember ever seeing.

On the seventh day no path could be found for the chariot. So they all rested while scouts were sent to find a passable path. Most of the soldiers and workers dropped into an exhausted sleep, but two of the young pups, almost too big for the chariot, had wandered off. Hallee had to go find them before a hawk or weasel did, but she didn't dare leave Chip alone. He was more of a pup than the two who were lost!

"Come on, Chip!" she said, and seizing his paw she dragged him after her into the woods, calling the pups by name. For a long time she looked and called. Finally, desperately tired, she sat down under a small fern, pulling Chip down beside her and almost weeping in desperation.

Just as she was about to pull herself wearily to her feet, she heard Chip's voice—a sound she had feared she would never hear again.

Chip said rather slowly and a little hoarsely, "I—I killed him, you know."

Hallee glanced up in amazement. Chip was looking into her eyes, and she could tell that he knew who she was. She almost began to cry tears of joy, but she was afraid that crying or even speaking might drive him back into his paralyzing grief.

"I killed him, you know."

She said very slowly, "Did you, Chip?"

He looked into her eyes very seriously and nodded. "Oh, yes. I killed him."

Hallee said gently, "It wasn't your fault."

Chip shivered and seemed to grow even more tense. "Yes, it was! I killed him!" He seemed to go limp, the light went out of his eyes, and he was as before.

Hallee waited for Chip to go on, but he dropped his head and said no more. "You wait right here, Chip," she said. "I'll go looking for those two pups."

Chip seemed not to hear, and when Hallee walked away, he did not move. For what seemed a long time he simply waited, and then a loud voice announced, "The Maker is with you, mighty mouse of valor!"

The words seemed to strike Chip like an arrow in his heart.

He leaped to his feet and lifted his eyes to the figure before him. For a moment he could not speak, then he gasped, "Maker, is it You?"

"Yes, Chip." The being drew closer and threw back the hood that covered His face. For the first time Chip saw the calm eyes, the slight smile, and the noble strength in the Maker's face.

"Oh, Maker, don't call me a mouse of valor!"

"And why not, My son?"

"Because I'm a miserable failure!"

The Maker drew closer, and Chip's vision grew dim with tears as he saw the love in the dark eyes. The Maker said quietly, "You are grieving over your friend."

"Yes! I killed him!"

"No, you did not."

"But I was the one who cut the rope!"

"But I was the one who told you to cut the rope." The Maker reached out and gently lifted Chip's face, then said, "You have risked your life many times for your people, My son. And many of your companions have died for their nation. Were their deaths all without meaning? Do you not understand that it was I who was protecting the white-feet?"

Chip thought of the many friends who had died in battle. "Indeed, their deaths were not without meaning. They died for what they loved—their brothers and sisters of the Burrow."

"And do you not see that Singer died for that same cause?"

"But why not *me*?"

"Each of My servants has a work to do. Singer has done what I asked of him. Your work is not finished, Chip. In a sense it has not yet begun." The Maker paused, and His voice suddenly grew louder. "Singer's death has meaning for you only if you are willing to obey Me. If you go on hiding from your calling, from My plan for your heart and life, all is lost. Your people are on My heart, as are all living things. I chose you for this time, My son. Will you refuse to be that for which I made you?"

A sense of shame flooded Chip, but he knew he could not refuse the plea of those dark eyes that were fastened on him. "I—I will do anything you command, Sire! But I am not worthy. I have often been selfish, always making myself the hero in my dreams. And sometimes my fear has kept me from behaving as courageously as I knew I should."

The Maker did not take his eyes from Chip's. "That is true, but I am willing to forgive you and to change you. Furthermore, you do not have the strength for the task that lies ahead of you. Thus far you have performed your duties in your own power. But if you would please Me, you must act in My strength, and for that, your heart must be changed."

"My heart?"

"Yes, for it is in the heart that I receive all true service. And only the heart that is given freely to Me can change. Will you let Me change your heart, Chip?"

For a long moment Chip didn't answer, but then he knew this was the moment that would change his entire life forever. He fell to his knees and cried out, "I want to love You, Maker! Please, forgive all my wrongdoing, and change my heart!"

Chip felt the Maker's hand rest lightly on his head. He closed his eyes, and time passed. Later he could not remember how long he knelt, but when he finally looked up, he saw joy on the Maker's face.

"Is my heart changed?" Chip whispered, but then he leaped to his feet. "It *is* changed! I know it!"

The Maker smiled. "Do you know what is different, My son?"

"I can't tell, but when I look at You—"

"You now love Me, Chip. That is what I want from you and from all My servants. It's not what you can do for Me that matters," the Maker said quietly. "What gives Me pleasure is when My creatures love Me."

"I'll always love You, Maker!" Chip whispered. "And I'll obey You all my days!"

†

Hallee came back, herding the missing pups. Chip had his back to her, and she said, "Come now, Chip. We must go home."

And then Hallee got the surprise of her life. Chip turned and said, "I'm ready, Hallee." His eyes were clear, and so was his voice. Coming to her, he took her paw and said simply, "You've been very good to me, Hallee."

Hallee stared at Chip, then said, "Chip! You're like your old self! What happened?"

Chip smiled and turned to pick up one of the pups. "I've just met Someone who gave me what I've always wanted deep inside."

"Someone out here in the woods?"

"Yes, but He's not only here—He's everywhere, Hallee," Chip said. He smiled and said, "I met the Maker, and I'll never be the same again. Now He lives in my heart, so that even if I can't see Him with my eyes, I know I'll never be alone! Let's get back to the others. They may be worried about us and about these pups."

They made their way back to camp, and Chip went at once to speak to Silver. The two of them walked away, Silver listening intently to the young white-foot.

Hallee could not hear their conversation, but later she pulled Silver aside and spoke of how changed Chip was. "What has happened to him, Silver?"

"He has met the Maker, and he now has a heart devoted to serving Him. In a way he always did, but now he's a new creature. I want you to stay very close to him. I think he will begin to talk more now that he's broken the silence. *That* was what concerned me. If he hadn't spoken, he would have died, I think."

"But he'll be all right, won't he, Silver?" Hallee cried.

"I think he will. It will depend on you, or I miss my guess. Other than myself, he has spoken only to you, so he must trust you. Stay close. If he speaks, try to get him to say as much as you can."

Chip didn't say anything more until late that night. As Hallee sat beside him she said quietly, "I think Singer saved us all, from what I have heard. I think he *knew* what he had to do, just as *you* would have done, Chip, wouldn't you?"

"I hope so, Hallee." He did not speak for a long time, then added, "You know, when I raised Durance and cut the rope, I heard—"

She saw that he had grown strangely calm, and she asked, "What did you hear, Chip?"

Chip looked into her eyes, and she saw that his madness was gone. He said in a voice of wonder, "I heard Singer calling out, 'Good-bye, Captain Chip! Don't grieve my departure!'"

"Did—did you hear anything else, Chip?"

"Yes. He said, 'I'll see you in—' But he never did finish that thought." Chip gave a little sob and went on, "Where do you think he meant, Hallee?"

She said, "I don't know, Chip, but I believe you'll see him again—somewhere in the West, Silver says."

Chip looked toward the West for a long moment, then whispered intently, "I'll see you, Singer! I'll see you in the Deep West!"

CHAPTER TWENTY-THREE
Trapped!

HE seems like the old Chip!" Major Meadows said happily one morning. He and Silver were watching as Chip and several scouts returned with news about what they had seen further ahead. Two days had passed since Silver found Chip and Hallee sitting at dawn by a dead campfire with Chip seemingly back to his old self. But he wasn't—not all the way.

"Haven't you noticed anything about Chip?" Silver asked Major Meadows.

"He seems fit to me."

"Physically, yes. But there's one thing Chip won't do now."

"And what's that?"

"He won't give an order."

The major looked quickly at Silver, then back toward Chip. "Oh, my word! That's bad! I've seen it before, of course. Good officers often discover they just can't bring themselves to order their troops into battle."

"I believe it's because he still feels responsible for Singer's death."

"Well, he's not much good to us then, is he—I mean, as a leader?"

"No. As it is, he may never give an order again. To get him back to what he was, it would take some sort of—well, I don't know what exactly. We'll just have to pray and keep our eyes open."

Their progress was now slower than ever. So many crows flew overhead during all waking hours that everyone was convinced the birds were searching for them. The land had given way to thick, almost impassable tangles of briars. Food was scarce and cold since they didn't dare make any fires.

Two days later the scouts finally came back with welcome news. "There's a break to this blasted thorn patch!" the scout said excitedly. "Not too far from here there's a plain—flat as your paw."

"That means the river is close by!" Silver said at once.

"Well, that's good news," the major snorted.

"Is it?" Silver asked as if to himself. "Well, at least we'll get out of this thicket."

Chip was with Budger and Trooper when they got to the plain the next day. One minute Porky was struggling to get the chariot through the thick briars; the next it popped out into the sand like a cork out of a bottle.

Budger waved his paw at the sand. "I never thought a piece of flat land would look so good."

"I too am 'appy that we are out of de jongle!" Trooper breathed in the fresh air in large gulps.

"Chip," Budger said, "go tell the others to stay out of the open as much as they can, will you? Those crows are overhead again."

Chip only stared at him helplessly, and Budger saw that his friend could not bring himself to give even such a simple order. So he said quickly, "Never mind. I have to go over there anyway. You keep an eye on things out here."

As he trudged away Trooper followed him and said, "Budger, what ease wrong weeth our captain? He ease not heemself, no?"

"He'll be all right, Trooper. Just be patient with him." Budger only wished he was as confident as he sounded.

Late that afternoon they gathered for a council, but Chip sat far outside the circle, seeming to pay little attention.

"Well, I suppose it's decision time," the major announced. "What's our next move?"

They all looked to Silver for answers, as they had for many weeks. The seer said, "I'm not sure, but we have to do something! This snow won't hold off forever."

"Sire, what are our choices?" Prince Hal asked.

"Well, we have to get to the river, and to do that we have to cross this open stretch. If we go in daylight, the crows will see us. If we go at night, the owls will be there."

"But what ease left?" Trooper asked.

Silver pondered slowly, then said, "I think we have no choice but to send out a scouting party tonight. If they can dodge the owls, and if they can find us someplace where we can take shelter, and if they can get back to us alive, we can chance crossing the plain and the river. Otherwise . . ."

"I weel do eet!" Trooper said at once. "I was born for such a mission, no?"

Silver smiled at the tiny fighter. "I thought you would volunteer, my son."

"And I must go also," Prince Hal said.

"No, you must stay," Silver said at once.

"Not this time, Silver!" Hal's face was intent, and he seemed a far different prince than so long ago when he had insisted on leading his troops into battle without understanding what he was saying or the risks involved. "I know what you will say: 'You are the hope of the white-feet, the future king.' And that is true. But the king must not be a king in words only—he must lead."

"But if you are killed—" Silver protested.

Hal looked at him, and a warm smile broke across his handsome face. "Silver, how strange it would be if I need to remind you that the Maker will not fail me. I have faith in Him. Do you?"

"Well spoken!" Budger brimmed with delight. "He's got you, Silver!"

Silver slowly nodded, then smiled at the prince. "I believe you are my teacher in this instance, My Prince." Then he did what he had never done before—he bowed low before Prince Hal and said, "You are my Sovereign and my King."

Hal was confused and grew quite embarrassed. "Oh, you needn't make such a big thing out of it!"

Silver said gravely, "It *is* a big thing, Your Majesty. The white-feet have a king over them at last." Then he grew very serious. "How many will you take with you?"

"The fewer the better," Hal said at once. "I think Trooper and I will do."

"Ah! We weel not share thees glory with anyone!" Trooper kissed Hal's paw delicately. "Let us go now, My Prince. I am ready for thees adventure!"

Hallee did not like this development, but she knew her brother had come into a new period of his life. So she simply said, "Be very careful, will you?"

†

Two hours later Trooper and Prince Hal left, and there was a nervous silence in the camp as they disappeared in the darkness, crossing the plain by zigzagging this way and that, taking advantage of every bit of cover.

Trooper was an old hand, of course, at this sort of mission, but he was not sure how well Prince Hal would do. However, the prince showed an aptitude for the work, and they covered much ground in the first hour. Time after time an owl would glide over, but they would duck into a crevice or behind a rotten log. Soon they felt they were getting close to the river. "Smell that?" Hal asked.

"Eet ease the river," Trooper whispered. Then he stiffened. "Wait! There ease somebody coming!"

Then Hal heard it too, and they waited breathlessly with weapons drawn. Someone was walking very carefully across the same ridge of sand they had just crossed. Trooper crawled out on a branch of driftwood under which the pursuer must pass and waited. Soon a shadowy form appeared in the dim moonlight, and as it passed between them Trooper yelled, "Get heem!" They both fell on him with a fury. There was a brief struggle, and then their victim said, "Trooper, get your paw out of my mouth! It's me—Chip!"

"Chip!" the prince said in amazement. "What are you doing here?" They released him, and the three of them stood staring at one another. "Did Silver send you?"

"No—I just came." They waited for more of an explanation, but realizing that he had indeed wandered after them on his own, they glanced at each other and shrugged.

"Isn't that a line of trees over there?" Chip said. He pointed into the darkness, and by the light of the moon the other two saw that he was right. "I'll bet that's where the river is."

Quickly they covered the rest of the journey, and soon they were standing on the banks of the most water any of them had ever seen. None of them could see across it, and that made the scene even more frightening to the animals, who had never seen anything wider than a small creek.

"I don't like this," Hal said.

"I don't like heem too!" Trooper said in a nervous voice. "But look at these beeg trees. There ease plenty places for cover, no?"

"That's right," Hal said. "Let's find a good place, then get back and give a report."

Chip was staring out across the river. He was fascinated by the mystery of it, and finally he turned to the others and said, "He would have made a poem about it." And they knew he was thinking of Singer.

A short while later they found an excellent campsite—close to the river but well hidden from the crows. They began their trip back to the woods, but almost at once Trooper called, "Watch out! Eet ease a dog!" They dove under a large piece of driftwood just in time to avoid the snapping jaws of a terrier who had seemed to appear out of nowhere.

His teeth almost closed on Trooper's tail, but the three wedged themselves under the log and began trying to burrow back away from the claws of the dog, who was now digging furiously.

"Can we get out that way?" the prince asked in a shaky voice, pointing to the back of the log.

"No. It's solid wood," Chip said.

"Let's make a run for it!" Hal cried and would have darted into the terrier's jaws if Chip had not held him back.

"No. He'd get us for sure on this flat ground," Chip said.

"We have to do *something*!" Hal whispered.

"We must die with honor!" Trooper said as he drew his sword, preparing to march out in glory.

"Stop right there, Trooper!" Chip's voice rang out over the clawing of the dog, and the power of his command was such that Trooper stopped in his tracks.

Trooper looked at Chip, and then a big smile split his face. He laughed out loud despite the danger. "Well, Captain Cheep ease in command, no?"

Chip himself smiled. "Well, I guess I am giving orders again, and here they are—you two get over there—see that opening at the end?"

"And then what, my captain?" Trooper demanded.

"When I get the dog's attention, you two can make your break. I don't think you'll have any trouble. There's cover right over that ridge, as I recall. Once you're there, he can't trouble you."

Hal said tensely, "And what about you?"

"I can take care of myself."

Hal said stubbornly, "We're not going to leave you here!"

"No, I weel fool the dog, Cheep, and you had better make a run for it."

Something happened to Chip then, something that neither he nor the others could ever explain. He seemed to grow larger, and he said, "I do not want any arguments. I am your captain, and I order you to get to that entrance—quickly!"

Against their wills Trooper and Hal found themselves moving in obedience to Chip's words. When they were at the narrow entrance, Chip suddenly smiled at them and cried out, "Rag-Tags forever! Now *go*!" And it was as if his voice pushed them out into the open. They tumbled out, half-expecting the dog's fangs to close on them immediately. And indeed, the instant they were outside, the scratching stopped, and they knew he had heard them! With hearts pounding and lungs pumping they raced madly across the sand, expecting to be swallowed whole any instant.

Instead, as they reached the cover safely they heard the dog give a short yelp as though someone had driven a pine needle into him! Then there was a cry of rage from the dog's throat, and they knew he had been challenged. They raced into the darkness where they would be safe, and in their ears came the horrible bubbling snarl of a meat-eating animal who had gotten his victim in his vicious fangs! They raced on until they could hear no more, and when they arrived at the camp they could say nothing at first.

Finally Trooper got his breath, looked around at the white-feet, and said, “That Cheep—’e was one brave white-foot, you know? I do not theenk I will ever see one like heem again!”

CHAPTER TWENTY-FOUR
The Darkest Hour

HALLEE kept busy feeding the invalids and keeping a sharp eye on the young pups, but often she would glance to the west hoping to see the patrol return. Finally when the work was done she sat down by a small holly tree and nibbled listlessly on some dried corn.

"Princess Hallee," a voice spoke behind her, "are you worried about your brother?" Silver sat down beside her, his eyes expressing kindness.

"I'm worried about all three of them," Hallee said. "Shouldn't they have been back by now?"

"There's no way of telling. They may have to hold up for a day or two. Perhaps they'll have trouble finding the right spot." He looked at her more closely. "You're tired, and perhaps all this strain has been too much for you."

"It's no worse for me than for anyone else."

"I think it is. Not everyone has the duties of being a princess. And I know you're grieving for your father and are worried about your mother."

"Well, I—I don't think so much about my father. I know I can't bring him back. But I can't help wondering about my mother." The queen had not been the same after the death of her husband, and they had not been able to convince her to leave.

"I understand how you feel. In times like these, we have to trust the Maker."

"I wish I had your faith, Silver. I wish . . ." After a few moments of uncomfortable silence, Hallee left and lay down, wrapped in her blanket. Sleep came quickly, only to bring troublesome dreams—nightmares about brown rats and awful monsters.

But after a while these ended, and slowly she became aware of a light right in front of her. Thinking it was someone with a lamp, she opened her eyes and at once sat straight up. "Who are you?" she gasped.

"A friend."

Hallee swallowed hard, for she had never seen such a person. He was tall, and light seemed to flow from his body. He was wearing some sort of robe, but the hood was thrown back, and she could see the warmth and love in his eyes. "I have come to grant your wish, Hallee."

"My wish?"

"Yes. You wished for more faith. I will grant your desire."

"You are the Maker!"

"Some call me that. I have many names, but that one will do until you are old enough to learn others."

Hallee gasped. "I just don't have faith, sire!"

"You do, princess—all who belong to Me have a measure of faith. But not all use it as they should."

Hallee pondered this slowly, and her face clouded over. "You mean I can *decide* to use my faith? Just like that?"

The Maker smiled. "Does that sound too simple? The true things are always simple, Hallee—faith, love, devotion. I have a special message for you: You will play a major role in the journey of the white-feet to freedom."

Hallee looked up in confusion and said quickly, "Me? I can't do anything! I mean, I can't fight or be a scout—"

The Maker held up his hand. "You can believe, and that is more important than all the rest. A dark hour is coming, Hallee, perhaps more than one, and when that time is darkest, when all else will want to quit, you must believe with all your heart! Will you do that, Hallee? Will you trust Me like that?"

Hallee realized she was being commissioned in a special way, and she answered very slowly, "Well, I suppose nobody knows exactly what he or she will do in a difficult time, but I—I *will* believe, Maker, no matter what!"

"Excellent," the Maker smiled. "Now there are two of you."

"What do you mean?"

"Why, you and Chip. My greatest joy during this war and the mad journey through the wilderness has been the growing faith and courage in the hearts of you two young ones. Remember, the power that keeps the sun moving in the great dance is working on behalf of the white-feet!"

Hallee drifted off to sleep, but when she awoke, she knew what had happened had not been a dream!

†

Many hours went by, but there was still no word from the patrol. Budger once began grunting to himself but was overheard by Hallee to say, "No need to worry, no sir! That Chip—there *is* something about that chap! He'll make it all right. I refuse to believe otherwise!"

Hallee finally dropped off into a fitful nap inside the chariot, waking up only when someone pulled at her shoulder and said, "Princess, the patrol's back!"

She scurried outside and found Silver, Major Meadows, and a few soldiers standing around the patrol. She could not see around them or over them, but she heard her brother as he finished his report.

"The river's there all right," Hal said. "We ought to be able to get there in one long march—" He broke off and seemed to be weary.

Hallee squeezed through the others and threw herself on Hal, crying, "You're back! I was so worried! Trooper, you took good care of the prince, I see."

The tiny shrew usually had a flood of words for Hallee, or anyone else for that matter, but now he avoided her look and muttered something no one could understand.

They were behaving very strangely, Hallee thought, as she looked around with a bright smile. "My goodness, why are you all so gloomy? You found the river, and you're back safe." She glanced around in sudden realization, and her heart leaped as she asked quietly, "Where's Chip?"

No one answered, and Hallee said again, "What's the matter? Did something happen?" She could not say any more because of the lump of fear in her throat. She looked at Hal who finally said, "Hallee, I'm sorry to—to have to tell you this, but Captain Chip is—well, he was—" The crown prince of the white-feet seemed to suddenly have some sort of trouble with his vision, for he blinked rapidly, and then muttered, "I—uh, I have something in my eye. You tell them, Trooper."

Trooper's voice was soft at first, but as he came to the end of the story, he became sad and dramatic at the same time. ". . . and then the captain, he make us ron! He look at us, and he say for us to move, and we do it, doan we, My Prince? And then, just as we get on the beeg hill and are safe, we hear thees 'orrible snarl that dog make—like when he ease really mad, you know? And that ease when we know—when we know that Cheep has come out to fight with heem! And I say to my own self, 'Trooper, that Cheep, he ease one brave white-foot!' The prince and myself were safe and soun', but Cheep . . ." The shrew whipped out his blade and cried out, "Here ease to Captain Cheep—he was the best of all of us!"

All murmured their assent, but there was no joy in their voices. " Could Chip have escaped somehow? Is there really no hope, Trooper?" Silver asked.

Trooper sheathed his sword, then looked around fiercely. "When a mouse takes on a beeg dog, there ease no end except death and glory."

†

The story of Chip's death became known to all the white-feet in no time at all, and the leaders quickly realized how much everyone's morale was hurt by Chip's loss. The next morning Silver and Major Meadows spoke about their next move. The major said sadly, "I tell you, sire, there's no heart in any of them! It appears that they don't care anymore!"

Silver had not spoken much after the report of Chip's death. Now he looked around and said, "I hadn't realized how much hope I put in Chip myself. The *one* thing I was sure of was that he was the one chosen to lead us to the West."

The major even grew more nervous when he heard the prophet express his own doubts. He leaped to his feet and said,

"We've got to do *something*! We can't just sit here like a bunch of sick pups."

"Yes," Silver agreed, pulling himself together. "You're right. We've all been feeling sorry for ourselves much too much. Get the leaders together right now." While the major gathered the council, Silver stared hard at the West. He seemed to be listening for a voice that never came. *Maker, I haven't heard Your voice in some time now. Help me . . .*

Once they were all sitting in a circle, the major took charge. "We must make a decision. We can't stay here. I say it's time to make a run for the river. We can make it if we don't give in to our fears!"

"I don't see how we can make it." Prince Hal felt weary, overwhelmingly so ever since the patrol. "There are owls at night, hawks by day—and that dog is still there, I suppose."

Budger said, "But the major is right—we have to do something. I think those crows have spotted us. You know what that means."

"If they have, we can expect a small army of rats here at almost any time." Silver nodded. "I say we must leave—though I confess I don't see much hope in it either."

For over an hour they discussed the whole situation. Some lost their tempers, and others seemed indifferent, as if it were too late to do anything anyway.

Finally there was a long silence, until Budger muttered, "I always knew it would come to this. We might as well have stayed in the burrow and died there as to die here."

"No!" Hallee was on her feet, and the fierce light in her eyes amazed all of them—except perhaps for Silver. "We aren't going to quit! We can't! That's not what the Maker wants. We must keep believing in Him and His kind plans for us. We're going on—all of us." She ran around the circle, shaking her delicate paw in face after face, pulling at Budger, shaking Ben, pushing others. She was a whirling princess with a flame in her usually mild eyes!

"But, princess, how?" Ben asked.

"What matters how?" Trooper's eyes shone with admiration for Hallee. "We weel go togethair to seek the West, eh, princess?"

They all stood up as Hallee's confidence swept over them, and they all began to talk at once. No one saw Silver go to Hallee and whisper in her ear, but if they had, they would have seen that she was very troubled by what the seer told her. But she did not tell anyone about it until much later.

Suddenly Ben shouted, "I've got it! I've got it! I know how we can all get to the river!" He danced a jig in excitement. "It's so simple! All we have to do is go in the chariot!"

"But we won't all fit inside it!" the major protested.

"We can make two trips—no, wait!" Ben thought hard and then said gleefully, "We don't even have to do that. We'll load everyone we can into the chariot, and the rest of us will walk *underneath* it! Don't you see?" he yelled. "No hawk or owl can get us there. I don't know why I didn't think of this before."

Major Meadows said quickly, "Well, I'll eat my sword if the little fellow hasn't come up with the answer!"

"But I see several disadvantages," Budger began. But he was drowned out, for the idea had swept them all like wildfire, and they were ready to try it right then.

Quickly the major organized them, declaring that they would move out as soon as all was ready. "No sense waiting around here for those rats!" he said.

All the food was stored in the chariot, along with the weapons and supplies, and when Porky was asked to pull them on this last perilous lap, he gave his usual response. "Ain't no bother to me."

Hallee insisted on making the trip under the chariot with the soldiers. She was flanked on one side by Trooper and on the other by Ben. Silver and Major Meadows were in the front. The white-feet stepped on each other's feet as they all crowded together. There was little noise, and Hallee could not see much. She felt secure enough though with the heavy metal chariot over her head, the bristling Porky in front, and brave Rag-Tags on every side of her.

Several times during the next several hours the white-feet (and one shrew) could hear owls sweeping down to investigate, but they knew better than to attack a porcupine, so they left the chariot alone.

They were all tired after three hours, but they kept going because they knew they were getting close. Trooper peered out and said, "I remember that beeg willow tree. Ease not far now, I theenk!"

All of them could smell the river, and though mice do not care for water as a rule, the river kept looming larger in their minds as the day went by. To them, it wasn't a river—it was an escape route, perhaps even a doorway to their true home—the West! They could feel the land turning marshy and damp under their feet, and their hopes rose.

Suddenly Porky gave a fierce snort, and then he began running at breakneck speed, at least for him! Porcupines are very slow, but to those in and under the chariot, they were moving very fast indeed. Those inside were thrown to the floor, and most of those underneath suddenly found themselves out in the open. It was a miracle that the jerking wheels did not run over anyone!

"Porky, what is it?" Ben cried, but the porcupine did not slow down.

"It must be some kind of animal!" Hallee said in fear. "But what kind of animal would dare attack a porcupine?"

"A fisher—that's what!" Budger snapped as a dark shadowy form shot out of the woods. "It *is* a fisher! Spread out, everyone!"

There was complete confusion as the fisher caught up to Porky, scrambling away as fast as he could. The fisher is the only enemy of the slow-moving porcupine, and the mice watched in horror as the predator slipped a paw under the clumsy Porky and flipped him easily onto his back, exposing his tender white underbelly.

That would normally have been the end of Porky, for the fisher is so fast that in one motion he can slash open the hapless porcupine's stomach. In this instance, however, the harness with which Porky pulled the chariot saved his life! Thanks to the harness, he only rolled two thirds of the way. So sure of his skill was the fisher that he began slashing at the vulnerable Porky anyway, leaving a set of bloody marks on the soft belly. Porky gave his tail a sudden twist that caught the foe full in the face. The fisher uttered a wild cry of pain and blundered into the harness, turning the chariot over and spilling white-feet all over the ground. Clawing and scratching at the quills in his flesh, the animal ran screeching into the night. Porky too fled the scene, wailing in great pain. When he didn't return that day or the next, his white-foot friends had no choice but to assume the worst.

The resulting confusion meant great danger for the white-feet. Pups and wounded and mothers-to-be were thrown suddenly out of their security into the perilous night, and if an alert owl had sailed over then, they would have been easy prey. But Major Meadows came rushing up with Silver, and they and the soldiers soon got the helpless ones into some kind of order.

"Head for the river!" Silver ordered. "Let's get these wounded ones to some kind of shelter!"

"Right!" the major agreed. He shouted orders right and left, and soldiers helped wounded comrades, carrying pups on their backs, make their way to the river. A party of scouts came dashing back almost at once, reporting that several burrows, none of them large, had been located.

"Anything!" the major snorted, and soon, in four separate cold, wet burrows, the remains of the white-foot nation shivered and clung to each other for a little warmth.

Prince Hal looked at the miserable mice, wet, tired, and

hungry, and said remorsefully, "So much for my supposed greatness. I guess you were right all the time, Budger. We'll never see the West."

Everyone was too exhausted to encourage the prince, and they all shivered until most of them drifted off into a restless sleep.

Silver looked into the darkness, considering their plight. He murmured to the major, "No food saved, I suppose? This is our worse hour, I think."

Hallee said out of the darkness, "Silver, do you still want me to believe—even now?"

Silver paused so long that she thought he had not heard her, but then she heard his faint answer. "I am old, princess, and I have believed in the Maker's goodness for most of my life. But here in this hole, with so many helpless mice, not knowing which direction to go, with enemies perhaps on our very doorstep, I—I am too tired to believe. I think this time *you* will have to believe for all of us. Can you do that, Hallee?"

At that moment Princess Hallee knew her visit from the Maker had been real. And she knew what she had to do.

There was no sound for a moment, but when Princess Hallee spoke, it was in a clear, bold voice. "Yes! I believe somehow we will be delivered from all this! No matter what has happened or may happen, I believe we will not be snuffed out of this world. I believe the Maker cares and that He has not forsaken us."

"That is a brave answer," Silver said, but he had no confidence in his own mind that there was any truth to Hallee's words. In his heart he feared that the great adventure was over and that all he had believed was nothing but a lie. He wanted to believe, but now it was just too hard. There would be no rescue, there was no Maker, and as far as he could see, the future held nothing but storms, with no sunshine at all.

CHAPTER TWENTY-FIVE

Sir Porky Gets a Medal

THE stirrings of winter brought grim fear into the hearts of the distressed white-feet, for they were far away from their familiar home. The pitifully small hoard of food they had managed to salvage from the chariot had been stacked in the damp burrows, but everyone knew that if more were not found they would starve. Any thought about crossing the river *somehow* was forgotten. Staying alive on this side of the river was taking up all their time and attention.

Silver and Major Meadows sent out several work parties

to bring in anything that could be eaten, but with little success. Budger and Trooper had found only a small supply of wild grain that the deer had overlooked, and they dumped it in the largest of the burrows.

"Well, we won't get fat on *that*!" Budger complained. "It's going to be a lean winter for us."

"Aye, eet ease so." Trooper sighed. "Already I am hongry, and you know how eet ease with us shrews—" He looked with a gleam in his fiery eye at Budger's bulk and added, "We have beeg appetites, eh, fran Budger?"

Budger drew his stomach in as far as possible and grinned sourly at the shrew. "Look to yourself, Trooper. I've often wondered what toasted shrew would taste like—not that there's enough of you to matter."

As they joked about their serious situation, trying to keep themselves and each other from worrying too much, Silver and the major talked, again, about all the danger the pack faced daily. They'd had many long talks, but no solutions, and finally they had to content themselves with hoping for some help from chance—or the Maker, if He still cared.

Seven days passed, and the food supplies grew slightly as the scouts found food here and there. One afternoon a cry from outside brought most of the white-feet to the surface.

"Why, it's Porky!" Hallee cried with delight as she rushed up to the shy creature, now surrounded by all his devoted friends. "Are you all right?" she asked anxiously.

"Ah, yes," Porky answered timidly. "I ain't hurt at all much."

"We thought that animal had killed you!" Prince Hal said in amazement.

"Aw, it wasn't nothin' much. He just scratched my tummy, and anyway *he* got the worst of it."

"I'm so glad!" Hallee squealed. "Oh, I could just hug you but—" She smiled and gestured at the needle-sharp quills with a gesture. "But there's no place!"

"Well, there is this, princess," Silver said softly, handing her something the others could not see clearly.

"Oh yes! I'm so glad we brought it with us from our home burrow. It's only a small thing, but we want you to have it. Porky, kneel!" The porcupine, a little confused, but obedient as usual, knelt in front of the princess.

"For bravery beyond the call of duty, and for services rendered at great personal danger, I name you Sir Porky—Hero of the Chariot! You may rise, Sir Porky, and accept from my hand the token of your office and the gratitude of the Nation of the White-feet!"

She draped a small medal on a slender chain over Porky's neck, and a cheer rang out from the entire pack, which embarrassed the porcupine no end. He rose up awkwardly and said in a very small voice, "Aw, now, it weren't no bother!" At that familiar sentence another cheer rang out. "Well, I just came to say good-bye," Porky said.

"You're leaving us?" Hallee asked.

"Yup. Time for me to be goin' back. It's been a real good thing—pulling your little chariot—but I reckon I'd best get home."

They tried to talk him into staying a while longer, but he felt his old territory calling him, and he waddled awkwardly back toward the east. They felt lonely as he disappeared into the timberline, muttering to himself, "It weren't no bother."

"He was a good friend," Major Meadows said simply. He began to cough and could not seem to stop.

Silver came to him at once. "You must rest, major. You've had that cough for several days. I'm afraid you're getting sick."

"Nonsense! A soldier doesn't have time for such foolishness." Nevertheless, he *was* sick, and the next day he had a fever and was unable to get up. "If I'm not up tomorrow, I'll be most upset with myself!" he exclaimed feebly.

Silver looked at Hal and shook his head. When they left the major's bedside, he said, "He's sicker than he knows, My

Prince. We will have to care for him. It will mean more work for you, I'm afraid."

"That's all right—I want to do whatever I can for the major. But that's not our only problem—I'm afraid it's snowing."

Silver shook his head wearily and said, "That's not good, but we must keep our spirits up, and we must not let the others know how serious the situation really is."

They went outside, and sure enough flakes were floating to the earth, leaving white streaks in the hollows of the ground. They went to all the burrows and did their best to cheer up everyone, but when they were finally back in their own place, it seemed to them very cold, dark, and wet.

Trooper and Budger had built a small fire. Looking around the dark burrow, Hal saw the affection in the faces around him, and he thought of the magnificence of the Royal Burrow and sighed. Hallee must have read his thoughts, for she took his paw and squeezed it tightly. He glanced at her and managed a small smile. "Not much like the Royal Burrow, is it, Hallee?"

"No, not much."

Budger's shrewd eyes took in the pair, and he passed his flask to them. "Have a little of this, you two. It'll warm you up."

They both tasted a little, but then Trooper, seeing their sadness, said, "Well, my frans, thees must look like a pretty bad time, no? But I'm telling you, many times thees fellow has been in much worse, you bet!" He began to tell an old tale of a most courageous shrew—himself—who cut his way out of a whole *army* of fierce enemies! Leaping to his feet he drew his sword and cut and slashed around the burrow so wildly that those sitting there had to duck to keep their heads on their shoulders. Finally he ended by saying, "So I jump up, and I fight my way out—and so I win dat fight, you bettair know eet!"

Hal laughed with the rest, and it was wonderful medicine for him. "You sure about all that, Trooper? Sounds like it would have taken a dozen shrews at least to do all that."

Trooper swept the ground with his feathered hat. "I'm de bravest fellow I know. Eet ease 'ard for me to be modest because I have so leetle to be modest about!"

They all laughed, and then Ben told them about a tremendous new invention he was planning, and then one by one they all joined in the campfire talk. Somehow their situation now seemed more bearable.

But slowly the fire died, and the bitter cold crept in and seemed to grip their hearts again. The talk dwindled, and finally they all sat there listening to their own thoughts. The difficulties of the past seemed light compared with the dangers of the future, and they dropped off into an uneasy sleep.

Princess Hallee's last thought was not spoken, for it would have done no good. It concerned a sturdy, young, white-foot soldier who had done much to save his pack but who would not do so again. Hallee bit back the words and blinked back the tears as the night and the cold fell upon them all.

PART FOUR

A Hero's Return

CHAPTER TWENTY-SIX

Rebellion in the Wilderness

"I'VE been trying to keep a history of everything, a sort of journal. But there's nothing to write anymore!" Princess Hallee threw down her tiny quill in disgust and went for the tenth time to look out at the frozen world. She returned and sat with a sigh beside Budger, who was trying to nap. "Don't you ever do anything but sleep?" she asked sharply as she poked him in the ribs.

Budger stirred and mumbled, "What else is there to do? We can't go outside in weather like this."

"That's exactly what I mean!" Hallee cried. "We've been stuck in these wet old holes for a week now, and the food is disappearing, and there's no end to this snow, and—oh, I don't know what we're going to do, Budger!"

Budger snorted and sat up, then looked the princess in the eye. She was, he decided, about as forlorn as he'd ever seen her. But then again, they were *all* sick of being snowed in. Everyone was getting grumpy and fearful, taking offense easily. It was obvious that unless something happened they would not make it through the winter.

"A suggestion's been making the rounds that we go back to the burrow." Ben made himself wake up and reached out for a well-polished bone, trying without success to find another morsel of meat.

"Back to the burrow? Why, that's the most idiotic thing I've ever heard of," Budger snorted. "What half-wit thought that one up?"

"Oh, nobody knows really," Ben said. "Rattle and Blackie are going along with it though, and quite a few of the mothers who have young pups. They think we'll all die if we stay here in this wilderness."

"What do they think they'll gain by going back to the burrow?" Budger asked sharply. "Murkon would tear the flesh off their bones!"

Hallee's eyes filled with tears, and Budger remembered too late that the princess was still worrying about her mother, as well as the other friends and family who had chosen to stay behind. She brushed the tears away quickly and said, "Well, we can't go back. We just have to keep going, that's all."

Later that same day there was a sharp conflict between the leaders of those who wanted to return and Silver. Major Meadows was still quite sick, so the old prophet stood alone against at least a dozen angry mutineers led by Rattle. He and Blackie had behaved themselves during the whole journey so far, but now . . .

"You've led us out here to die!" Rattle shouted, and the others urged him on with loud cries of agreement. "But we ain't going to do it, see!"

Silver did not answer for a moment but then said with an irritated edge to his voice, "What exactly do you propose to do?"

"We're taking all the food we can carry, and we're going back home where we belong. We never should have left there in the first place!"

"What about the deep snow and the hawks? The wolves will be hungry too—you can be sure of that! And how do you propose to carry all the wounded, the sick, the elderly? What about the mothers with pups? How will you get everyone back safely?"

Rattle was struck silent by these reasonable questions. Not having any logical answers he began shouting, "Never you mind how we'll do it. Are you coming along or are you going to stay by this blasted river and die here?"

Hal moved close to Silver, and the remaining Rag-Tags—Budger, Ben, Trooper, and a few others—joined them. Battle seemed unavoidable; there seemed to be no workable compromise. Silver knew that Rattle's proposal was suicidal, and yet he had no encouragement to offer the white-feet for the present dilemma. Always there had been a last-minute reprieve, but now it seemed there was no hope. On previous occasions Silver always had a clear picture of what the Maker wanted them to do or how the Maker would help them. But now . . .

As the two groups stood there, practically at sword-point, they heard a noise over by the entrance. Silver said softly, "Quiet! Someone's trying to break in."

Instantly every white-foot forgot the quarrel and turned to face the danger. It was night outside, and they were sure that whoever was digging through the blocked entrance was not a friend.

"Do we have any sentries or patrols out there right now?" Hal whispered to Silver.

"No. It's been too cold."

"Maybe it's just a stray muskrat looking for shelter," Hallee suggested, but everyone knew all the animals were already holed up by this time. They all waited nervously as the digging grew louder.

As they waited in the darkness, Silver said in an urgent whisper, "As soon as they get in, whoever it is, we must try to take them alive."

"Can we not keel them a leetle?" Trooper said in dismay.

"No—alive," Silver demanded. "Be ready—they're almost through!"

They could hear dirt flying and rocks falling very nearby now, and a section of the walled-up burrow suddenly fell in. A dark shadowy form fell into the burrow, then another, and the defenders fell on the invaders with wild cries!

"I have heem!" Trooper shouted.

"That's me, you fool!" Budger grunted. "Here! I've got this one—grab that fellow there, Silver! Ben, get some rope!"

The invaders were buried under a mass of bodies and were uttering muffled protests.

"All right, let them up—but keep your blades ready," Silver ordered. The white-feet began unpiling one by one and standing with their swords ready. Finally at the very bottom Budger, Ben, and Hal uncovered the uninvited guests. "All right! On your feet whoever you are!" Hal cried loudly. "Let's have a look at you!"

It was too dark to see much, but the two on the floor were apparently not weasels or anything so dangerous. One of them was a mouse, and the other was what seemed to be a rat—a fact that made them all extend their swords toward him.

"Who are you, and what do you want?" Silver demanded. The larger animal did not move, but the mouse jumped to his feet and shouted at the top of his lungs, "I'm Captain Chip of the Rag-Tag Brigade! Rag-Tags forever!"

After a moment or two of disbelief, they all recognized that it was indeed Chip! A cry went up, and instantly he was swarmed by his comrades, who began to beat his shoulders to reassure themselves that he was not a ghost. Everyone was talking at once. Hallee's eyes outshone the stars.

They pulled him this way and that. "Chip! It's really you!" "We thought you were dead." "Where in heaven's name have you been?" "Chip, you're back!" They welcomed home the one they had thought they would never see again, and then it grew very quiet as Silver approached, his eyes glistening and his chest heaving hard. He put his paws on Chip's sturdy shoulders and looked deeply into his eyes.

"Well, mighty mouse of valor," he said slowly. "We meet again, eh?"

"Yes, sire," Chip said quietly. "The Maker has been with me."

Hallee rushed to him and cried with joy, 'But, Chip, where have you been? We—we all thought you were dead!"

"Yes, and Hallee has been the chief mourner," Hal said. "But tell us what happened."

Chip stared at the faces of the ones he loved most in the whole world—Budger, Trooper, Ben, Silver, Hal—and Hallee, of course. He searched for words, but none came for a minute. Finally he said so quietly that only those closest to him could hear him, "I've come home." Then he shook his shoulders and said, "I want you to meet a friend."

He turned aside, and they saw that the other new arrival was indeed a rat—but not one of the dreaded brown rats who had driven them from their home. He was black, sleek, and muscular, with a black patch over one eye and a red kerchief over his head. A long coat covered his broad-bladed sword. He stood up and nodded as Chip said, "This is my friend Sailor.

He saved my life, and I hope you'll learn to trust him as I have."

Hallee came quickly and curtsied before Sailor, saying sweetly, "Sir, you are welcome—and you have our gratitude for saving the life of our captain."

"Well, now, missy," Sailor said in a deep voice with a strange accent, "I take that as right good of you to say so." He looked around curiously and said, "The captain has been telling me about you, and I'm right pleased to lay eyes on you all."

Everyone began talking again, but they finally settled down to hear Chip's story. Silver noticed that the hopelessness they'd all been battling seemed to be gone now, but not entirely. Rattle and his crew said nothing but just sat quietly with frowns on their faces. However, everyone else listened intently as Chip told them how he had come back to them.

"I suppose the prince and Trooper told you about the dog?"

"How did you ever get away from that monster?" Hal demanded.

"Ben got me out of that one," Chip said with a smile as he looked at Ben's astonished face.

"I wasn't even there!" Ben protested.

"No, but one of your inventions was," Chip said. "Remember that idea you had to put leaves and branches that had been sprayed by skunks into some sort of bag so it could be sprayed on an enemy?"

Ben grinned with delight. "That was a long time ago, Chip, and it was too messy!"

"Yes, but I kept it on hand anyway, just in case. Thank the Maker, I had it with me when we went on our patrol, and it *worked*!" Chip smiled. He held out a little pouch, now empty and flat for them to see. "There it is. Of course, it was full of terrible skunk smells when I used it, but it saved my life."

"Tell us all about it, Chip!" Hallee urged, leaning closer to him, making Chip feel a little nervous.

"Well, I have to tell you, I was more frightened than you can imagine—I really was!" They smiled at him though they couldn't picture Chip ever being overcome with fear. "Anyway, the dog snapped at me and got me right in his jaws, and that's when I let go with Ben's invention. I never knew anything could smell so bad. It got in both of our eyes—not a pleasant experience. But that's what made the difference, I tell you. That monster dropped me and ran around in circles trying to scratch his eyes. And I was doing the same thing, I tell you!" He rubbed his eyes at the memory. "Well, the dog ran off, but I was blind and did not know which way to go. Besides that, he had bitten me rather badly on the leg. So there I was . . ." The memory seemed to overwhelm Chip for the moment.

"What did you do then?" Silver demanded.

"I started crawling, toward the river I hoped, because all I could think of was washing the skunk smell out of my eyes and washing my leg to ease the pain. So I crawled and crawled, and it was by the Maker's mercy that no owl spotted me."

"So you did find the river?" Budger asked as he gave his little friend another comforting pat or two.

"Oh, yes, *finally*. I got my eyes cleaned out, but my leg was in bad shape, and I couldn't walk, so things looked pretty hopeless. I kept out of sight for two days and nights, hiding by the river. I had nothing to eat, and I was getting weaker all the time. On the third night—I was out of my head with fever—I was lying under a bush, and I suddenly saw two eyes staring at me. I was too sick and tired to run, and I just thought, *I suppose this is the end of my life*. I was just lying there waiting for the mink or whatever it was to slit my throat when I heard a voice say, 'Ahoy, there, mate! What's the trouble now?'"

"Aye, that was me!" Sailor nodded in delight. He continued the story, already feeling welcome among new friends. "I'd been watching him for a day or so, and he had courage, he had! Seen that right off, I did! So I says to meself, there's a chap who would be a good shipmate in foul weather! So I goes over and meets up with the bloke, and I took him to me little place, I did."

Chip nodded with a smile at Sailor. "He saved my life, that's what he did. Fed me and bound my leg and pulled me through. I made him a Rag-Tag at once. We can count on him, no doubt about that."

"I don't think so," a voice interrupted, jarring the harmony of the moment. Rattle stepped out of the dark corner where he'd been listening to Chip's tale. "We don't even know this rat, do we? I say we make an end to the beggar!" He drew his sword but stepped back hastily toward his companions when Sailor pulled out his sword and was joined by Chip, who had drawn Durance.

"Come along then, if you wants a taste of steel." Sailor's good eye gleamed in the darkness.

"He's a friend of mine," Chip said angrily. "And he's a water rat—not one of those brown rats."

"I say let's finish 'im off right now!" Blackie snarled as he moved up to stand beside Rattle.

"Yeah!" Rattle said. "So Chip's back, and a suspicious pal with him. That don't change nothing, it don't! We're still going back to the burrow!"

Chip lowered his sword in surprise and stared at Rattle. "Back to the burrow! What for? Don't you know they'll make slaves out of you there, if not worse?"

"No, they won't. Some of the brown rats were telling us before we left that if we join up with them, the Dread Deliverer will—"

"Do not speak that name!" Silver's voice rang out like thunder. "You do not know what strange fire you play with! He will deliver you right enough—to his own evil purposes!"

"That's what *you* say," Blackie snarled. "But we know that whoever serves the Dread Deliverer gets the best of everything. And that's why we're going back, ain't we, Rattle?"

Just as they again held out their swords, ready for action, Chip cried out, "But we don't have to go back!"

"What else can we do?" Rattle demanded shrilly. "We'll starve if we stay here."

"That's right," Chip said. "But we're not going to stay here. We're going to continue our journey."

Even Silver was stunned at that announcement. "But, Chip, how can we go on? It's deep winter, and many of us are sick. We can't travel even a short ways without losing most of us to one danger or another."

Chip did not at that time give any details of his plan. He knew they didn't need information right now—they needed a leader. As he and Sailor had traveled in search of the white-feet, he had prayed to the Maker for guidance and courage. And as Rattle and Blackie had given voice to their rebellion, Chip knew what he was meant to do, and that now was the time. "We'll go on all right. I know it looks impossible, but there's a way—one I'd never have thought of in a thousand years. But now I know it's the right thing. Whoever wants to come, let's go—I have something to show you."

Before they could protest he rushed through the entrance and out into the night. The others followed immediately, except for Rattle and his companions who followed reluctantly. As Hallee scrambled to keep up, she managed to say breathlessly to Budger, "Well, we're on our way somewhere."

Budger smiled. "I'd follow that lad to—well, I guess to the end of the world. Strange how an old doubter like me can get so caught up with a young fellow who believes like him."

"I guess we're all ready to follow Chip," Hallee said.

So they plunged blindly after the leader of the white-feet, trusting in him and in their Maker.

CHAPTER TWENTY-SEVEN

The *Victory*

FOR over an hour the small band of white-feet followed Chip and Sailor along the frozen bank of the river. There were only a few trees close to the water, so they darted from rock to bush, avoiding the open spaces. There was something ghostly about the silence, and all of them kept a close watch for great owls and any other hungry predators.

Finally Chip said, "There it is." They all stopped and in the first light of dawn they saw a long, low building next to the river.

"Step lively, mates," Sailor said, leading them to a spot at the base of the wall. He moved a large rock with a grunt, then disappeared into a hole. They all crowded after him, anxious to be out of the open and away from any hungry enemies.

As their eyes adjusted to the darkness of the shed, they saw a long line of various kinds of boats side by side. The white-feet did not know what they were, having never seen any before. But as they followed Sailor and Chip down a heavy wooden walkway to which the craft were all docked, Sailor lectured them on the uses of the strange objects.

"These are what men call boats, mates. They use them to travel over the water. See that one there? I've been on several trips in that one meself, I 'ave."

"Where do you go in them, Sailor?" Hallee asked mystified.

"Oh, missie, I'm a water rat, and I've been on the rivers since I was a pup. I've even sailed before the mast—out on the Big Water. Sailor's my name, and the sea's my game, I tells you! Now then, take a look at this one, mates—this is me home!"

Sailor had stopped before a strange-looking ship that was different from all the rest. For one thing, it was *much* smaller than the others. It was, in fact, a large model of a sailing ship complete in every detail. Sailor led them across a gangplank and into the ship.

"See that name?" He gestured at the gold letters on the front of the ship. "Well, I can't read, o' course, but I've heard what they calls it many a time. It's called *HMS Victory*, it is!"

"The *Victory*!" Silver said suddenly. "I like the sound of that!"

"Well ye may, governor! The way I understand it, it ain't no real ship atall—it's like a tiny version of the real big ones. Why, I've seen those ships myself, so big you couldn't believe it, with masts so tall you can't see the top of 'em! But this smaller ship was made just like one that was famous, don't you see? I've seen the men take it out in the summer, and they let it float on the river. It's just like a real ship, mates, but it's mouse size."

"You live on this thing?" Budger asked cautiously. "Don't the men mind that?" Since white-feet mouse, unlike house mice, keep far away from men whenever possible, they all felt a bit fearful at the moment.

"Why, they ain't no men here, mate!" Sailor cried. "That's the beauty of it! They closes this boathouse down in the winter, and nobody comes around until spring. And on board the *Victory*, no owls nor foxes can get in. It's a perfect winter home!"

"Give them a tour of the ship, Sailor," Chip suggested. He had been over every inch of the *Victory*, and he wanted his friends to share his joy. So he and Sailor led them around the deck, pointing out the wheel, the anchor, the rigging. When someone asked what the tall sticks with the white cloth were for, Sailor said, "Them is the masts and the sails—the sails make the ship go." This puzzled most of them, but Sailor said, "The wind blows against 'em and pushes the ship through the water."

"I see!" Ben yelped. "Why, it's the greatest invention I've ever heard of!" He immediately began investigating the ropes and lines that worked the sails, asking questions as fast as he could talk.

"Plenty of time to explain all that," Sailor chuckled. "Let's go below." He led them to the lower decks, and they were amazed to discover cabins with tiny windows, bunks, and stoves—with everything just their size so living there would be very comfortable indeed.

"Why, it's like it was made just for us!" Prince Hal exclaimed. "Look, I fit just right in this bed!"

Silver said, "In a sense, perhaps it was made for us." He was watching Chip carefully, sure there was more to his plan. "What's all this about, captain?" he asked.

Chip said, "Let's all go up on the deck. You can see the

rest of the ship later." They went up the stairs and gathered around Chip and Sailor, waiting expectantly.

"I propose that we bring the whole nation here to the *Victory*." He spoke with a new, more determined authority, and Blackie and Rattle, who had come reluctantly, ignored his sudden glance in their direction. "This place is like a huge burrow. Everything we need is here. There's even a place, Sailor tells me, where we can get plenty of food. It will be safe here."

"For how long?" Blackie asked skeptically. "What about when the men come back?"

"We won't be here when they come back." Chip looked at them and said slowly, "We're going to travel west in the *Victory*!"

That announcement took their breath away! Some began to shake their heads. White-feet in a boat? Others looked at each other, then at the ship. The first to accept the idea was, of course, Trooper. He leaped agilely onto the rail and waved his tiny sword in the air with a shrill cry. "We weel do eet, my frans! We weel sail on thees *Victory* toward the West. I doan care eef eet keel us all—at least we will die trying to find our true home!"

"Can it be done?" Silver asked Chip. He looked up at the sails and gear, all totally meaningless to all of them except Sailor.

"I believe it can be done, sire," Chip said. "Sailor can show Ben how to work this thing in a couple of days, and they can both teach us how to help. You told us we are to go to the West, right, Silver? Well, we can't do it on land, but we can in the *Victory*! This is a special provision from the Maker—I just know it!"

A cry of approval broke out from everyone except Blackie and Rattle. Even Budger said, "Well, I'll be—he's done it again! Captain Chip, if you don't get us all hanged or sunk in the river or into some other disaster, we just might do it!"

"That's the most positive comment I've ever heard from you, Budger," Silver said with a smile. "You're right, it will be dangerous, but we can do it—with the help of the Maker. For a while I was doubting the Maker myself, but He's still watching out for us!"

"Humph! I *knew* you'd say that," Budger mumbled. "Why doesn't this 'Maker' show Himself? Why is He so bashful?"

"My friend," Chip said with a friendly paw on the huge white-foot's shoulder, "you have to admit that finding the *Victory* was more than just luck."

"We'll see, we'll see. We have a long way to go yet!"

"Eet weel be a piece of cake!" Trooper kissed his own paw eloquently.

†

Despite Trooper's entertaining confidence, it most certainly was *not* a piece of cake. In fact, it was a tremendous amount of work. First, they had to convince everyone to move to the *Victory*. Prince Hal was most helpful there, and the princess too. But Chip did even more. Not that he did much talking, but his amazing reappearance had made him into a hero, again, and almost everyone became excited about their new home and new adventure. No more was heard about going back to the burrow, though Rattle and his buddies continued to grumble and criticize.

It took many trips and several days to move all their supplies, for they had to move very quietly and could only take a little bit at a time. "We could have done all this with just one trip in the chariot!" Ben moaned wearily. But Silver knew Chip had a purpose for doing it this way. The white-feet were gaining courage and stamina for all the formidable dangers they would face, and working together was certainly better than the despair they had been living in.

"This is going to work, isn't it, Silver?" Hal asked one day.

They had just brought a load of food from the old burrows, and now he sat beside the seer, resting before making another trip.

"Yes, My Prince. I believe it is the way that was meant for us. Not only by Chip but by the Maker."

Hal stirred restlessly, then added, "I want to tell you something—I—I've been a spoiled pup, Silver! And I've decided—I will not be a king!"

"No?" Silver asked quietly, never taking his eyes from Hal.

"No. I am not worthy, and I'm not a leader. It's obvious that Chip is the leader. So I'm going to renounce the crown." He looked at Silver with a trace of sadness in his fine eyes.

Silver put an arm across his shoulder. "You cannot do that, My Prince. Chip is—well, he is many things, but he is not a king! *You* will be the king, and this willingness to give up your rights is evidence that you *are* the proper ruler of the nation." Silver paused, then smiled. "Anyway, Chip would not accept it."

"He wouldn't?"

"No. He has his role to play, just as you have yours."

"What *is* he, anyway, Silver?"

"Chip?" Silver murmured with a smile. "Well, I guess he's an average white-foot mouse who's had to become more than he ever thought he could. And so will you, Hal! So will you!"

Finally the task was done, and the entire tribe now lived in the cabins of the *Victory*. They began to live like sailors, even using some of the names Sailor taught them—*deck* instead of *floor*, *topside*, *aft*, and other terms. They loved their new home at once, for the ship was like a large burrow, only more comfortable. "Perhaps it is now," Silver said one day. "But once we lift anchor and the ship starts to move, some of you will be sicker than you can imagine."

For the next month while the cold bit and roared outside the boathouse, inside the white-feet were being made into a crew by Sailor and Ben. They learned to scurry up and down the tiny rope ladders quicker than any human sailor could have done it. And Trooper was in his element. He loved to scamper to the highest sail of all, look down on the massive vessel far below, and cry out strange battle cries that Sailor had taught him. Slowly they mastered all the gear, and Ben learned from Sailor how to handle the wheel, until finally they were ready. Or so they thought.

"We have to keep practicing," Sailor said when some complained about being tired. "It's one thing to scamper up a mast here where it's quiet, but what about when it's nighttime, and the wind is whistlin' through the rigging, and the sail is frozen—and your paws too. Then if you miss a step, into the sea you go!" They all shivered at the thought of going into the water.

"But don't worry—I think you'll be a good crew." He smiled fondly. "We'll have a fine voyage, mates."

"When will we leave, Chip?" Ben asked one morning.

"I hope we can wait until spring, but that may not be possible," Chip said.

"That would be best," Sailor agreed. "With an inexperienced crew and this ice, it would be too risky to leave now."

"Maybe we can wait, but we may have to leave suddenly too." Chip started to say more but changed his mind. "Let's make sure the *Victory* is ready to go at a moment's notice, just in case. How are we going to get that door open, Ben?" He pointed to the huge door that would have to swing open to let the *Victory* onto the river.

"No problem there, captain," Ben said smugly. "There's only one little latch, and I can slip that any time you say."

"Budger, do we have enough food and water, all the supplies we'll need?"

"All ready, captain." Budger grinned. "With Sailor's help we managed to just about empty a storage chest in a little room down at the end."

"We need to have guards on duty at all times," Chip said.

"Guards?" Budger asked. "Looking for what?"

Chip didn't answer, but from then on he insisted that sentries patrol the area outside day and night.

Only to Silver did Chip express the reason for his fears. "I won't feel safe until we're well away from the shore. None of you know that Colonel Murkon like I do. He's insane, Silver, and cruel! I don't think for one moment he's given up looking for us."

"Do you think he can find us here?" Silver asked.

"Yes! And this Dread Deliverer he serves—I'm afraid he's even more evil than Murkon!"

Silver nodded. "I of all people should not have forgotten that, Chip. The Dread Deliverer *is* powerful—more than any of us knows. The whole world lies in darkness, it seems to me, and if we are to escape this evil, we must pay any price to escape it!"

"Maybe we'll get away without any more trouble," Chip said. "But let's be ready to leave if we have to. I think I'll never rest easy until we get to the West."

"Yes. All of us are like that," Silver agreed. "But most of us have to cross some stormy seas before we get there."

CHAPTER TWENTY-EIGHT
Cavern of Evil

SOMEWHERE in the thick darkness an animal was struggling for its life, and Chip was drawn out of a deep sleep by the faint moans that seemed to come from deep within the earth. He thought at first he was dreaming and tried to ignore the cries. But the cry of fear seemed to grow louder, and he opened his eyes in protest. He felt sick and helpless as if he'd been ill with a fever; but when he took his first look around, such fear shot through his heart that he awoke at once.

He was not asleep in his neat little bunk on the *Victory*. He looked around wildly for his clothes neatly folded on the small chair by the wall or the familiar figure of Budger in the bunk next to his. But everything was changed!

He was in some sort of high vaulted cave, and by a greenish light he made out a group of figures who were watching him. He tried to jump up and defend himself, but he found he could move only slowly. Finally he managed to stand upright, but when he tried to run he seemed rooted to the spot.

From deep in the earth beneath his feet the cry that had awakened him echoed again and again. He could not understand a word, but he easily understood the helpless agony and terror that were part of the screams. Somehow he knew that the dim figures were responsible for the nameless agony, and he was suddenly aware that they had brought him here to put him in that place of torment, wherever it was!

Chip had been afraid many times—afraid of hawks, owls, and many other natural enemies. But this fear was different. This time the enemy was evil itself, and like a foul sickness it ate away at his mind until he wanted to scream in panic. And perhaps he would have done so, but just when he felt himself slipping away, he also felt deep within himself a sense of power. He also heard within himself a song of some sort that was growing louder. The song spoke of courage, and soon Chip saw a light. It was feeble at first, but it grew until it was brighter than the foul darkness of the cave. Chip drew a deep breath and then, instead of screaming in fear, cried out in a clear voice, "Who are you? And what do you want from me?"

At his sudden challenge, the figures seemed to waver and grow dim, as if they were not accustomed to any victim standing against them. Encouraged, Chip called more loudly, "I do not care who you are! You cannot frighten me with your shadows! Show your faces if you are not afraid!" Chip was aware that he was not speaking with the usual white-foot language but rather one that he did not know. It was as if someone else spoke through his lips, in a forgotten tongue of spiritual life and power.

Again the figures wavered, but then one of them separated himself from the others. He seemed to move through the green darkness like a serpent gliding through a swamp. It was Colonel Murkon. And yet he was different, even more hateful than before. Chip had not forgotten the colonel; in fact, he remembered every feature. But this face was not the one he remembered. Murkon's face had not been pleasant, but this face was like a nightmare!

In the reddish eyes that seemed to glow in the darkness like coals of fire, Chip saw the most awful hatred he had ever seen. The sounds of the agonizing screams that Chip could still hear brought some sort of awful pleasure to this being, and he listened with his head turned as if those cries were pleasant music. Hatred, violence, greed, and a multitude of other foul desires played across his face, and when he spoke, his voice was full of evil.

"You have been summoned, white-foot! And you will not leave this place again. Not until you have surrendered your will to the Dread Deliverer of all the earth!"

A moan went up from those who waited in the darkness, and the cries from the pit grew louder and more desperate. "Oh, yes, you will surrender," the sinister being cried loudly. "You have won a small victory or two, but there will be no more! Now you must become one of us!"

The fiends on the outer circle began to move closer, and they echoed with one deadly voice the words of this evil foe: "One of us! One of us! You will be one of us!"

The cavern echoed with their hellish chant, and to Chip's horror he found himself tempted to join in with them. "I will be one of you! I will be one of you!" he was tempted to say. But then he saw the horrid smile on Murkon's evil face, and he shook himself and cried aloud, "No, I will not! Never!" The circle of evildoers seemed to draw back, and Murkon's face grew more obscure. Chip thought with huge relief that he had won, but then he heard another noise.

He thought he heard Murkon chanting some kind of awful song, and though he could not understand the words, he felt that some huge presence was entering the cave. It was a heavy thing, massive and overwhelming with evil. The thing grew heavier, and Chip felt that a tremendous mountain was resting on his frail body and that if he did not give in, he would be crushed by the weight of it. He heard those surrounding him speak together in some sort of worship, and then the presence grew so powerful that he could almost see it. He shuddered under the force of the most evil presence he had ever imagined.

There was no voice, but the tiny light that he had sensed almost went out, and his ears could no longer hear the song that had cheered his feeble heart, for it was drowned out by what seemed to be the howling of millions of lost, mad creatures.

"What—what do you want?" Chip whispered faintly. He heard no voice, but something was putting thoughts inside his head. *Why do you struggle so? You're tired, but I will wipe your fears and trials away. You must give in. See how easy it is?*

Chip began to find a strange attractiveness in this. Why struggle indeed? It *would* be easy to just give in, for the thing had muted the anguished cries, and the white-foot could no longer see clearly the face of Murkon. What he felt now was a little like being very cold and very tired. How easy it would be to just slip into the pleasures of sleep. How very easy. *Why struggle? Just join me.*

But join who? Chip came awake with a sudden shock, and he saw that he had almost fallen into the trap, for the entire circle had moved closer, like wolves around an almost helpless victim. There was an unholy light in their eyes, and their foul smell was overwhelming. Chip summoned all his strength and with all his might shouted, "Away from me, Dread Deliverer and all you evil powers of darkness. In the name of the Maker of all that is good, I command you to leave!"

There was sudden confusion, and Chip saw the forms

waver like flames quenched by a sudden wind. There was a roaring like a tornado, and he felt himself being carried away.

Even as he was drawn away he felt the dark, massive power that had sat upon him grow wild with rage, and a message was forced upon him, clear as stone: *For this you will pay! I will take the life of the one dearest to you!*

Then Chip seemed to feel himself driven through the air like a leaf in a windstorm, and he was so afraid that he found himself crying to the Maker, to Silver, to Budger. *Help me!*

"Chip! Chip, for heaven's sake, wake up!"

Chip opened his eyes to find himself in his bunk on the *Victory* with Budger and several others standing around him.

He sat up in bed and said in confusion, "I—I must have been dreaming."

"Ho! You have been 'aving an awful nightmare, mate," Sailor chuckled. "Must've been that salt pork we 'ad fer dinner."

"Are you all right, Chip?" Budger asked. He saw the confusion in his young friend's eyes and realized that he had not had a normal dream.

"Yes, I'm all right now, Budger. You all better get back to sleep. I need to rest alone." He got up and herded them all out of the room, then sat down and found that his paws were trembling. "It was no dream! Not that!" he muttered. For the rest of the night he sat upright in a chair and thought deeply about the evil being who had confronted him. And many times that night the Dread Deliverer's warning came back to haunt him: *For this you will pay! I will take the life of the one dearest to you!*

The light of the rising sun soon lit the cabin where he sat, but Chip's heart was dark indeed as he stood to face the day.

CHAPTER TWENTY-NINE
The Coming of Deedee

LIFE on the *Victory* went on so smoothly for the tribe that the hardships of the past were almost forgotten. Outside the weather grew bitter cold, but inside the boathouse the winter sun streamed through the high windows as Sailor kept training a crew to operate the ship. At his command the various changes of sail and steering were carried out eagerly and efficiently by the young white-feet. Ben was learning the fastest and quickly mastered the sails and the steering. He even took apart the cannons on the gun deck.

After one of the drills most of the Rag-Tags sat in the forward area of the upper deck and lazily sipped a drink invented by Trooper. He steadfastly refused to reveal the formula, but it was potent enough for even Sailor, though it didn't make anybody lose self-control like the beverages men liked to enjoy.

"Well, mates," Sailor sighed after he took a sip of the spicy brew, "this *is* the life, ain't it now? Plenty of food, warm bunks, and no hawks to watch out for. Can't be better than that, can it?"

Mutters of agreement were heard. Budger grunted and said, "Aye, but what's next, I want to know."

"Why worry about that?" Ben asked

"We can't stay here forever!" Budger said irritably. "What will we do when spring comes and the men come back and get their boats out?"

"That's too far away to worry about," Ben sniffed.

Chip said nothing, but he'd been thinking about the future for weeks. The strange dream was still strong in his memory, and he had been troubled over the dire warning that had ended it. He wanted to get away from the area as soon as possible. "Maybe we can leave soon. I mean we can handle the ship, can't we, Sailor?"

Sailor said, "Oh, we can do that, but look at that weather! She'll be snowing again soon, and it's no lark to manage a mainsail in heavy weather."

"Besides, what's the rush?" Hal asked lazily, draped over the rail. He turned and said to Chip in a teasing tone, "You're such a fire eater—you can't stand a little peace and quiet like the rest of us!"

Chip grinned at the young prince. The best thing about their time on the *Victory* had been the comradeship that had grown between Hal and himself. Despite a bad beginning, they were now well on the way to becoming close friends. The pair of them, with Hallee making a frequent third, had spent many hours talking about the past and planning for the future. Hal's arrogance was gone, it seemed, and he was now accepted by all the Rag-Tags as one of the crew.

Chip started to answer, but before he could a white-foot came scrambling up the plank and fell onto the deck stuttering in excitement.

"S-sir, w-we've f-found something! I mean someone—"

"What is it, Winkle?" Chip asked. "Take your time."

"Well, we were on patrol, and you know that part of the woods just south of the chariot? Well, we had almost gotten past there when this female white-foot ran out and stopped us."

"A white-foot but not one of our tribe?" Chip asked.

"That's right, sire!" Winkle said, "She's from around here somewhere, I reckon."

"Didn't she say where she was from?" Hal asked.

"Well, no, sir. I think she was too scared, and she was just about worn out. She did say she'd been lost in the woods for a long time."

"Where is she, Winkle?" Chip demanded.

"Oh, we brought her back with us, of course. Had to carry her the last part of the way. Shall I have her brought on board, captain?"

"Yes, at once," Chip ordered. "Hal, would you ask Hallee to make a room ready for her? Sounds like she may need a little nursing for a while!" He watched Hal dash down the ladder, then hurried over to the plank. "Bring her up here—quickly!" he called. The two husky soldiers bearing a stretcher made out of leaves and thick twigs came aboard. Chip and the others gathered around and looked at the young mouse. When she opened her soft, dark eyes, the sight of so many strangers frightened her, and she uttered a forlorn little cry.

"All right now, stop gawking at the poor thing!" Hallee had arrived and shoved the curious onlookers rudely aside. "Do you want to frighten her to death? You two follow me—and be careful going down these steps, you hear me?" They left, with Hallee making little comforting sounds. Instantly a hum of conversation began on the deck.

Winkle was asked so many questions that his head swam. Finally Chip said, "Hal, let's go see if we can have a talk with her."

"Right," Hal agreed. "If there are any others out there, we ought to know it."

They scurried below deck, but Hallee would not even let them into the room. "Go someplace and swig that awful stuff Trooper's been making," she sniffed impatiently. "The poor thing is asleep already."

"But we need to speak with her," Chip argued.

"I'll come and get you when she's able to talk. Now out with you!"

The ship was soon humming with rumors, but none of the other patrols had seen anything. A few hours later Hallee sought out Chip and Hal saying, "She's awake now." They followed her eagerly to where the young mouse lay. As they hurried into the room, both of them were suddenly speechless, for sitting on the bed looking at them was the most beautiful young mouse either of them had ever seen. "Hello. My name is Deedee," she said. Her fur was golden with a reddish touch around her face, and her stomach was a snowy white. Hal and Chip just kept staring.

Hallee glared at them and snapped, "Have you both gone to sleep?" She turned to Deedee and added in a gentler voice, "This is my brother, Prince Hal, and this is Captain Chip."

Chip swept off his hat and said, "Ah—yes—well, do you think you could tell us about yourself?"

Hal stepped forward quickly and said, "If you feel like talking, that is. It wouldn't do for you to overstrain yourself."

Deedee's smile seemed to paralyze both Hal and Chip. "Oh, I'm fine now," she said. "But if you hadn't found me, I don't think—" Her voice dropped to a whisper. She sat up straighter. Her voice went higher, and her tiny paws twisted the bedcovers. "Oh, it's been so dreadful! My—my whole family—the whole tribe—they're all trapped!"

Chip looked above Deedee's head so he could concentrate and asked, "Trapped by whom?"

Deedee shivered as she said, "The rats! Those awful brown rats!"

Hal and Chip exchanged glances, and now Chip's voice grew more urgent. "The brown rats have invaded your burrow? How long ago?"

"It's been over a week now," Deedee said. "They came on us all at once during the night. They put every burrow under guard. And our king—he's dead! They just—killed him." She began to weep. "My poor father—and my brothers—they're all slaves! Everyone was so afraid—and—"

"How did you get away?" Chip asked.

"I slipped away when we were supposed to be working," Deedee said. "But they followed me—I saw them in the woods looking for me."

"Are there many of them?" Chip inquired solemnly.

"Not over twenty," Deedee said. "But they're so *big*! And they're all armed with terrible swords and daggers and whips!" Her face clouded again, and she moaned, "My poor family! What will become of them?"

Hallee said quickly, "I think that's enough for now. You need your rest, Deedee. You two get about your business!" She paused and looked at Chip who was staring at Deedee with his eyes wide open. "If you can tear yourself away, that is, captain!"

Chip hurried out, followed by Hal. They went topside and called for a meeting of the Council at once, an easy task since everyone was anxious to find out what they had learned.

As they sat on the deck and listened to Chip's and Hal's report, Silver was especially moved. "You see what this means, of course?" he asked.

"Yes," Budger answered. "It means what I've said all along. We're not safe here."

"I think that's right," Chip said. "We can't stay here."

Sailor asked at once, "Shall we weigh anchor then, captain?"

"No, I don't think so," Chip said. He spoke slowly, and the look on his face made the others pause.

"What are you thinking, Captain Chip?" Silver asked. The prophet was looking keenly at the young white-foot. He, more than any of the others, knew how closely the destiny of the nation was tied to this young soldier.

"Well, I know this may sound crazy, but I think we ought to raid Deedee's village before we leave."

"What!" Budger said in shocked surprise. "That's too dangerous, Chip. What in the world would that accomplish, except get some of us killed?"

Trooper threw his fancy hat in the air and waved his sword in the air dramatically. "My frans, let us dare to be brave! Glory—she will be ours, no?"

Most of the crew felt they were somewhere between Trooper's wild impulsiveness and Budger's stubborn resistance. They argued for hours, but finally Chip said, "I don't like the risk any more than any of you, but we are going! That's an order!" The others looked at him in shocked surprise. Usually Chip *suggested* things, but his flashing eyes told them he would not be talked out of this! But he did add, "No one *has* to go. I'm taking a rescue party there, and we're going to bring back any white-feet who want to come. We can't leave Deedee's family there as slaves."

Hal frowned when he heard Deedee's name. "Wait a minute, Chip. If you're doing this because of what you think of Deedee—I mean, she *is* pretty, but that's not a good enough reason to risk our lives." Actually Hal was sorry he hadn't thought of it first. He was already wondering if he was falling in love with the delicate creature, and suddenly he saw Chip as a rival. But then an idea occurred to him, and he said eagerly, "*I'll* lead the party. After all, Chip, you are our true leader, and we can't risk losing you. I'll lead the rescue."

Chip was surprised at the prince's offer and was not pleased with the obvious motive. But he saw at once that Hal's jealousy did accomplish one good thing—it settled the fact that they *were* going. Now all he had to do was persuade Hal that he was too inexperienced to lead such a difficult patrol.

"There's something we have to take care of first," he said briskly. "We must make sure we can set sail as soon as we return. Sailor, can you and Ben have the *Victory* ready to leave by the time the raiding party gets back?"

"Sure, we can, captain," Ben answered. "All we have to do is pull her out with these lines, and then the current will take her and then—"

"All right, all right, you two be ready," Chip said hurriedly. He had been thinking about the raid and Hal's stubbornness. He turned to the prince and said, "Hal, I think we both better go—one of us in the front and one to cover the rear."

This seemed to satisfy Hal, and he said quickly, "Fine. I'll go tell Deedee—if that's all right with you?"

Chip shrugged, and Hal scurried off to see Deedee. As Chip gave orders quickly, Silver stood to one side, a calm smile on his face. The raid was organized so efficiently that soon Chip and the old seer were alone on deck.

"Well, Chip," Silver said quietly, "another adventure, eh?"

"Do you think I've chosen the right thing, Silver?" Chip asked, looking in the face of his guide and friend. "It's so hard to decide things like this. What if someone gets—well, what if we lose some of the party? It'll be my fault." He hesitated, then told Silver about his nightmare, including the fatal last words. "I'm afraid someone will get—hurt."

"Command is a lonely work, as you know already. And I fear you'll learn other hard lessons as well, Chip. But I'm not afraid for the pack—not with Captain Chip in command!"

"Captain Chip!" he sniffed. "I'd rather be the lowest recruit."

"I'm sure you would. But we aren't left to choose those things for ourselves."

Chip looked hard and long into Silver's wise old eyes. Finally he sighed and said, "Where will it all end, Silver?"

Silver put a thin paw on Chip's shoulder and gave it a little shake, as close to showing affection as he ever got, and murmured so softly that Chip almost missed it. "Why, it will end where all good things end, my boy—in the Deep West!"

"You keep using the words 'the Deep West.' Exactly where is the Deep West, Silver?"

"Chip, there is for all of us a *west*, a place on earth where we will find what we long for."

"But what's the *Deep* West?"

"Ah, you will find, my Chip, that no place on this earth will ever truly satisfy our longings. The richest land in all the world, if we came to it, would not make us really happy. But there is *another* west—I call it the Deep West—that all of us long for."

"You mean heaven?"

"Yes, I mean heaven. Men call it that, but it is a place for all of the Maker's creatures. I believe there will be mice and men and lions and hummingbirds in the Deep West."

Chip was silent, then he whispered, "We may or may not get to the west on this earth, but I believe one day we'll all be with the Maker in the Deep West."

"So do I—and so do all who love the Maker!"

CHAPTER THIRTY
The Raid

GRIM-faced, they approached the burrow ready to fight to the death if need be. Deedee had given them careful directions on how to reach her home, as well as a map showing where the brown rats were quartered—one of the finest private burrows in the settlement. Chip had told the soldiers simply, "Hit them hard—protect each other—bring the captives to the *Victory*."

Fortunately, they attacked the burrow at just the right time, for the majority of the brown rats were away on a mission. Only four of them were in the guard room as the Rag-Tags struck at the light of dawn, and all of them were captured almost at once under the fierce onslaught of the Rag-Tags.

"Waste no time!" Chip whispered. "Gather the villagers and bring them here as quickly as you can." They separated into squads and went their various ways. It soon became apparent that the brown rats had posted no guards at the individual burrows. Within two hours about thirty adults and at least as many youngsters were standing before Chip, their belongings on their backs as Chip had directed.

"Which is Deedee's family?" Chip asked, and at once an aged but healthy pair of mice stepped forward. "Deedee is all right," Chip assured them. "You'll be with her soon. We have to get away before the rest of the patrol gets back. Is everyone ready? Hal, lead the way. I'll cover the rear with Trooper. Let's go!"

The captives needed little urging, for the rats had treated them harshly. Within a few moments the entire procession had disappeared into the woods, headed with all speed for the *Victory*.

Trooper and Chip kept well behind with a careful eye out for pursuing enemies, but there was no sign of them. "My fran Cheep, I wonder why they left their camp so unguarded?" Trooper asked.

"I can guess," Chip said. "I think they're out looking for us." Trooper protested, but Chip added, "Why else are they here, so close to the place where Murkon knew we were headed? They haven't forgotten us, Trooper. I don't think they ever will."

They got back to the *Victory* without incident, but as they came aboard Chip suddenly felt two slender arms around his neck and a delicate kiss on his right cheek. "Captain Chip, you did it!" Deedee shouted, clinging to him. "You've saved my family! How can I ever thank you!"

Hallee, observing this joyful outburst, didn't like what she was seeing. She was glad the rescue had been a success, but she most definitely did not like the idea of another female showering attention on Chip. "I'm sure you'll find a way,

Deedee!" she snapped, then said loudly, "Captain, if you're not too busy, we'd like some instruction on getting away from here."

Chip tried to remove himself from Deedee's grasp and muttered something to her about having duties to attend to. But she clung to his arm firmly, chatting on and on about how she would *never* forget his courage and his kindness. Chip tried to explain that the triumph was due to everyone's efforts, not just his. Looking aside, he caught a glimpse of Prince Hal and saw the same gloomy look on his face that he'd worn in earlier days, and that saddened Chip.

Finally getting himself loose from Deedee's grasp, he began directing the final preparations for departure. Most of the supplies were in place, but there was a constant stream of activity as Ben and Sailor helped everyone with a flurry of last-minute chores.

"We'll travel by night," Chip told Silver and his little group. "There's too much chance of being seen by day—by men and by rats! We'll leave at sundown, when there's just enough light to get the *Victory* into the channel." He looked around and said grimly, "I don't know where we're going any more than you do, but one thing is sure—we can't stay here. Any questions?"

"Just one, captain," Ben said. "Did you know that the last patrol hasn't come in yet? They're overdue by two hours."

"Whose patrol is it?" Chip asked.

"Well, Rattle has been asking and asking to go, so we finally gave in and let him lead it."

"And I suppose Blackie went with him?"

"Yes. Was that a mistake?"

"I'm not sure," Chip said slowly. "It's just that—well, they've been trying to get us to turn back for a while now."

"You don't think they'd desert?" Silver asked. "They wouldn't be fool enough to take that kind of risk—with the rats in the area and all!"

There was an uncomfortable silence, and then a young soldier who was working closely with Ben said, "I guess I should have mentioned this before, but . . ."

"What is it, Trot?" Ben asked him.

"Well, it's just that Rattle has been having meetings with some of the younger fellows. They asked me to come, and I went once."

"What was he up to?" Chip inquired.

Trot shifted uncomfortably and reluctantly said, "They said we ought to sort of make friends with the brown rats. Said we could get in with their leaders, and then we could have power over the rest. And they said—" He halted, glanced at Chip, then said bravely, "They said that if we got rid of the captain and his bunch, things would be a lot better. That's when I left! Blackie said if I mentioned it he'd slit my throat, but maybe I should have said something anyway."

"Well, Trot, you'll know better from now on," Silver said with a nod. "Perhaps they've joined up with the enemy, or maybe they just lost their way a bit. What will we do if they're not back by the time we sail?"

"Leave the blighters right 'ere!" Sailor said with raised voice. The rest agreed with him. Lately the pair had been a continual irritation to the whole nation, and they were not sad to see them go.

Budger said slowly, "It might be worse than that. They just might lead the enemy right to the *Victory*."

Chip said, "Indeed! Sailor, are you ready to launch the ship soon?"

"Yes, captain," Sailor answered with a grin.

"Then let's get some guards on duty—*lots* of guards," he insisted. Soon able-bodied soldiers all around the ship were watching for the brown rats, and a patrol was sent to keep searching nearby woods in order to give early warning of any approaching enemies.

The tension made the hours drag by, and in the late afternoon Chip paced nervously on the deck, ready to announce that it was time for departure. He was just about to call the patrol in when he heard them coming. Then he saw them, and he knew at once that they had seen something. They dashed across the open ground and almost fell into the narrow entrance into the boathouse shouting, "Captain, they're coming! The brown rats are coming!"

"How close are they?" Chip demanded.

"There they are now!" Silver said grimly. He pointed across the field, and it seemed to Chip that the ground was alive with brown rats. He began shouting orders. "Ben, tell Sailor to launch the ship. Use every hand to get it clear! All you Rag-Tags, they'll have to come at us through this entrance, so I want all of you except five to help with the ship! Trooper, and you, and you two, and you, stay with me! The rest of you go!"

They had to haul the *Victory* into the channel by means of the ropes Ben had rigged up. Otherwise they could never have budged the huge ship. Chip heard the creak of the far door and knew that Ben had sprung the latch. The door swung open, revealing the swollen river in the approaching darkness. He heard Ben call out, "All right now, pull! Put your backs into it!" Chip glanced back to see the bulk of the *Victory* begin to inch forward.

But then he heard the wave of rats arrive, and he joined the small group waiting at the door. They had piled boxes and anything heavy in front of the entrance into the boathouse, but the battering of the large rats and their cries of rage made it evident that they would soon break through. Chip said, "They'll have to come in one at a time, and they're big and fat. That's why we made the opening so small. But if even one gets inside, he'll be able to cause us enough trouble to let the rest squeeze through. So don't show any mercy!"

"What you theenk, my captain? They will ne-vair get through that opening! Me, Trooper, I promise you!" He danced excitedly around waving his tiny sword in the air.

When the first brown rat shoved through, it was Trooper, of course, who had the honor of killing him with one quick thrust. "Eet ease a piece of cake, my frans!" he cried.

But it was not, for no sooner had one brown rat fallen than two more struggled to get in. The rats broke down part of the wall to make the opening larger, determined to accomplish their evil plans. Their eyes were red with fury, and the possibility of death seemed to mean nothing to them.

Then Chip heard a familiar voice crying out his name. "You inside! Chip—I've come for you!"

"Murkon!" Chip said with a grim smile. "I thought it would come to this." He looked over his shoulder. "Is the *Victory* free yet?"

"It'll take maybe ten more minutes," someone said, and Chip was surprised to see Budger standing there, his sword red.

"I thought I told you to help with the ship."

"I guess I'm getting a little hard of hearing," Budger said, looking over Chip's shoulders. "I didn't hear you."

"Well, you hear me now, Budger!" Chip waved toward the ship and said, "We can take care of this."

Budger ignored him. "You say that's Murkon? Why don't you talk to him?"

"What for?" Chip demanded.

"To use up a little time—so we can get the ship launched," Budger said calmly. "If you can slow them up, we'll have a better chance of getting away."

Chip had not thought of that, but he saw the wisdom of it at once. "Murkon!" he called out, and the yelling on the outside grew quieter.

"I am here," Murkon said. "Clear the entrance, and we will accept your surrender."

"What are your terms?" Chip asked. He already knew the terms—death. But giving the *Victory* more time to break free was *his* goal.

"You will be treated fairly," Murkon said in his deceptive voice. "Unblock the entrance at once or you will all die."

Chip whispered quietly, "All of you, get to the ship! I can keep him talking until the *Victory* is free!"

"What about you?" one of them asked.

"I'll jump onto the *Victory* just as she clears the end of the boathouse," Chip said. "Now go, all of you."

All of them left at once, except for Budger. He calmly wiped his sword on the uniform of a dead enemy and said, "Keep talking, captain."

Chip was familiar with the stubbornness of the huge soldier, and he knew it was useless to argue. He raised his voice and said, "Well, I'm afraid you may be right, but we need to agree on the terms."

Murkon cried out, "Agree on the terms? We will give you nothing! Nothing! I give you two seconds to surrender!"

Chip knew his plan wasn't going to work, so he cried out, "To the pit with you, Murkon! You've lost! Do you hear me? I am Chip of the Burrow, and I tell you, you've lost *again*!" He looked at the ship, then turned to Budger. "All right, my friend, the ship is clear—get started!"

Just then two things happened so quickly that there was no time to prevent either one. Colonel Murkon must have been standing just outside the entrance, for as Chip finished his challenge, the head and shoulder of the enemy officer shoved through the opening. Budger and Chip were caught off guard, and the enraged Murkon threw a glittering blade straight at Chip's unprotected back. Budger gave a cry and threw himself in its path, then fell to the floor in sudden pain, the enemy's knife in his back.

Chip stepped across his friend as Murkon drew his sword and lunged straight at him. The white-foot had no time to think, but his training had prepared him for such a moment. With one smooth turn of his wrist he parried the rat's thrust, and in another motion he buried Durance in Murkon's chest. The enemy colonel looked down at the blade unbelievingly, then cast a gaze of furious rage at his enemy. A glaze came into his eyes, and he fell backwards as Chip pulled Durance free.

Chip knelt beside Budger, who was struggling to his feet. "Budger! How bad is it?" Chip cried.

For the first time since Chip had known him, Budger expressed confidence rather than skepticism. "Not bad, Chip. Not bad, my boy." But his back, Chip saw, was already covered with blood, and his eyes were beginning to close.

"Come on," Chip wept, "I'll get you to the ship. We still have time."

"No, Chip. I'll not be making this voyage with you," Budger said faintly. He motioned toward the entrance. "I'll keep them busy until you're safe."

Chip, mourning the way the Dread Deliverer's prophecy had come true, stood there weeping and could not move.

"Go, Chip! The *Victory* is almost gone, and they're calling for you."

Chip could not see clearly through his tears, but he heard voices urging him back to the ship. "I won't leave you, Budger," he said brokenly. "I won't!"

Budger straightened up and put his heavy paw on Chip's heaving shoulder. His voice got a little stronger as he said, "You have to go, Chip. They're all depending on you. Go now—I think more enemies are coming."

Chip heard the voices of the rats beginning to grow louder, and he felt like he was being torn in two. "I can't leave you! I can't!"

"Chip, I have a little confession to make." Budger gave a small grin though his eyes were glazed with pain. "I—I have to tell you—that all this talk about the Deep West, the Maker, and all that . . ."

"What about it, Budger?" Chip whispered.

"Well, the thing is, I've—I've found myself believing in Him—the Maker, that is." Budger grinned and nodded happily. "What a thing for a logical fellow like myself to admit, eh?" He gasped for breath, then said, "Chip, they're coming! Run—run, my boy!" He gave Chip a hard hug, then shoved him toward the ship. But just before he turned to face the final attack of the rats, he gave a confident, bright smile and said cheerily, "The joke of it is that all this time you and Silver have been bragging about this Deep West of yours—" The rats broke through, and Budger turned to meet them with his last bit of strength. As Chip turned and fled blindly toward the *Victory*, he heard Budger's last words. "The joke of it is, I'll see this Deep West before you do! Run, oh, run, my friend!"

Then the rats fell upon him.

CHAPTER THIRTY-ONE
Smooth Sailing

FOR over a month the *Victory* had made its way down the river, traveling only by night. It had become a way of life to the white-feet, an easier life than they had ever known, for they had plenty of food and no natural enemies. Every evening Sailor piloted the ship out of the hiding place chosen the morning before, and they would glide silently along close to shore. At first the white-feet found the cold air uncomfortable, and they were afraid of the river. But now it was getting warmer as they moved further south.

Just before dawn they would head into a cove or bay well

covered by massive overhanging branches, then drop anchor. The more adventuresome would go ashore to seek food, although there was no shortage. Every day brought a sense of wonder over what the next bend in the river would bring.

Now that Rattle and his crew were gone, there was complete unity among the white-feet. They enjoyed their friendship and often praised the Maker together.

They had entered warmer waters, and a group was sitting around Sailor as he guided the *Victory* downstream one fine evening.

"Isn't Chip ever going to laugh again?" Trot asked. "It's been over a month now, and anyway it wasn't his fault that Budger died."

No one answered for a long time, then Sailor said, "Well, I've not known the bloke that long, but 'e ain't the same as when we met. Why, even when 'e was chewed up and left for dead by that huge dog 'e wasn't like *this*."

The others nodded, and Ben said, "He never talks to anyone much these days. Spends most of his time up there." He nodded up at the mainmast, where high above the deck the crow's nest, a platform used by lookouts, could barely be seen in the darkness. "I'm worried about him."

High above, Chip watched the lights of the stars reflect on the smooth river far below. The wind was still cold, but he had grown to like the nip of the air and the smell of the river. Every night he went at once to the perch and sat there until almost dawn.

Chip was deeply hurting in ways he could not put into words. Budger's death had shocked him terribly, and others' lack of understanding afterwards made him feel isolated. Perhaps they had not really grasped how vital a part Budger had played in his life. He had spoken to almost no one for several days, partly because everyone had been busy learning to actually sail the *Victory* rather than just going through practice exercises. Chip felt very much alone. He even felt cut off from Major Meadows and Silver, perhaps because of the difference in their ages, though from past experiences with them he should have known they would understand. But his grief was so deep, he didn't want to talk with them. He wanted someone to share his burden with, and yet he preferred to remain alone in his sorrow.

†

One evening Chip wandered toward the part of the deck where Hallee usually stood for a while, but she was not there. He heard a light step and turned to greet her, but it was Deedee instead. She came to him and began talking in her usual chatty way. "My goodness, captain, where have you been hiding yourself? I declare—I've looked all over this old ship for three days for you."

"Well, I've been pretty busy, Deedee," he began. He started to tell her about his intense grief and the burdens he was carrying, but she interrupted him with a light laugh.

"My goodness, I think you'd better come with me, captain. We've having a party downstairs, and you'll have the *best* time!"

She pulled at him, but he said quickly, "I would rather stay here and talk if you don't mind, Deedee."

"Don't be such an old stick in the mud!" Deedee laughed, and her smile was so beautiful that it took Chip's breath away for a moment. "You've just got the blues," she said. Deedee had not known what close friends Chip and Budger were. "You come with me, and we'll have us a *fine* time."

She put her arm under his and was attempting to drag him down the ladder when Hal and Hallee stepped onto the deck.

It would be difficult to say who felt worse—Hal, Hallee, or Chip—but Deedee was not at all embarrassed. "Look who's coming to the party," she cried out. "He just *insists* on taking little old me! Isn't that nice?"

Hal's face clouded over. "That's just peachy!" he growled and rushed off toward the back of the boat.

"Why, whatever is wrong with Hal?" Deedee asked.

"Nothing," Hallee said sarcastically as she turned to leave.

"Hallee," Chip said quickly, "if you have a minute, I—I'd like to talk to you."

"Oh no, you don't," Deedee said with a smile. "You need to laugh and have a good time, and that's what we're going to do! Come on, captain! You too, Hallee."

Short of tearing himself away from her by force, Chip had no choice. But he did not like the sudden frown on Hallee's face as they went below, leaving her topside.

At the party he tried to listen to Deedee's constant chatter, but he really didn't feel like being at a party. So at the first opportunity he left. He found Hal and Hallee staring out over the carved figurehead on the bow. He could not think of what to say. Hal glared at him, then turned and left.

Hallee did not say a word, but Chip couldn't remain quiet. "Hallee, I don't know what's wrong with me." He started to tell her how lost he felt without Budger and how responsible for the other white-foot's death he felt, but Hallee's jealousy about seeing Chip and Deedee together kept her from being a sympathetic listener.

She waited until Chip finished and then said, "We all have problems, captain, don't we? But I'm sure that if you attend enough *parties*, it will all work out." The look on Chip's face made her sorry for what she'd said, but before she could try to undo the damage, he clamped his jaw shut and left without another word.

She stamped her foot on the deck and said, "*That* was a wonderful speech to make to him, wasn't it, Hallee?" She thought about all the difficulties Chip had faced on their behalf and how he had given himself for all of them with no thought for himself, and her anger at herself grew even greater. "What a nitwit you are!" She gritted her teeth and set out to find him. But Chip had already climbed into the crow's nest, and she did not see him again for two days. By then he had built a wall of anger around himself that neither she nor anyone else could break through.

Thus their hearts grew colder as the weather grew warmer.

†

The weeks wore on, and from time to time they had experiences that brought a little excitement into their otherwise routine lives. Early one morning they nearly ran into a rowboat with two men in it. They were pulling up some sort of line with hooks on it, and they didn't even see the *Victory* until it drifted over their line. One man called out, "Hey, Ed! What's that?"

Chip was, again, in the perch above the deck, but the situation happened so suddenly that he could do nothing about it. He saw the boat shift as the men straightened up, and he heard one of them say, "Ah, that's jest an ole log, I reckon." The men went back to their fishing.

"That was a close one!" Sailor said quietly when Chip came down. "We'll have to be more careful." He sniffed the air and said, "I figure we ain't too far from the Big Water now. I'd hate to get us caught after coming all this way."

"What's the Big Water like, Sailor?" Chip asked. He was used to the river now, but he could not picture a body of water that was much, much larger.

Sailor scratched his neck and answered, "Well, I can't exactly tell you, captain. See, you ain't never in your whole life been able to see much. Always trees and hills and stuff in your way, so to speak. But imagine you're on a piece of ground as flat as this here deck, and there ain't nothing at all on that ground for as far—for as far as we come already in the *Victory*. Nothing at all but green waves and sky that seems to go on forever!"

Chip wrestled with his thoughts and said faintly, "I can't

picture it, Sailor, but what little I do see of it—well, it scares me a little."

"You're not alone there, captain!" The water rat grinned. "Everybody's at least a little scared of the Big Water, includin' meself."

"How do you ever find your way around in it?"

"As to that, I wouldn't know. Guess they's a way, though. I've been on ships that stayed away from land for months, and they finally got where they was goin'. I don't rightly know how though."

That night Chip went to talk to Silver. He found the prophet in the major's cabin. The old soldier was still ill and was much weaker now than when the voyage had begun.

"Major Meadows," Chip grinned, "you're looking fit tonight," wanting to encourage his friend.

"Why not?" the major answered with a light in his eye. "Never think I won't be up on that deck when we get to the West, Chip."

"I'm sure of it," Chip said as cheerfully as he could, though secretly he had doubts. "That's what I wanted to talk to you and Silver about. When we leave the river and go into the Big Water, how do we know where we're going, and how do we get there?"

He had expected Silver to have the answer, but the seer said at once, "I don't know, Chip. Sailor may know something about it."

"No, he doesn't. I've already asked him."

"Well then, it will be a voyage of faith, won't it?"

"A voyage of faith!" the major chuckled. "I'd like to hear what our friend Budger would have said to *that*!" Then he paused, and his face softened. "Sorry, captain. No offense?"

"Of course not, major." Chip smiled bravely. "And I know what he'd say if he was still with us. He'd say, 'Sail on!'"

"I think he would, Chip." Silver nodded with a gleam in his

sharp eyes. "He died with a real faith—and now we have to live in it."

They talked about the dangers for a long time that night, and Chip went to his cabin feeling more lonely than ever. He was almost asleep when he heard the lookout cry, "There she is—the Big Water!"

He leaped off his bunk and ran topside, then scampered up the mainmast where Trooper was sitting in the crow's nest staring forward. "I never see nothing like *that*!" he breathed.

The river had ended, and it opened like a fan into the tall waves of the mighty sea, beautifully reflecting the bright moonlight. As far as Chip could see, there was nothing but green water tipped with whitecaps that reached up toward the endless blue sky. As the rising sun shed light on the scene, he looked and looked but still could not take in all the immensity of the Big Water. The *Victory* would be a mere speck on this rolling, endless mass of water fathoms deep and many miles across.

"I didn't theenk I would ever be afraid of anybody," Trooper said slowly, "but thees ees one beeg feller!"

Chip looked across the water and tried to picture their voyage across the trackless, watery wastes. He gulped and said bravely to Trooper, "Just think, Trooper, we serve the Maker of all of this! Certainly He will guide and protect us!"

CHAPTER THIRTY-TWO
The Big Water

THE *Victory* thrust out into the sea so unexpectedly that they all felt a twinge of fear. Since Sailor felt they weren't prepared to handle the open sea quite yet, he had some of the crew set the sails for the first time. They had just used the current of the river for the past two months, but now they had to put themselves in position to let the wind blow them back up the river, at least for now.

Sailor was pulling on the wheel, and Ben was high overhead, driving his crew with a vengeance. Sailor bellowed out the appropriate navigation commands. It would all have been nonsense to the mice a few weeks earlier, but now they obeyed without a question. Gradually the topsails caught the wind, and the *Victory* began to reverse direction, gathering speed as she did so. The large waves showered the deck with bursts of spray. The ship was rising and falling in time with the ocean waves, and soon they drove the vessel up the river to a safe spot where they could rest and get ready for the challenge of the Big Water.

They gathered on the deck under some cypress trees, and as the sun spread its brilliant light over the coast they talked for a long time about what they should do now.

There was a difference of opinion among them. That was clear from the start. The sight of the ocean had shaken the courage of many of them. None of those from Deedee's pack were ready to risk leaving the shore, except for Deedee herself, and many of Chip's own burrow felt the same way.

Late that afternoon, when most of the others were taking their rest, Silver, Ben, Chip, Sailor, Hal, Hallee, Major Meadows in a comfortable chair, Trooper, and a few trusted officers continued to struggle with the decision.

"Maybe we ought to wait a few days," Ben suggested.

"Wait for what?" Chip questioned. "If we wait for a week or a month, we'd still face the same decision."

"Right," the major said, "although we might be discovered in the meantime, and after a month we'd be out of food."

"We have no choice, do we? I say let's go on to the West—right away," Chip said strongly.

Suddenly Hal spoke up, not looking at Chip. "Go *where*? Does anyone know where we're going? Or how to get there?" He looked around and continued, "I say let's make a new home right here. This is good country, and far away from the brown rats. We can make a good life for ourselves, with no risks."

There were murmurs of agreement, but Silver said, "Do not deceive yourself, My Prince. There is no safety here—or anywhere else—except in the West. The decision is simple—go there or perish here."

A lengthy debate followed, Hal speaking eloquently against

the voyage, while Silver and Chip steadfastly argued that they should go forward. At one point Hal started to claim his royal birth as a way of settling the argument, but a glance around convinced him that would not be successful. He finally just shrugged. "Well, if you're determined to get us all killed, I suppose that's what will happen!" He stalked off in a rage, and everyone felt very uncomfortable.

"Let's wait a day. We can at least do that," Silver said, and they all quickly agreed.

They began to go their own ways, but Hallee, who had not said a single word during the whole discussion, went swiftly to Chip and said, "Chip, do whatever you think is right." With those few words she was gone. But Chip's heart felt less heavy, and he had a gleam in his eye that had been missing for a long time.

That day the tides rolled the *Victory* gently, and the rigging made a quiet rustle in the air. The boards creaked alarmingly, but the ship was well built, and they soon grew used to it. The sun began to fall in the west, and several of them watched it go, wondering if they too would soon disappear in that same west.

Just as the last rays of the sun were lighting the green water in the mouth of the river, Silver called for the entire company to assemble.

In no time everyone on board was crowded onto the deck. It was very quiet as the old prophet ascended the upper deck where the wheel was and faced his people. He waited until the last pup had grown still, then began to speak in a calm voice.

"You have come far, my friends. If you had not, you would either be dead or in slavery. The burrows are no more, nor will they ever be again. A dark and terrible shadow is falling on our world, and most of those alive will fall under it. There will be suffering and death such as no one has ever seen.

"But now this little band, for a reason known only to the

Maker, has been permitted to find a place of peace. I cannot tell why you were chosen while others must stay and face the terrors of the Dread Deliverer. Someday we will perhaps know these things, but not now. Now is the time for you to have courage, to trust the Maker in greater ways than ever before and cast yourself into an adventure!"

Silver paused and pointed toward the west, shouting, "There—there you must go! To the West!"

His words had stirred some of them, and they felt a little more confident, but others looked afraid. Silver nodded slowly. "I know you are afraid. But to feel fear is not defeat. Defeat is to let your fears rob you of your dreams, to allow them to hold you back from being what the Maker has always meant for you to be!" He raised his voice. "You must go—now! There is your captain." He pointed at Chip, who was staring at him in amazement. The old seer seemed to have fire from heaven coursing through his thin frame.

Silver walked to the rail and stepped out on the plank that stretched over to the ground. He turned and looked at them. "You will find the West. The Maker has led you safe thus far. You will not be lost."

"Silver!" Chip cried out as he ran to him. "What are you doing? You're not leaving us?"

"My time is over, Captain Chip." Silver put his paws on Chip's shoulders and said so quietly that few could hear, "I told you from the first—you are the mouse of valor. Now be strong and of good courage. And believe this, my son, we shall meet again." Without hesitation he ran lightly down the gangplank, and when he set foot on the earth he called, "Pull in the plank, captain. Go now—use the cover of darkness to hide from any enemies on shore. It is the time of Captain Chip!" Then he seemed to fade into the undergrowth. It was getting dark, and Chip could not see too well, but it seemed to him that the seer did not so much walk away as fade into thin air.

Taking Silver's words seriously, knowing the prophet had

never given him wrong advice, Chip whirled and called out, "Weigh anchor, Sailor! Ben, get every inch of sail you can on those masts! All hands, work quickly now!" There was a flurry of activity as the crew sprang to their tasks and the passengers hurried below.

Almost at once the *Victory* began to move back into the Big Water, and as the dark, open sea rushed toward them with all its mystery, Chip seemed to hear a small voice in his mind saying, *Chip, do what you think is right.* That would be a comfort to him throughout that long night.

Most of the white-feet had thought an ocean voyage was like a river voyage—easygoing, gentle, and pleasant. But they soon discovered that the river and the Big Water had little in common.

Trooper was the first to discover this, for as soon as the *Victory* left the shore and came off a gigantic wave only to dip far down again, then rise rapidly up the crest of another smooth green wave, Trooper's face turned yellow, and he said faintly, "I do not theenk I like thees Beeg Water much." Knowing he was about to be sick, he quickly held his head over the rail. Almost all of them were sick, except for Sailor, and for a few days it was difficult to find enough crewmen to set the sails properly in order to drive the *Victory* westward.

In addition, no one had told them about the noises that a wooden ship makes—creaking and groaning at every seam. The frightened white-feet feared the ship might break apart at any moment.

They were also learning that it is one thing to work on a steady deck in a river but quite another to balance yourself while carrying a tray of food on a deck that slants sharply one way, then without warning tips the other way!

Those working the sails from one day to the next were now aware that as the ship rolled from side to side, if they fell, they would hit the deck or, just as likely, fall into the threatening sea.

Chip, though he had spoken so bravely earlier, now often looked toward the endless ocean and sometimes asked himself if he had done wisely. Who was he to risk the lives of all these in his care? Should they turn back, as some were whispering?

As they drove deeper and deeper into the sea, the fear became more intense, and Chip and his leaders enjoyed little sleep. They believed they were in the hands of the Maker, but seeing the huge waves and hearing the powerful winds, it was difficult to continue in that assurance.

Even so, all would have been well if they had not hit a vicious squall ten days into their ocean journey. It came upon them when Sailor was resting, and unfortunately the novice at the wheel did not realize the danger until the ship was tossed like a toy on a suddenly raging wave, and water began pouring out of heaven like a mighty waterfall.

Sailor ran to the wheel and began shouting for the crew to take the canvas in before the winds tore the *Victory* apart. With the sails in, they were safer, though the ship was tossed about until the winds died down. Most of the white-feet had bruises where they had been thrown against a wall or to the deck.

It was a short but vicious and deadly storm, but they did not discover the real danger until two days later. Chip was on deck when Ben approached him, and Chip could tell he was afraid.

"Captain, we have a serious problem," Ben said. "You know that storm we had two days ago? Well, some water got into the lower compartments."

"Didn't you pump it out?" Chip asked.

"Yes," Ben said, "but that was where we kept our supplies. Now most of the food is ruined—soaked with salty seawater. And—and that's not the worst—all our fresh water is spoiled too."

"No!" Chip shouted, for he saw at once that such a situation would mean certain death. "Wasn't the fresh water in kegs?"

"I guess they weren't very good kegs," Ben said. "They're all ruined."

"How many have you told about this?" Chip asked.

"Just you."

"All right—here's what I want you to do. Get a squad of the best men we have. Search every cabin. I want every drop of water on this ship that isn't ruined placed in my cabin at once!"

"Yes, sir!" Ben said. He quickly carried out Chip's orders, ignoring the cries of protest that followed the search of every cabin.

Two hours later Chip and Ben were sitting in his cabin measuring the water Ben had salvaged. "How much is there?" Ben asked.

Chip looked at the small barrels and vessels and shook his head. "Not enough, Ben." He said in a hard voice, "No one must know how little there is. Do you understand that, Ben? No one at all!"

"But, Chip, they'll have to know, won't they?"

"They'll know about the loss below decks, but they don't have to know how bad off we are. We can't let them lose hope, Ben. That's important. Any day we may have a rainstorm or hit an island or the mainland. But until we do, I and I alone will give out this water!"

Ben had never seen Chip like this, and he was a little afraid, though he made no protest. At Chip's command he called everyone on deck, and Chip told them bleakly what had happened to the kegs of fresh water.

"How much is left, captain?" someone asked.

"There's enough to last—if we're careful. It's going to be a hard time—a thirsty time. But we must work together. Once a day you will send one of your group, and I will give that one the water allowance for that day. Make it last, for under no circumstances will anyone get any more until the next day." He looked over his friends' faces, which were beginning to look a little suspicious. "Every drop of water that is drinkable is in that cabin. It will last, but we must be very cautious. That's all I have to say. Send your representatives to get today's water as soon as you can."

There was a murmur of anger, and he heard someone say, "Who does he think he is anyway?"

Chip stood outside his cabin with one large container of fresh water, and when the first applicant approached him and gave his name, Chip asked Ben, "How many rations for this one?" When Ben told him, Chip said, "Hold out your vessel." He slowly poured five medium-sized cupfuls of water into it and said, "That's it. Next!"

The white-foot did not move. He looked at the small amount of water and said, "That's enough for me, but there are *five* of us."

"That *is* the ration for five for one day," Chip said. "Move on now."

Anger rose in the eyes of the white-foot, and Chip said at once, "Trooper, move this one along. He's blocking the way!" Trooper made him leave. And so it went. Most of them did not say anything, but there was a sullen look in their eyes.

One heavy, middle-aged mother of six said angrily, "And how large is *your* ration, I wonder!"

Chip did not answer. He tightened his lips and said, "Next!" Finally they had all received their water. Chip and Ben went inside, and Ben said, "Chip, this isn't going to work! They think you're holding out on them—using the water for yourself."

"I can't help that!"

"But they'll hate you, Chip!"

"I can't help that either," Chip said. "It has to be done this way. Ben, set all the sails—every inch! We've got to find *something*!"

Those were difficult days. The sun beat down uncomfortably, and every day seemed to last forever. The miserly sip of water was only enough to make the white-feet even more thirsty, and daily the murmurs against Chip grew louder. There were even mild threats now. So Trooper never got too far away from the captain. His black, poisonous teeth kept troublemakers quiet—at least while he was there.

The worst time for Chip came on the sixth day. Hallee came to his cabin, and he stepped outside to face her. She was thin, and her lips were white and parched when she spoke. "Captain, I wouldn't ask for myself, but Major Meadows is very sick. He's had a fever for two days now. He needs an extra drink of water. Will you let me have it?" She looked at him, begging him with her dark eyes.

Chip was torn inside. He loved the old man, and he wanted to please Hallee, but he alone knew there was not even one more day's ration for everyone left. He could not give in!

"I'm sorry, Hallee. I can't make any exceptions."

She stood quietly for a minute, then turned without a word and left. He watched her go, then went inside the cabin and looked long into the few inches of water in the last keg. "Now she'll hate me forever," he thought as he sat down heavily.

The next day when the white-feet came for their rations, some of them barely able to stand, he said through dry lips, "The ration will be cut in half today."

A cry of anger went up, and then Chip knew what hatred was. They were ready to rush him and beat him to the deck. Trooper stood near, but he too was suffering from the lack of drinking water and so was weak as a kitten.

What would have happened no one would ever know because just at that moment Sailor cried out, "Ship off the port bow!"

They all rushed to the rail and saw a few miles away a boat with men on the rails pointing at the *Victory*.

"They've seen us," Chip said. Then he said in his old voice, "Everyone get into the cabins. Stay quiet no matter what happens! They'll take the *Victory*, but we'll get free, I promise you!"

They all scurried below and hid themselves in the dark cabins just as the small medium-sized motor launch pulled alongside. They heard men's voices saying, "Will you look at this!" The *Victory* rolled heavily as the voices got louder, and then some of the men were pulling on it. Trooper, hidden in one of the open upper cabins, saw a huge eye peering in and heard a voice he could not understand say, "Why, it's a model of the *Victory*. Must have got loose from someone and drifted out to sea. It's a miracle it wasn't sunk this far from land."

There was a sudden cry, and if they could have understood the language of men, they would have heard, "Look at this, for crying out loud!"

"What is it?"

"A mouse! A live mouse! Well, ain't that a caution!"

"How'd he get here?"

"Dunno. But I guess the *Victory* had a captain this time. Look at 'im. A regular little Nelson, ain't he, mates?"

"What'll we do with 'im?"

"I know," someone answered. "That bird of yours that died, Tommy—you still got his cage, ain't you?"

"Sure, I have. Gimme that little feller. We'll make a regular pet of 'im. I ain't never 'ad no captain for a pet afore!"

They all laughed, and then one of them said, "We'll take this ship back with us. She'll tow behind us nice as you please. Put that nylon line on her bow, will yer, Harry? Now, then, let's take the captain to his new 'ome."

Chip, trying to get everyone below deck before the men arrived, had been forced to hide in one of the small lockers on the deck. Unfortunately, it was this locker that one of the sailors had opened, then pulled Chip out by his tail.

So now the *Victory* was being towed at the end of a blue nylon cord, and Captain Chip was a prisoner in a birdcage where he suffered the most hopeless thoughts of his life. *Maker, where are You now, when I need You most?* he cried silently. But there was no reply.

CHAPTER THIRTY-THREE
An Unexpected Deliverer

"WELL, at least now there's plenty to eat and drink," Chip said sadly. He had been in the cage for two days, and now he sat picking at the large chunk of fragrant cheese the sailor had put in there.

Escape had been his first thought, but a quick examination of the cage showed that to be impossible. It was a heavy metal cage, and the door was fastened on the outside with a bar, and over that was a u-shaped wire lock.

"I can't squeeze out, can't eat the bars, can't reach the

lock." He named the impossibilities grimly. He was in an agony of suspense concerning those still on the *Victory*. Were they alive? Were they starving to death? He shook the bars futilely, then slumped down on the tiny piece of blanket they had shoved into the cage for his bedding. He would give anything for one look at his friends who were bobbing up and down in the *Victory*.

The sailor entered and poked his finger through the bars, as he often did, trying to make friends. But Chip pulled away, as he always did. The sailor shook the cage in anger, spilling the small bowl of water onto the blanket, then left swearing loudly, having plunged the room into darkness with a flick of a switch.

For long hours Chip sat there, and then he thought he heard something—a faint rustling sound near the door. There it was again! Something was moving near the bottom of the door. Then he heard a tiny voice whispering his name! "Chip! Chip! Are you in there?"

"Yes!" he shouted. "I'm up here. Who is it?"

"It's me, Chip—Hallee." There was more rustling, and then he heard her climbing the chair that was close to the table on which the cage sat. "Where are you? I can't see you."

His eyes were more accustomed to the darkness, and he could see her clearly. He answered, "Above you, Hallee. In the cage."

She looked up and waited until her eyes adjusted to the darkness so she could see. "There you are. Well, sir, you're in a pretty fine mess, aren't you?"

"Well, I guess—"

"Captain Chip of the Rag-Tag Brigade in a birdcage!" she scolded as she clambered up the chair and leaped onto the table.

"Hallee! How did you get here?" Chip thrust his paws out of the cage, and she took them in her small ones.

"No questions. *I'm* the captain—for a little while at least.

Where's the door—oh, here it is." She easily moved the wire off the bar and moved the bar aside. In one leap Chip was free!

He grabbed her, held her close, and cried out, "Hallee, you're wonderful!"

She smiled. "Well, it is good to have your better qualities appreciated, but we'd better get out of here."

He followed her gladly down the chair and under the door without a word. She led him down a dimly lit passageway, through another door, and finally up a flight of steps that led up to the deck. They saw none of the crew. The ship was not moving at all, being anchored for the night. They came to the bow, where the Rag-Tag Brigade was waiting for him with huge smiles. They all tried to talk at once, but Hallee said, "Let's get away from here, then you can talk all you want."

They all jumped onto the *Victory*, and Trooper cut the blue line with his sword. At once the *Victory* began to drift away, and they set the sails without delay. The wind filled the sails, and the ship seemed to skim over the waters, putting the other vessel far behind in no time.

What a party they had then! Everyone on board had to pound Chip on the back and welcome him a thousand times! There was a feast in the dining room with beet wine to spare. They all drank and laughed and danced with greater joy than they'd ever experienced before.

Finally, when they were too stuffed to move, Chip said, "Where did you get all this stuff?"

They all tried to answer, but Trooper said firmly, "All pleeze shut the mouth! *I* will tell eet. I tell you, Cheep, you see thees gorl—thees Hallee? I tell you, she is soch a one! If I want a fine wife, I take her for my own self!"

"Oh, Trooper," Hallee protested warmly. "I wish you'd hush—"

"She do it all, Cheep," Trooper cried out, lifting his tiny glass to her. "We are all dying of thirst, and this one she say, 'Why you lie there like cheeldren!' And she make me so ashamed that I get up, and she go up the blue rope, and we follow her. Then we get water and we make many, many trips, and we all eat and drink and get strong plenty queek!"

"Oh, Trooper, you did all the work!" Hallee protested, a bit embarrassed by the look of warm admiration for her that she saw in Chip's eyes.

"She's the one, laddie," Major Meadows said. "I'll eat my sword if she didn't plan the whole thing! Got the ship stocked with water and food, and then off she goes and comes back with you in tow! She's one in a million, that Hallee girl is!"

They went on like this for some time, but finally the crowd began to wander away, and Chip had time for a quick word with Hallee. They were standing almost in the same spot where she had told him to do whatever he thought was right. He stepped close to her and said, "Hallee, I can't ever find words to thank you. I would have died in that awful cage if you hadn't come."

"Oh, Chip, you've done so much for all of us. After you were taken, Ben explained about why you were rationing the water. If you hadn't kept it quiet and taken all the abuse we poured on you—it makes me ashamed to think of how we treated you."

"Hallee," Chip said, "there's something I want to tell you—something I've been meaning to tell you for a long time."

"Yes, Chip," Hallee whispered eagerly.

"Well, it's just that—"

"Chip, here you are!" Deedee gushed as she hurried up to the captain. "I declare, I haven't had a minute alone with you all night. Now you just come with me and tell me all about what you've been up to, you hear!" She dragged him off so forcefully that whatever he was going to say to Hallee didn't get said that night. And whatever she might have said about Deedee on that occasion would not bear repeating!

The next day there was little time for talk, for the major had grown worse, and Hallee spent most of her time caring for him. She did have a moment with Chip just before supper. "He's very ill, Chip. I—I don't think he can last much longer."

For the next two days they set the sails to get as much speed as possible. Many began to experience that strange feeling that animals sometimes have just before something important happens.

"It's not far, Chip," Ben said. "I can smell the land!"

Sailor agreed. "See them birds? Them is land birds. Never too far out, they ain't."

On the third day just at dawn the lookout shouted, "Land ho! There—in the west."

Chip was sitting with Major Meadows, and they heard the cry together. The major had been unconscious, but now his eyes opened wide, and he smiled with delight. "There it is, Captain Chip. The West. I told you I'd see it. Get me on the deck—be quick now!"

He was so light that Chip picked up his withered body without effort and carried him topside. "Hold me up, boy, so I can see it."

Hallee and Chip helped the old soldier hold on to the rail. "There it is—the West!" the major said with relief. They saw the hills of the new land rising out of the sea before them. Even as the major gave a cry of joy at the sight, Chip felt him slump, and he knew that his dear friend had left this life. They laid him down gently, and Chip said softly, "Well, he's found more than he expected—he's in the Deep West, Hallee."

They joined hands and looked at the new land as it grew clearer and sharper in the morning light.

CHAPTER THIRTY-FOUR
Safe at Last

AND they lived happily ever after. So all the old stories go, and this one is no exception. They never were really sure where they were, but after a while it didn't matter. The land was a paradise—almost. There were owls, weasels, and many natural enemies. But there was good climate and good food, and they had each other. It seemed to be a land that was made to be a haven for wanderers. They built a Royal Burrow, and before long there was a coronation and Prince Hal became King Hal. And he had a queen by his side. To nobody's surprise it was Queen Deedee. She was foolish and light-headed, but he loved her, and that is enough reason for making anyone a queen.

Sailor, wanting still more sailing adventures, had gone off with the *Victory*, but the Rag-Tags kept together—after a fashion. One by one, of course, as is the nature of mice and men, they began to pair off with young females. Of course, those who did not pair off were rather lonely.

Chip was sitting on the beach with Trooper one afternoon many months after the landing, and Ben came hopping along the beach with excitement. "Chip, Trooper, guess what?"

"You're going to set up your own burrow with that young white-foot you've been chasing all over the place," Chip said wearily.

Ben's jaw dropped open. "How did you know?" he asked.

"Everybody's known except you—for weeks now." Chip realized he was being harsh with his old friend, so he smiled and said, "I think that's wonderful, Ben. I pray the Maker's best for you."

"You'll come and see us often, won't you, Chip?" he cried, but he was already moving off to tell someone else his "secret."

Chip sighed heavily and said, "Well, Trooper, that leaves you and me—just the two of us out of the whole Rag-Tag Brigade."

Trooper made a peculiar noise, and Chip thought he was choking. "What's wrong?" he asked.

"Well, the theeng ease, my fran Cheep—what I mean to say ease that I—that ease we—you might say—" Here Trooper, who had never been speechless since Chip had met him, simply raised his paws helplessly.

"Trooper!" Chip cried out. "Not *you*!"

The little shrew grinned broadly and gave a laugh. "Ah, eet ease so, my fran. There ease a leetle one I have met, and we theenk eet weel be best if I—that ease if we—oh, Cheep, you know how eet ease!" he cried suddenly.

Chip smiled and struck the little fellow on the shoulder affectionately. "No, I don't know how eet ease—but you do. So get to it, I say."

Trooper left, and Chip felt very much alone on the beach. "All of them?" he mused. "Nobody left but me."

Feeling quite miserable he began to walk down the beach. But then he saw someone walking toward him—the one he most wanted to see.

"Hallee!" he said quickly.

She smiled at him and said, "Hail, mighty mouse of valor!" She had often teased him about his first meeting with Silver, but now she seemed serious.

They walked on in silence for a long way, it seemed, and then she said, "Well?"

"Well what?" he said weakly.

"Well, are you a mouse of valor or not?" He was so quiet that she said in exasperation, "I should have left you in that cage!"

Then he laughed and took her by the shoulders. "Hallee, I'm just a common white-foot, and you—you're a princess of royal blood."

"You are Captain Chip of the Rag-Tag Brigade. That's royal enough for anyone. Now will you say what you meant to say to me that time on the deck or not?"

She pulled away from him and fled down the beach, but she didn't run very fast, on purpose, so he could easily catch her. Then Captain Chip told Princess Hallee what it was he had been trying to say to her for such a long time. You can probably guess what that was.

AFTERWORD

TIME sometimes seems to move very slow; at other times it goes like the wind. In any case a great deal of time had passed since Chip told Hallee something on the beach. Now, very close to that spot, an ancient white-foot was talking to a bunch of young pups who were crawling around his feet. Many of them were his own flesh and blood—not grandchildren—great-great-great-grandchildren.

He had been telling them about his youth, as he often did. Now they were begging again, "Tell us about the *Victory*—no, tell the one about the fight in the ravine." They never got tired of his stories, and if he tried to leave out part of one, there would be a chorus of protests—"No, no, you left out part of it!" And so he would go over it all.

"Captain," one of the very young mice said, "tell us about Princess Hallee."

He looked down into her eager face and placed a grizzled paw on her fresh young head. "Well," he said slowly, "you are very much like her."

"Me?"

"Yes, very much. I remember the day on the *Victory* when we saw this land for the first time—she looked exactly as you do now."

The young white-foot was amazed and listened intently. Finally the aged storyteller shooed them off and shuffled into the little burrow they had made for him so he could be near the beach he loved so much. A middle-aged white-foot cooked for him, and tonight she had left him a warm drink on the table. "Will you need anything else tonight, captain?" she asked.

"No. I'll just have one pipe and then go to bed. Good night."

"Good night, captain."

The air was warm, and the smoke was pleasant. He thought now so often of the past, hardly ever of the present, and not at all of the future.

The hum of night insects made him drowsy, and there was a strange warmth in the air. *That drink must be a little of Trooper's brew*, he thought to himself. He smiled as he thought of the little fireball—dead now for many years.

"Well, he was a good one. So were they all—indeed they were," he muttered. He thought he ought to go to bed, but suddenly he was aware that he was not tired at all—very strange.

Besides, there was a very fine looking white-foot coming up from the beach right to the front porch. A most impressive looking fellow!

The hum of insects seemed to have grown louder, or had his hearing gotten sharper? The visitor came up the steps, and the ancient white-foot looked at him. There was *something* about him—what was it?

"Good evening, Chip," the visitor said. "Are you ready tonight?"

Chip's eyes felt moist, and he felt so *strange*. "I—I know you, don't I?" he asked.

The imposing visitor smiled and said strongly, "I should think you do. It's been a long time, but I think you'll remember if you try—you mighty mouse of valor."

Chip's heart skipped a beat, and he stood up suddenly. "Silver? It's really you?"

"Oh, yes. I told you I'd see you again. Do you remember?"

"Yes! Yes, I do remember. Silver, you've come back!"

"I didn't think you'd forget me," he laughed. Then he asked again, "Are you ready?"

Chip looked at Silver, and a wild light gleamed in his eye. "I was born ready!" he cried out.

Silver laughed in delight. "You're just the same as always! Let's be going then." He walked down toward the beach, and Chip followed him quickly.

He noticed that his legs were not trembling as they had for quite a few years now. He walked strongly as if he were young again.

"How bright the stars are tonight!" he said suddenly. Then he realized that he was seeing as he once had—keenly and sharply.

"Silver," he said, "you look so young. It's been years, but you're not old at all."

"Neither are you, Chip," Silver said gently.

Chip looked down and saw that he had the strong limbs of his youth again. He looked around the world wildly and cried out with a mighty shout, "I *know* now. Oh, I *know*! We're going to the Deep West, aren't we?"

Somehow they were rising over the massive cliff that towered over the beach, and even as they rose, Silver said, "Yes, Chip. Now is the time for you to enter into the real West—the Deep West."

Chip heard him, but he was looking at the land as it lay beneath him. It was the world he'd known, but it was different. Now they were passing into a long valley, and at the end of that valley there was a mighty hill, and they were somehow walking toward it.

The air rang softly with musical chimes, it seemed to Chip, and he stopped suddenly and said, "Do you hear that?"

"Yes, I hear it."

"What is it?"

"I think it's your coronation call, Captain Chip."

They turned and walked together toward the crest of the

hill. There was a golden door with silver hinges, and out of it stepped a very small figure. Now Chip heard his name called again, as he had heard it once so long ago.

"Chip! I stood up for you that time, didn't I, Chip?"

"Peedee!" Chip cried out as the small figure ran toward him and fell into his arms. "Peedee, it's really you!"

"Certainly, my boy! What did you expect?" He heard another familiar voice, and then he saw Budger.

And then there were many others—Singer and Hal and Major Meadows and Trot and a hundred others, all calling to him with voices like silver bells.

"Welcome home, Chip! Welcome! Welcome!"

Then there was one more voice, clearer than all the rest. It was Hallee, and she looked just the same as she had before—and yet even more beautiful. "Welcome home, my darling Chip," she said. She smiled and motioned ahead. "Look who's waiting to welcome you."

Chip stared at the bright figure who stood with open arms, smiling with great joy. "My son, welcome home after your long journey."

"Maker, is it really You?" Chip cried.

"None other. Now come and we will begin."

Hallee took him by the paw, and they went through the door together to the sound of silver chimes and golden trumpets.

THE END